A LUCY HOWARD MYSTERY

FALSE CLAIMS

LIES IN LOVE AND INSURANCE

KATHERINE NICHOLS

*To Church
and Joanne,
Thank you
for taking
care of our body
and for being
a reader.
Katherine
Nichols*

D1600926

Black Rose Writing | Texas

The author grants the final approval for this literary material.

First printing

This is a work of fiction. Names, characters, businesses, places, events, and incidents are either the products of the author's imagination or used in a fictitious manner. Any resemblance to actual persons, living or dead, or actual events is purely coincidental.

ISBN: 978-1-68513-269-9
PUBLISHED BY BLACK ROSE WRITING
www.blackrosewriting.com

Printed in the United States of America
Suggested Retail Price (SRP) $21.95

False Claims is printed in Calluna

*As a planet-friendly publisher, Black Rose Writing does its best to eliminate unnecessary waste to reduce paper usage and energy costs, while never compromising the reading experience. As a result, the final word count vs. page count may not meet common expectations.

PRAISE FOR
FALSE CLAIMS

"In her latest novel, Nichols takes readers on a wild ride with a charming protagonist who discovers honesty may not always be the best policy when it comes to murder. But when it comes to love, truth matters."

–Gaby Anderson Author of *South of Happily*

"Nichols creates a cast of funny eccentrics who are in way over their heads when it comes to fraudulent antiques dealers, deadly doctors, and cold-blooded murderers. "

–Kim Conrey Author of *Stealing Ares*

This book is dedicated to truth in writing, even when it's fiction.

ACKNOWLEDGMENTS

Unlike my protagonist Lucy Howard, I'm not obsessed with complete honesty. After all, I'm a writer. We borrow from real events and use them to create our own brand of chaos on the page. And we rely on friends and family to keep us grounded.

My husband patiently counts and carries my books from launches to bookstores and back, without a single complaint. My daughters and sons-in-law show up for me despite their busy lives. The Wild Women Who Write, my critique and podcast comrades—Gaby Anderson, Kim Conrey, and Lizbeth Jones—inspire me to keep going whenever I get overwhelmed. And members of the Atlanta Writers Club and Sisters in Crime support and encourage me.

Black Rose Writing gives me the confidence to keep developing characters I love.

As always, I want to thank my talented photographer, compassionate counselor, and great friend, Madonna Mezzanotte, for my headshot.

FALSE CLAIMS

CHAPTER 1

After spending most of the morning studying photos on the whiteboard in my office, I was no closer to understanding how the tiny woman, lying on the floor next to a gigantic wheel of Gouda cheese, had become a criminal.

A horizontal row of pictures taken on the day of Elsie Ericksen's accident told a sad story. For at least the third time in an hour, I inspected each one of them. The first, a still from store video footage, captured the agony of a frail, elderly lady flat on her back in front of a display case filled with international cheeses. In the second, her wrinkled little face was twisted in pain, but she sat upright, cradling her right arm. The last featured her, pants streaked with dirt, being hauled away on a stretcher.

The rest of the photographic evidence, taken during the weeks after her disastrous fall, told a very different story. Photos ranged from the woman line dancing in cowboy boots to hurling a bowling ball down the lane to sitting high on a riding lawn mower with a beer in her free hand. Most striking was Elsie standing at the water's edge like a forgotten goddess, arms raised, head tilted to the sky. Sunlight illuminated her stylish silver bob and formed a halo around her creased but lovely face. This woman bore almost no resemblance to My Lady of the Gouda.

"Dammit, Elsie." I stepped away from the board for a look at the big picture. "I was rooting for you."

A part of me wanted to rip down the photos and tear them into tiny pieces. From my research, I learned she was a sixty-five-year-old widow living on Social Security and a meager pension from the railroad where her husband had worked until his death four years ago. When pitted against Ollie's Organic Grocery, where a small carton of yogurt went for $4.50, Elsie made the perfect victim.

But the evidence against her—the photos on my whiteboard, videos of her in yoga and Pilates classes and swimming in the senior citizen pool—created an airtight case for insurance fraud.

It was no wonder that when my boss, Hugh Farewell, assigned Elsie to me, I had been certain poor Elsie was the real deal. One interpretation told by those images was that her fun-filled lifestyle had been cut short by a terrible accident. With only the photos of her injury in my possession, I believed that version was the true story. But Hugh smelled a rat and instructed me to dig deeper into her life.

Despite my reluctance, I began digging. In her statement, she said she had slipped on a wet spot, either from mopping or a spill. The problem was her black pants were dry and dusty.

Dirty slacks proved nothing, so I turned to social media. It took longer than usual to track her down, but I located Elsie on the alumni site of Creek Meadow High in Smyrna, Georgia. I registered on MyClass to gain access to more of her graduating class. I located a woman who wasn't a member of the group, set up a quick profile for her, and signed up. Then I sent friend requests to the reunion people. Elsie hadn't been foolish enough to post the incriminating photos, but several friends had tagged her, including a fellow bowler on her team No Time to Spare.

The damning shots had been taken during the six-week period immediately after Elsie filed her claim against Ollie's. She insisted her arm was severely, perhaps permanently, damaged. The reality was the elderly huckster had missed her calling. Over the past four years, employees had found her flailing on the floors of stores throughout the entire state of Georgia and into southeast

Tennessee. Through my contacts in other agencies, I discovered she had received $150,000 from various companies. I suspected I had only scratched the surface.

The tiny con woman's secret for success was to ask for the minimum in damages. Most adjustors took one look at pictures of the pitiful old lady lying crumpled on whatever floor she selected and counted their blessings.

I tried to resign myself to the fact that Elsie was no victim, perfect or otherwise. Despite all I knew about her and the hard evidence displayed on the whiteboard, I was certain there was more to her story.

My boss would have told me to get my head out of my ass, face the facts, and close the case. I had no intention of telling him I wouldn't sign off until I spoke with the woman in person. That would require field work, a plan, and more time than I had. So, I set the file aside.

After the intensity of the Erickson case, I welcomed the less challenging task of filling out paperwork. I reached for the spiral notebook filled with to-do lists and flipped through it, looking for a clean sheet, where I could write *review EE*, check it off, and outline the rest of the day's activities. Some people keep diaries, I maintain past and present lists of tasks, so I can see what I've accomplished and congratulate myself.

I landed on a page from over four months ago and made the mistake of reading it. In addition to items like *Finish the Wilson spreadsheet*, it included more personal ones. Some were harmless reminders to pick up dry cleaning or call my parents. The last was a memory minefield.

It began with instructions to order from my boyfriend's favorite Chinese place, a dinner I planned to surprise him with at his law office after hours and continued with a list of personal grooming items designed to make me irresistible to that boyfriend.

Flashbacks of the evening hammered me, and I ripped the sheet from the notebook. I was tearing it into pieces the way I'd imagined doing with Elsie's photos, when the receptionist buzzed through the ancient intercom system.

"You've got a very handsome visitor in the lobby. He says he's your uncle, but I don't see how he could be old enough for you to be his niece."

Buddy's laugh boomed through the receiver, filling me with a familiar delight. The youngest of Mom's three brothers, he was the only grown-up who'd been consistently forthcoming with us kids. Even his voice was nothing like a typical adult's that conveyed half-truths to children—downbeat followed by up with a sing-song regularity. No, my uncle was a master of syncopation. His shifts in rhythm were vocal magic tricks that promised and delivered unexpected honesty.

"Too damned much honesty," according to my father after I came home from my uncle's raving about all the beautiful dresses in Buddy's closet and how I wanted to be a female impersonator when I grew up.

Mom had shrugged and said, "He is who he is; God love him."

Dad had left the room muttering.

Then and now, I loved the man without reservation and buzzed with the same excitement I had as a kid stumbling around in his size thirteen high heels.

On the way to the lobby, a twinge of apprehension came over me as I realized Buddy had only been to my office once before. And that had been to tell me my grandfather had passed.

My anxiety lessened when I reached the waiting area to find my uncle joking with the receptionist. At least thirty pounds overweight, his choice of wardrobe walked the line between eccentric and thought provoking. Today, he wore designer jeans and a T-shirt with Mick Jagger's tongue spread tight over Buddy's generous belly. The look startled me until I remembered he had been working as a front man for the band his live-in love played in.

"Baby girl! You are even prettier than the last time I saw you."

I stopped several feet from him, struck by an off note in his cheerful greeting. Before I could pinpoint the exact spot of variance, he pulled me into his bearlike grasp. I breathed in the aroma of English Leather with a touch of canine in the mix, courtesy of his three Chihuahuas: Pepe, Paco, and Doris.

He loosened his hold but stayed close. "Is there somewhere we can talk?" His shaky tenor, with its unexpected ups and downs, convinced me his entire greeting had been forced.

"Of course." My uncle's usually rosy cheeks were pale. "We can go to my office."

He followed me down the hallway but paused at my door and whispered, "If you don't mind, honey, let's go someplace more private." He pointed at a stained ceiling tile. "You never know who might be listening."

A child of the sixties, my uncle had been arrested once at a protest march, and from then on, had been certain Big Brother was keeping tabs on him.

"Sure. I just need to clean up a few things first."

I took Elsie's adventures off the board and placed them on my desk. While retrieving my purse from my file cabinet, I brushed against the stack and knocked the photos to the floor.

"Let me help you with that." Buddy stooped and began picking up the pictures. He stopped and examined the shot of Elsie on the riding lawn mower. "Who is this sassy little lady?"

"Just someone from a case I'm working on." I held out my hand.

"She looks familiar."

"I shouldn't have left them lying around since they're part of an active investigation." As soon as the words were out of my mouth, I recognized my mistake.

"An investigation, huh?" He reached into his pocket for his reading glasses and lined up the photos on the desktop, then studied each one. When he got to Lucy in the bowling alley, he picked it up and squinted. "Wait a minute. Maybe Norm's team the Rocking Pins played against her in last year's tournament." He took a closer look. "No, darn it. That's not it. Don't worry; it'll come to me."

I sincerely hoped it wouldn't. I scooped up the images and stuck them in Elsie's folder.

"There's a coffee shop around the corner." I ushered him out of the office to the front desk, where I stopped to see if the receptionist wanted anything. After taking her order for an iced mocha latte with an almond biscotti, we walked outside.

On the way, I worried that even the short walk might be rough on him and slowed my pace.

September in Atlanta is beautifully unpredictable. One minute it's hot enough to bubble asphalt; the next, breezes fill the air, making you want to wave a scarf while riding in a red convertible.

Today was a scarf-waving day, but the cooler temperatures didn't offer my uncle much relief. By the time we reached the shop, sweat dripped from his receding hairline into his heavy-lidded eyes.

I got him situated in a booth, then ordered iced coffees and watched him while I waited. Whatever cheer he'd been spreading to the receptionist had evaporated. His sagging shoulders and dejected expression worried me.

My unwavering need for transparency served me well in the career I had fallen into. But that quality had its drawbacks. One of them was the tendency to see the potential for catastrophe in every situation. Was my uncle sick, dying even? Or was it Mom or Dad? Surely, he wouldn't have come to the place I worked to deliver such devastating news.

Before I conjured additional tragic situations, the barista called my name. I carried the frothy drinks to our booth where Buddy sat with his head resting on the table, fast asleep.

I took a sip of coffee and glanced around the room. We were the only customers in the shop, and the kid behind the counter was busy texting on his cell, so there was no reason to disturb his snooze. I noticed a thin line of drool at the corner of his mouth and dabbed at it with my napkin, then stirred my drink and waited.

Well into his adult life, Buddy's doctors diagnosed his condition as narcolepsy with cataplexy. The poor man's internal rhythms were all confused, causing him to stay awake most of the night and drop into a sound sleep at random times during the day. While asleep, he often experienced frightening visual or auditory hallucinations so strong they slammed him into consciousness and left him unable to determine reality from his terrifying visions. If he happened to be standing at the onset of an episode, instead of dozing off, he might only lose muscle control and slide into what looked like a slow-motion drunken fall.

Most of the one in three thousand narcoleptics in the US who suffer from the condition have no more than two of the symptoms. Lucky Buddy hit the trifecta starting in his mid-twenties.

His family and friends alternated between thinking he was just lazy or a walking drunk. A few months before his thirtieth birthday, he dozed off at the wheel late one night and drove his car off the road. He escaped with a broken arm and multiple gashes and bruises. His doctor discovered a pattern of accidents in his records and ordered a series of tests that revealed an abnormally low level of hypocretin, the chemical that regulates wakefulness.

I suspected his life before being diagnosed had been a living nightmare.

Yelping, he jerked upright and sent his coffee rolling across the table. I caught it before the lid popped off.

"How long was I out?" He rubbed his hand through his bristled buzz cut and shook his head.

"Only a few minutes." I squeezed his arm. "The new medicine isn't helping?"

"Guess not. The doc's got me on a combination of antidepressants and a stimulant, but we can't seem to get it right."

I wanted details on the ongoing quest to find a treatment plan, but his sudden shift of expression stopped me. His countenance morphed from mournful to what I could only describe as fearful.

"I didn't come to see you about my sorry medical state." He glanced around the coffee shop and lowered his voice. "I've got a problem, baby girl, and I thought what with you being a private investigator and all, you might be able to help."

Dad believed I was a badass version of Nancy Drew and had obviously shared this misconception with his brother-in-law.

Before I could explain my job was much less exciting, my uncle leaned forward and covered my hands with his. "I'm afraid I may have killed someone."

I snorted icy coffee through my nose. "You what?"

He responded with a frantic shushing sound before whispering, "I may have killed someone. At least, that's what it looks like."

"Who in the world could you have killed?" I could not imagine sweet, harmless Buddy hurting anyone. "And what do you mean looks like? Wouldn't you know if you had, uh, you know, actually killed someone?"

He shook his head. "It's not that simple. I can't talk about it here, but honey, I need your help."

"My help? What can I do? Should you maybe, I don't know, call a lawyer?"

Other than his brief imprisonment for activism, my uncle had a clean record. But he maintained a distrust of the legal system.

"Please, Lucy, I've got complete confidence in you. Just stop by the house, and I'll explain everything."

"Well, you shouldn't have complete confidence in me. You shouldn't have any confidence in me. I work in claims, which is nothing like real police work. And I've only been doing it for a few months. Plus, I—"

"Please, Lucy."

I turned away from the tears welling in his eyes.

"Okay. I'll come. But this is way over my head, so I'm bringing my boss. He's a licensed private investigator."

Buddy protested, but I held firm, and he agreed to let me share the information with Hugh, our lead and only investigator.

"But I don't want to involve the police."

"I can't guarantee I'll be able to make Hugh do anything." I left him sitting at the table while I got Darla's order.

No longer gentle, the breeze whipped the scattered leaves into whirlwinds of gold and orange and red. He plodded through the leafy turmoil like the sleepwalker he occasionally was. We stopped by his Outback wagon, where he kissed my cheek, then slid behind the steering wheel.

"Hold on a minute. I thought you weren't supposed to be driving."

"I'll be fine." He took a pill bottle from his pants pocket. "I take one of these right before I get in. Then I keep the windows rolled down, and the radio cranked up."

The car lurched away from the curb, and I watched as the *Life is Better with a Chihuahua* bumper sticker disappeared into the distance. I closed my eyes and offered up a prayer for Buddy and anyone in his path.

CHAPTER 2

Still in a daze from my uncle's revelation, I placed Darla's order on the front desk and asked if Hugh was in. He wasn't. She promised to let me know when he arrived.

I returned to my windowless office, unable to get Buddy off my mind. Always dramatic, both on and off stage, he did love to be the center of attention but never fabricated crises in his life.

I planned to continue examining Elsie's case, but my heart wasn't in it. So, I picked up the file on another slip-and-fall that looked legitimate. Righteous cases validated me. They restored my faith in the system and gave purpose to the tedium that made up much of the job.

After four, Darla buzzed. "Hugh's back. You might want to wait awhile. He's in a crappy mood."

I resisted the urge to ask how she could tell the difference between his current state of mind and his normally prickly attitude. After returning everything to the appropriate folders, I walked to his office and tapped on the door, then entered without waiting for a response.

He scowled at me from behind a mound of printed forms. "I don't know how the hell anything ever gets done." He shoved the papers aside, opened the bottom drawer, removed a bottle of Wild Turkey, and set it in the middle of the desk.

"Hand me a glass," he commanded in his rumbling voice, then pointed to the bookshelf near the door. "Grab one for yourself while you're at it."

Not much of a bourbon drinker since my college days when Wild Turkey and diet soda almost killed me, I needed to get Hugh into a more cooperative mood, so I brought two glasses. He filled his to the brim.

"About half that for me, please." But he kept pouring.

"Take a load off, Princess." The only seat in the room was an old leather one from his former office; it was stacked high with piles of paper that looked as if a sneeze would cause an avalanche. I spotted a folding chair in the hallway and dragged it in.

He raised his drink. "Here's to nipples. Without them, boobs would have no point."

"I think you missed the *point* of the HR meeting about inappropriate sexual remarks."

He rolled his eyes, and I sighed, then lifted the bourbon to my lips. The smell reminded me of the fraternity bathroom and my last bout with the golden poison. Bracing myself, I sipped and shuddered as the liquid burned its way down my throat. Hugh grinned.

"You must need a pretty big favor." He took another gulp. "Okay, spill it—the request, not the drink. That's expensive stuff."

I told him about Buddy. I expected him to interrupt with questions or snarky comments, but he kept quiet. Concluding with my uncle's fear he might have killed someone, I waited for a reaction. Other than sipping bourbon, propping his feet on the desk, and staring at the ceiling, there was none.

Urgent to fill the silence, I said. "I wanted to call the police, but Buddy has a problem with the authorities, and he didn't want to, but maybe we still—"

Hugh held up a meaty index finger. "It might be a little early for that. First, we have to find out if he really did knock someone off or if he's just some kind of delusional whack-job."

Despite having wondered the same thing myself, it irritated me to hear him disparage Buddy. "My uncle is most definitely not a whack-job. He's as sane as the next person."

If the next person were a hallucinatory narcoleptic.

He handed me a small notebook, tightened the top on the Wild Turkey, and put it back in his drawer. "Write down the address. I'll try to make it around 7:30. But afterward, I'm going to need something from you."

"And what would that be?" Although I didn't know what he wanted, I doubted I would like it.

"It's not that big a deal, just a little surveillance work."

He'd been pushing me for months to expand my role at the agency. He insisted my attention to detail would help in the field, but I resisted. Now, I had no choice other than to say yes.

He downed his drink, finished mine, and began thumbing through the forms scattered across his desktop.

"Okay, then." I scribbled Buddy's information in the notebook and rushed for the door before he reconsidered.

"One more thing," he said as I was making my exit. "You might want to change into something you don't mind getting a little dirty."

. . .

On the way home, I called Buddy to let him know when we would be stopping by.

I imagined different scenarios for their upcoming meeting. None of the possibilities were encouraging. My uncle had dealt with macho men all his life, but Hugh was different. What the hell. My boss could be a major asshole. And a little Buddy often went a long way.

In less than twenty minutes, I reached the curving drive that wound around a gray stone Georgian home. Behind the sprawling mansion with its proud white columns, sat a detached garage my landlords converted into an apartment. I parked on the small square of pavement in front. The door groaned in protest as I pushed it.

While the owners, an elderly couple who spent most of their time in Boca, kept up with the demands of maintaining their historic home in Roswell, Georgia, they were less meticulous about upkeep on my place. The original intent was to let their wayward grandson live there to keep an eye on the main house while they were away. After complaints from neighbors and citations from the police, they realized their property would be safer without him and helped the boy relocate to Colorado, where he would be among kindred souls.

Renting the apartment to me had been something of an afterthought, a proposal from the couple's accountant. My ex-boyfriend Lance called it a dump and pressed me to move in with him. But I loved the place, despite the many repairs it needed. Plus, I hadn't been ready to make such a big commitment. Things might have turned out differently if I had.

Normally, coming home made me feel safe and in control. Tonight, the shiny red Porsche Carrera in the driveway destroyed whatever calm I reclaimed after Buddy's visit. The overpriced little car belonged to my ex. Just knowing he was close quickened my heartbeat. A flash of heat came over me, not unlike the one generated by Hugh's bourbon. Lance Crawford, however, was potentially far more intoxicating. In fact, he made me act like a bigger fool than any excess of alcohol and diet soda had.

"Get it together, girl. You do not need this jackass in your life." But want and need are two very different things, and if I were being totally honest, I still wanted Lance.

It wasn't as if I had trouble attracting men. My wavy brown hair is long with highlights that mimic streaks of sunlight. My eyes are an interesting shade of greenish-gold, and I've grown to like the freckles sprinkled across my nose and cheeks. I never kidded myself that I was beautiful, but I wasn't bad to look at.

But I hadn't been particularly lucky in love. The inquisitive nature that was such an essential part of my personality proved to be too much for the boys and men I dated. What I saw as healthy curiosity, past boyfriends saw as unrelenting suspicion.

One potential suitor complained I turned every date into a test he hadn't studied for. (He failed.) Another accused me of gathering information for a background check. (I was.) Closing in on thirty, I feared I might be completely unsuitable for any long-term relationship.

Lance Crawford was different. My best friend Bethany called him the Abercrombie guy because he looked like the bronzed blondes pictured in the store ads. Slender with wash-board abs and broad shoulders, he was ridiculously handsome. We met at a fancy midtown Atlanta bar she dragged me to. She spotted Lance immediately.

"My, my, my. Now that is one fine-looking man," she growled.

I didn't waste my time turning to check him out. The woman had identified her prey, and I knew better than to get in her way when she pounced.

She picked a table near his and crossed her long legs in his direction. I waited for the inevitable. Bethany Reinhardt, my best friend since ninth grade, was one of those women whose presence cannot be denied. With her creamy complexion, perky breasts, and auburn hair that cascaded down her back until it almost touched her perfectly formed derriere, she commanded center stage. And I faded into the background.

There was no reason to suspect tonight would be any different. Any minute now, that fine-looking man would saunter over and hit on my companion.

As predicted, Lance approached. When he asked if he could buy us drinks, I assumed he was speaking directly to her. I requested white wine and prepared to disappear. But it wasn't Bethany who interested him; it was me. His brilliant smile and twinkling light brown eyes, his double bass laughter—were all for me. He made me feel like the most fascinating woman in the world, no longer the

Lucy whose cautious philosophy about life and incessant need for truth and transparency sent men running for cover.

Despite the typical barroom sounds in the background—clinking glasses, high-pitched giggles—his voice wrapped me in rich velvet. Charm oozed from the rhythmic melody, and his words flowed so smoothly I forgot I hated never ending improvisation.

Together, our names were alliterative perfection: Lance and Lucy, so catchy a younger version of myself would have scrawled it over and over on my high school notebook. When he asked if he could drive me home, I didn't react like the old Lucy. I became the person this charming, sexy man seemed to think I was. Not only did I let him drive me home, I let him spend the night. Lucy Howard, who avoided kissing on the first date, did a lot more than kiss Lance Crawford.

I should have been furious about seeing his outrageously expensive car parked at my place, as if he had the right to be there. But the memory of his lean, hard body in my bed made it difficult to maintain the appropriate level of rage. I made myself revisit the night I discovered the truth about Lance.

Even now, I burned with humiliation and fury. Armed with dinner from our favorite takeout place, I sweet-talked the security guard into letting me go up to Lance's floor unannounced. I teetered past the reception area in frighteningly high heels, wearing a tan raincoat and very little else. Early in our relationship, Lance revealed his office-sex fantasy: I would show up nearly naked, and he'd be so turned on he would clear his desk and throw me on top of it in one hot, fluid movement. Then we would make wild, crazy love fueled by the possibility someone might catch us.

The X-rated scene I planned hadn't unfolded the way I hoped. By the time I reached my destination, the container of cashew chicken had sprung a leak. My sexy thong panties had traveled up well beyond the point of no return, and the lacy push-up bra had turned deadly, threatening to crush my ribs in its vice-like grip. But I was determined to see it through. I would knock on the door and flash my delighted boyfriend the second he appeared

I hadn't factored in how I might look holding a soggy sack of Chinese food with brown sauce dripping down the front of my raincoat. I put the bag on the edge of the secretary's desk just outside his office and swiped at the spreading stain. Muffled voices from within confused me, and I was tempted to abort the mission, but something pushed me forward until I stood with my hand poised over the knob.

"Oh, God!" The throaty cry sent me scrambling back; my heel caught on the thick carpet, and I tripped. To steady myself, I grabbed for the doorknob.

Later, I would wonder what would have happened if Lance had taken the time to lock the damn door. Hell, if he'd simply shut it all the way, things might have turned out differently. But he and his sleazy associate Janelle were in such a hurry the door wasn't even completely closed. When I leaned against it, it gave way, and I wind-milled into the room.

The credenza stopped me from tumbling onto the carpeted floor. I held onto it and regained my balance, but the blonde sitting atop Lance with her back to me caused me to lose my emotional equilibrium.

Known for his constant composure both in and out of the courtroom, Lance had a momentary lapse of cool. He popped up from his rolling chair, sending the topless woman on his lap flying sideways, where she landed on her generous behind.

"Lucy, honey," Lance said while tucking and zipping. "What a surprise. Janelle and I were just going over some notes for tomorrow's trial." His erratic tempo and discordant tones sounded nothing like the voice of the man I'd fallen for.

"Guess I should have called ahead," I murmured, still not completely processing the scene. It wasn't until Janelle scrambled to her feet, holding a bright yellow blouse in front of her, that reality dawned. My stomach lurched, and my throat constricted as I bolted out the door.

"Please, Babe." He took my arm. "Let me explain."

Part of me desperately wanted to let him explain away the scene, to return to the dream I'd lived since we met. But even a master of spin like Lance lacked the power to turn back time.

"Don't. Even." I pulled out of his grasp and noticed the grease-stained paper bag on the secretary's desk. I reached inside and picked up a carton marked Mongolian beef. "I brought dinner," I said, opening the box. "You should eat it before it gets cold."

Before he could respond, I flung the container, sending chunks of meat and slimy noodles airborne. When I replayed the scene, as I often did, it was as if the gooey ingredients flew in slow motion until they landed with a satisfying plopping sound on his head and face. My only regret was that I had thrown the entrée instead of the hot and sour soup.

CHAPTER 3

I don't remember leaving the building or driving home or changing out of my disagreeable underwear. I recall swallowing a sleeping pill my doctor prescribed for an earlier bout of insomnia. And I would never forget how alone and miserable I was waking up the next morning.

It was days, no weeks, before I managed to close my eyes without conjuring up the image of Janelle astride Lance and his face when he saw me career into the room. But, with Bethany's help, I almost convinced myself I was better off with him out of my life.

I recycled his stupid running magazines and tossed out an assortment of health food and hair gel. I photoshopped him out of all the selfies of us and replaced him with various sexy movie stars.

Finally, I told my parents and my boss about the break-up. My mother surprised me by smiling and attempting to console me with an article about women who were having babies well into their forties.

Dad grunted, "Good riddance."

And Hugh said, "I wondered how long it would take you to dump that self-satisfied little prick."

About a month ago. Lance called to ask me out for coffee. "To clear the air." I explained I'd rather have a colonoscopy, and he hadn't contacted me again. Until now.

Parked beside the empty sports car, I surmised he must have used his key to let himself in. For a moment, I considered backing down the drive and getting the hell out of there. I got as far as reverse.

"No, Lucy Howard," I told myself. "You are a grown-ass woman, and you will not allow that minor league douche-bag to keep you out of your own home."

I shut off the engine and reached into my purse for a tube of lipstick, hesitating before applying it. It wasn't as if I wanted to impress Lance. But it wouldn't hurt him to see what he was missing.

Shoulders back, head held high, I walked from the car into my house. Standing in the foyer, I dropped my stuff on the oval table with a built-in umbrella stand, a purchase from Buddy's antique store. The entire apartment was furnished in a combination of cast-offs and period pieces my uncle helped me find. A Victorian fainting sofa reupholstered in blue-striped fabric and a matching undersized scroll-armchair fit perfectly in the area that opened into the kitchen. The owners had gone with mint-green appliances and pink and black tile to create a retro look. Lance said it looked like something from a 1960s movie set.

I smoothed my hair and took a deep breath before walking into the living room, where he sat on the edge of the fainting sofa.

He jumped to his feet and stepped toward me.

I extended my arms, palms facing him. "Don't come any closer." I knew I was being dramatic, but I didn't trust myself alone with him. Dressed in a light-weight navy plaid suit with a pale blue shirt that heightened the color of his eyes, he looked even better than I remembered.

"Babe, you look great," he said with a smile that revealed his impossibly white teeth.

Was that what he called Janelle, too? Or was she *honey* or *sugar* or something slutty?

When I refused to return the smile, his face morphed into an expression I suspected was meant to reflect sincere concern—the look I imagined he used to charm jury members during high-profile cases. Cases such as the one he and his associate were working on. "I didn't mean to scare you. I just wanted—no, I needed—to see you."

"Well, I don't want or need to see you," I lied. "What I do want is my key back."

"Please, don't be like that. At least hear me out. Then I promise I'll give you your key and leave."

I scooted my chair farther from him before sitting.

"What could you possibly have to say that would change anything? But if it will get you out and keep you out, go ahead."

He relaxed his shoulders and leaned forward. "I can't tell you how miserable I've been and how much I miss you."

He didn't look like a man who had been living in extreme distress.

He clasped his hands in front of his chest. Once again, I was reminded of a carefully choreographed address to the court. "I screwed up bad, real bad. But what you saw that night meant nothing. It was just sex. It's just when you work so closely with somebody, sometimes things get a, uh, complicated. And she's a very aggressive woman. Almost bloodthirsty. Frankly, she scares the crap out of me. But you're the only one I've ever loved. You know that, don't you?"

Was that a real tear in the corner of his eye?

"It seemed pretty straightforward to me. And if you were afraid, you did an excellent job of hiding it."

"I said I messed up." He stiffened into a straight back. His expression darkened, and his voice dropped an octave. "But is it really all my fault? I mean it's not easy the way you've always been so, um, well." He looked down for a minute, then directly into my eyes. "So suspicious."

I struggled to keep my composure, but the memory of one of our first nights together swam to the surface. Still glowing from his touch, I shared my past relationship issues. I explained how the men in my life thought I worried too much, almost to the point of paranoia, when all I wanted was to be able to trust someone completely.

And now, he was using my insecurities against me. But wasn't that what lawyers did?

He fidgeted in his seat before resuming. "I don't blame you for what happened."

I wondered what it would sound like if he were blaming me.

"I just want you to understand my side. Then maybe you can start to forgive me. Because what we have is too real to give up without a fight. And that's what I'm doing: fighting to get you back."

Before I could react, he slipped from the sofa onto his knees, trapping me in my chair. The move was so sudden and smooth I had no time to recoil in disgust. Truthfully, I hadn't felt disgusted at all. And I had no desire to pull away. The unsolicited memory of Janelle's fake blonde hair cascading down her naked back, however, served to reinforce my determination to resist his charms.

"Lucy Howard." He took my hands in his and gazed into my eyes. "I love you, and I plan on spending the rest of my life proving it to you." He brought one hand to his lips, then rose to his feet.

"Don't say anything. Just promise me you'll think about it—about us." He kept his gaze focused on me as he stepped back, then turned and walked to the door, where he paused to take the key from his pocket and place it on the table next to mine. Then he was gone.

. . .

I don't know how long I sat there, staring straight ahead. Lance had this power over me. With him, I became a woman who deserved a man as handsome and sexy as my ex. It was a kind of black magic. But it wasn't strong enough to destroy the memory of his betrayal.

My first impulse was to call Bethany. Then I noticed it was already 6:30. A typical conversation with my best friend rarely ended in less than an hour. She would need about twice that amount of time to remind me what a genuine asshole Lance was and how much better off I would be without him.

Besides, I was perfectly capable of composing a mental laundry list of the many reasons I had for being relieved the cheating bastard was out of my life. Only that wasn't exactly how I felt standing alone in my apartment.

Lance's visit had destroyed what little appetite I had left after talking to Buddy, but I needed fortification for the meeting with him and Hugh. A quick search of the refrigerator yielded some warty-looking strawberries, a bruised peach, and a carton of vanilla yogurt. After peeling and pitting the peach, I threw it all in the blender, added some ice and a squishy banana. I took a tentative sip, pronounced the concoction tolerable, and brought it to the bedroom.

Hugh's warning to wear something I didn't mind getting dirty came back to me. So, I changed into old jeans and a torn Willie Nelson sweatshirt.

The drive to Buddy's, with its cluttered antique shop in the front rooms, would take less than thirty minutes, but I gave myself extra time, time I would need to prepare my uncle for Hugh. Plus, the void from Lance's departure created a silence so overwhelming I couldn't stand it.

Once again, I anticipated how things would go with Hugh and Buddy. Was my concern another example of my over-worrying pessimism? The two men might surprise me and hit it off.

"In what universe?" I muttered.

There wasn't enough optimism in the state of Georgia to conjure a happy version of an encounter between my flamboyant uncle with his boyish charm and my grumpy colleague with his total immunity to charm, boyish or otherwise.

By the time I arrived at Buddy's, I had worked myself into a frenzy. What the hell was I thinking getting Hugh involved? I should have made Buddy call a lawyer, or at least pushed for details before inviting my boss to join me on what would most likely be an epic clash of personalities and lifestyles.

"Get a grip," I told myself. "It's too late now. Besides, what's the worst that can happen?"

Before I could concoct visions of disaster that might erupt from something as innocuous as shoe choice—Buddy's the latest in sneaker chic, Hugh's scuffed loafers with run-down heels—to the more dangerous territory of politics, I hopped from the car. Seeing the pink sign with Past Perfect written in bold black always made me smile. And, despite my jagged nerves, today was no exception. The name of the antique store Norm and my uncle owned was a tribute to Grandma Taylor, Mom and Buddy's mother. The woman had spent thirty-five years as an English teacher and had been a stickler for good grammar, which she considered on par with good character.

The shop occupied a corner lot, and Buddy and Norm lived in a spacious apartment in the back. As usual, the eclectic window display was an attention-getter. Currently, an elegant, elaborately carved writing desk was by a rickety table, laden with kitschy ceramic cows wearing hats.

Normally, I would have taken more time to enjoy my uncle's creative efforts, but today I couldn't spare it. I needed to prepare Buddy for Hugh.

I took the path to the backyard, where a chaotic assortment of whacky, tacky, and occasionally valuable objects greeted me. A pale green toilet with spindly ferns cascading from its tank sat next to a cracked claw-foot tub filled with floating rubber ducks. Plastic pink flamingos congregated in front of a row of grimacing garden gnomes. Sunlight flickered across the brow of a grinning marble caricature of Venus rising from her clam shell. I could have sworn her eyes were following me. I picked up the pace, pausing at the small screened-in back porch, packed with more outdoor treasures.

From within, Patsy Cline warbled about walking after midnight. I sang along as I rang the doorbell and waited. Worried my uncle wouldn't hear the buzzer above the singer's mournful voice, I raised my hand to bang on the screen door but stopped when a tall man with a full head of salt and pepper hair and a matching beard appeared.

"Lucybird! You're looking pretty as a peach." Norm flipped the latch and greeted me with his honey-laced baritone. He wrapped his rangy arms around me and pulled me inside.

Buddy met Norm Pinochet at an antiques convention in Nashville over fifteen years ago. Their long-distance relationship evolved into a live-in one when Norm agreed to move to Roswell, a small city north of Atlanta, and start a shop with my uncle.

Originally, my family considered them an unlikely couple. Norm was the hardy, outdoor type: hiking, camping, and flannel shirts. He was almost as macho as the brothers who had tormented Buddy throughout his childhood. Even though Buddy's idea of roughing it was staying in a Motel 6, and Norm wanted to climb every mountain, for them, it worked.

"You're looking pretty darn good yourself. I think somebody's been working out." I squeezed his bicep.

"Sure as hell's not me." He laughed and led me past a pink pig in a witch's hat sitting in the middle of a pile of pumpkins. "Sorry about the mess." He gestured to the conglomeration of Halloween-themed items surrounding us. "Our guy's got big plans."

Buddy had big plans for every holiday, but Halloween was his favorite. His enthusiasm for costumes and haunted houses made him a huge hit with me and my cousins when we were little. It still did with me.

We stepped into the kitchen where the spicy aroma of Buddy's famous beef and bean chili filled the air. Most of the cheerful yellow wall in front of me was covered with shelves loaded with intricately patterned blue and white serving plates. Light wood cabinets to the right held volumes of cookbooks.

Like Buddy, I had a strong interest in history. My uncle assumed it would translate into a passion for the antique business. The poor guy tried his best to convince me that joining him in his passion was the perfect way to satisfy my love of studying the past. To him there was nothing more fulfilling than the joy of discovering treasure in a pile of junk. It helped him make a personal connection with people he'd never met.

He didn't understand how I could get excited about looking at documents protected by glass or examining objects no one had cared about in centuries. I didn't have the words to explain my need to keep a dispassionate distance between myself and the rest of the world, past and present.

"I'm glad you came, Sugar. I'm concerned about our boy." Norm hugged me again, then asked, "How 'bout a bowl of chili? I got your uncle to tone it down, but it's still a one-and-half alarmer."

My stomach was already churning over the Hugh and Buddy encounter, so I declined the chili but accepted Norm's follow up offer of a beer.

"I'll give you two some alone time."

"You mean you're not joining us?" My voice came out squeaky.

"Of course, I will in a little bit. You know I'd never throw you to the wolves."

Bottle in hand, I headed to the sitting room where my uncle waited. A high-backed sofa, covered in a rose and yellow floral pattern, took up most of the right side of the room. Norm had been appalled at the cost of the fabric, specially ordered to replicate pre-Civil War decor, but Buddy proclaimed it was more than a piece of furniture. It was an investment.

An investment my uncle was currently passed out and drooling on. A fat tan and black Chihuahua reclined in his lap. When she saw me, the little dog bared her teeth and growled. I skirted around her and took a seat on the Louis XVI knock-off chair across from the two of them. It was uncomfortable but not as bad as getting my hand taken off by the diminutive beast. I sipped the cold beer and waited for Buddy to wake up.

Norm ambled into the room, carrying a dish towel. "I knew it was too quiet in here." He ignored the dog, who continued to snarl, and gently tucked the cloth under the sleeping man's chin to staunch the flow of saliva.

"He's been doing this more and more frequently and takes longer to wake up." Norm looked at his partner and shook his head. "I'm worried."

Before I could press for details, Buddy snorted and started into an upright position. He rubbed his eyes and yawned, and the dog began licking his face in a pantomime of ecstasy.

"That's a good girl, Doris." Buddy scratched the joyful creature behind the ear before scooping her up and planting her back in his lap.

"Dammit, Norm," he grumbled. "You were supposed to make sure I was awake when Lucy got here. I don't want her thinking her uncle is turning into an old man."

"You are an old man, but you're all mine." He smiled and added, "Guess Cinderella here will go clean up the kitchen." He winked at me before leaving.

"We need to talk before Hugh gets here," I said.

"Sure, honey." Buddy pushed an indignant Doris off his lap and stood. He ambled across the room to the roll-top desk and picked up a folded newspaper. "Did you see this article about Alistair Darrow?" His lip curled a little when he spoke the name of his antiques-dealer nemesis.

He handed me the paper, sat, and invited the dog to join him, but Doris shook herself haughtily and waddled away.

When I unfolded it, a baleful-looking Darrow glowered up at me. The first time I met the craggy old coot had been at the opening of Past Perfect almost ten years ago. I'd seen him a few times since then, once at an auction Buddy had dragged me to, another time at an estate sale Norm and I attended. With his long square jaw, narrow-set eyes, and bushy black eyebrows, he had the kind of face it was hard to forget. But it was his smug attitude and bearing that grated my nerves. As much as I disliked the man, however, I didn't enjoy reading about his demise.

Responding to a call from a concerned relative, police went to the home of Atlanta business owner Alistair Darrow Tuesday at 8:30 p.m. in his downtown Roswell antique store, A Better Tyme. Darrow was unresponsive when paramedics arrived. The cause of death has not been released.

The victim's nephew discovered the body after his uncle failed to show for dinner. Authorities are asking anyone in the vicinity on the afternoon of September fourteen to come forward.

I finished reading the article and turned to Buddy. "Is this the person you're not sure whether or not you killed?" Spoken aloud, the words sounded ridiculous. "Maybe you better tell me exactly what happened."

He tapped a staccato beat with his foot and shifted in his seat. "I know it sounds crazy," he began.

Norm returned from the kitchen, sat beside him, and put an arm around his shoulders.

"He has it in his mind he had something to do with that shitbird getting himself shot. I've explained to him there's no way he could be involved, but your uncle can be a real hard head." He patted Buddy gently on the back. "Just tell her what you told me."

"Well, you probably remember Al and I haven't been on the best of terms since he skunked me on that estate sale down in Gainesville. That sneaky son of a bitch convinced the Wheeler kids to sell him the entire contents of their mama's house. He got one of his lackeys to pose as an independent appraiser and under-value the good stuff. Acted like he was doing the family a favor by taking the junk off their hands for what they must have thought was a great price. Then the sleazeball turned around and tripled his profit."

I recalled how angry Buddy had been after driving to the home of Amanda Wheeler, only to discover the place had been emptied out by his rival.

"I know you were pretty pissed at him, but that was over four years ago, right?"

"It wasn't just that one time. Al Darrow was a lying, cheating phony-maroni. A Better Tyme! Who the hell spells time with a y?" Buddy's face turned red. "Plus, the nasty little weasel passes off repros with fake letters of authenticity."

He taught me the difference between repros, copies designed to fool buyers into thinking they were originals, and reproductions, commissioned pieces for people who weren't able to afford the real deal. The sale of repros was not only illegal, it was also viewed in the antique business as immoral and unethical since it tended to cast a bad light on honest dealers.

"I understand why you didn't like Darrow."

"Didn't like him?" Buddy shrugged off Norm's arm. "I hated the miserable bastard." He began pacing back and forth in front of the sofa. "I won't lie. I wanted to kill Al Darrow more than once. With his phony British accent. Shit. The man was born in South Pittsburg, Tennessee, around the corner from where your mama and I grew up. His name wasn't even Alistair; it was Alvin, after the goddamn chipmunks. I know because his brothers were Simon and Theodore. His drunken daddy's idea of a joke, I guess."

Norm planted himself in Buddy's path, forcing the agitated man to stop his crazed ranting. "Get hold of yourself."

Buddy covered his eyes with his hands. I thought he might be crying, but he straightened up and looked directly at me, clear-eyed.

"I may have wanted to kill him. But I could never have done it." He fell back on the sofa and hung his head. "At least," he whispered so softly I had to lean in to hear him, "I don't think I could have."

CHAPTER 4

Before I asked why Buddy wasn't sure about his own homicidal tendencies, the buzzer to the shop sounded, and a chorus of high-pitched barking signaled the approach of a stranger. Doris, along with two smaller Chihuahuas, shot past me toward the hallway separating the apartment from the store itself. I heard toenails on the hardwood floor, followed by a soft thud and a loud yelp. One of the guard dogs had hit the door hard.

"Dammit!" I hopped from my seat and joined the frenzied little pack. "I forgot to tell Hugh to use the back entrance." I hadn't had time to prepare my uncle and his partner for my boss's less than tolerant attitude toward life in general.

Buddy shouted for the dogs to stop barking and started to follow me, but I waved him away. "You sit. I'll go. Better yet, why don't you wheel in the drink cart? Hugh's a big bourbon man if you've got it."

I scooted past the little creatures, who paid no attention to their owner's commands for silence, then slipped through without a canine escort. A narrow shaft of soft light from the old-fashioned streetlamp Norm installed helped me navigate the distance to the switch a few feet away. I moved as quickly as possible, trying to avoid bumping into accent tables, ancient wicker chairs, and baskets filled with silk flowers.

Through the window I saw Hugh shifting impatiently from one foot to the other foot. I let him in as he pushed the buzzer for the third time.

"Sorry about that. I meant to tell you to—"

"Forget it." He entered, strode past me, and stopped to take in his surroundings. "Jesus! What a load of crap."

I shuddered, thankful I'd come alone.

"I guess one man's *crap* is another's treasure." Like his crazed pups, Buddy paid no attention to my request for him to stay behind. He gave Hugh the once-over, starting with his scruffy shoes and ending with his faded black t-shirt. "Of course, there's no accounting for taste, is there?"

I took a deep breath. "Uncle Buddy, this is—"

"Hugh Farewell." My boss stuck out his hand. "Sorry about that remark about your, uh, your treasures. All this shit looks the same to me."

He hesitated before reciprocating the gesture. I was relieved until I realized the two men appeared to be locked in a grip turned deadly. Both maintained neutral expressions, but my uncle's left eye twitched and my boss's cheeks reddened. I tugged on Buddy's sleeve.

"Come on, guys. Let's go someplace where we can talk."

The men released each other's hands and followed me through the back of the store and into the apartment.

The yapping trio of Chihuahuas retreated at the sight of the burly stranger but continued to express concern with a series of glass-shattering howls. Norm came running through the kitchen door.

"Settle down, little girl." He scooped up the lead dog. "Paco! Pepe! Enough." With their leader held captive, the smaller dogs lost their nerve and cowered behind him.

"Norm Pinochet. And this is Doris." He extended the squirming animal to Hugh and said in a trembling falsetto, "I'm just dying for somebody to pet my head."

Apparently, my boss did not come from a family familiar with humans voicing their pets' concerns. Instead of acknowledging the dog, he stood with his mouth hanging slack for a second before reaching over her and patting her owner's thick crop of hair.

Norm shot me an unreadable look, then smiled. "Come on, boys," he said to the other pups. "Let's get you some treats." They danced along beside him as he stumbled through the door. "I'll be back for drink orders in a minute." The rumbling sound of laughter followed him.

Buddy, who had watched the exchange with an enormous grin on his face, pointed to a chair. "Have a seat and take a load off."

He was still smiling as Hugh eased his bulky frame onto the fragile-looking armchair.

Since he considered small talk a complete waste of time, I decided to jump right into the main event. I showed him the newspaper article, and when he finished reading, gave him a brief account of the family history with Darrow.

"Buddy was just getting ready to tell us why he's concerned about his, uh..."

"What my niece is trying not to say is why I'm afraid I may have killed that sorry jackass."

With his thighs spilling over the sides of the chair, he looked as out of place as I imagined he felt. But he kept his cool and nodded at Buddy, who continued.

"Darrow was the kind of antiques dealer who gives the rest of us a bad name." He told the same story he shared with me, minus most of the invective.

Then he picked up where he left off before Hugh arrived. "Al closes, I mean closed, early on Tuesdays. He left a message asking if I could stop by at two o'clock. I got there about 1:45 and walked around back like he told me to. He stuck a note on the door saying he was running late and to make myself at home if I beat him there."

Norm slipped back into the room carrying a big glass of sweet tea and passed it to Buddy.

"You're a lifesaver." He gulped half the glass, wiped his mouth, and sighed.

We declined Norm's offer for tea, and my uncle continued.

"I spent the next fifteen or so minutes wandering around that tacky shop. Good God Almighty, the shoddy assortment of junk that man tried to pass off is more than shameful. It's criminal."

I took the brief silence that followed and the twisted expression that crossed his face as a sign he remembered a real crime had taken place, and it was a bit more serious than a violation of aesthetics or ethics.

"All of a sudden, I started getting a little weak in the knees and I thought, well shit. I'm about to have one of my sinking spells." He fanned himself in an exaggerated manner. "Did my niece tell you about my cataplexic narcolepsy?"

"No," I answered. "But I'll explain after you finish."

Buddy shrugged and stuck his lip out. "Just saying he might need a little background information to understand my predicament."

I glanced at my boss, who had been uncharacteristically silent during the narrative. Something about his calm observation of my uncle made me uneasy, like when you're watching one of those nature shows where the snake slithers toward a fat little mouse who doesn't realize the acorn he's eating will be his last meal.

"As I was saying," he continued, "my eyes were getting mighty heavy, so I sat down on this tattered old horsehair sofa. I bet my clothes are loaded with dust mites."

He stopped and asked Norm if we might have something a little stronger to drink.

"You betcha." He touched Buddy's shoulder before heading for the kitchen.

"After an episode, it takes a while before I return to normal. I checked my watch and saw it was after three. My ears started ringing, and I sensed one of my premonitions was coming on. Lucy, did you tell him I'm clairvoyant?"

"Guess I forgot," I said, even though I hadn't. His supposed ESP was a source of conflict and amusement in our family. Mom considered it a possibility since Grandma Taylor had the gift. His brothers laughed it off, and Dad refused to comment. As for Norm, if Buddy believed it, so did he, but he never seemed troubled by pronouncements of impending doom or impressed with predictions of lucky days.

"Well, I am. But back to my story. I stood at the bottom of the stairs to Al's apartment and called his name a few times. When there was no answer, I started shaking. All I wanted to do was get the hell out of there. Going there was a shitty idea in the first place."

"That's what I don't understand. The way you hated the man, why did you go?" I asked.

"Because of Jefferson Davis."

"Jefferson Davis?" I repeated.

"Right. That suck-ass fool used poor old Jeff to trick me into coming. Al was perfectly aware of my opinion of him and the trash he sold, so I was more than a little surprised when he called to ask for my help authenticating a wooden cutting board supposedly belonging to Jefferson Davis. My first instinct was to tell him he could stick it where the sun don't shine and see how authentic it turned out. But then I thought what if it was the real thing, and I missed the chance to see it? It's not too hard to verify the age of something like that, but provenance is a lot trickier. That asshole knew I wouldn't be able to resist it."

He had explained how important provenance was in the antique business. Just because a piece was old didn't necessarily make it valuable, but if it was an owned by some historical figure, its worth could go off the charts.

I addressed Hugh directly. "When Buddy says provenance, he means—"

"He means a record of ownership or the place of origin." Hugh finished for me.

My attempt to disguise my surprise must have failed.

"What?" Hugh bristled. "Just because I didn't graduate from some fancy-pants law school like your hotshot ex-boyfriend doesn't mean I can't sling around a few fifty cent words, including narcolepsy, by the way."

"You broke up with Lawyer Lance?" Buddy stood and shouted into the kitchen. "Norm, Lucy finally threw that pretentious son of a bitch to the curb. Bring out the good stuff." He turned to me. "Why didn't you tell me?"

"I figured Mom would have passed on the information. But wait. I thought you liked him."

"Oh, honey." Buddy sat back down and put his arm around my shoulders.

"How could anybody like that asshole?" Hugh asked as Norm rolled in a vintage 1960s drink cart.

"Well, he wasn't always an asshole." I had no idea why I felt the need to defend the man who had broken my heart. "Sometimes, he—"

"Sometimes he was an arrogant son of a bitch," Norm finished for her. "Sorry, but everybody hated the guy. We just pretended to like him because we didn't want to hurt your feelings."

Hugh leaned toward the cart and exclaimed, "Holy shit!" He pointed to one of the bottles. "Is that Pappy Van Winkle?"

"Who?" I asked.

"Not who," he corrected. "What. The best damn bourbon I've ever had. That's what!"

The three men spent the next ten minutes extolling the virtue of bourbon in general and Buddy's selection in particular, while I stewed over the reaction to my breakup. If one of them had spoken up sooner, I might not have suffered through the humiliation of catching my ex bouncing his half naked assistant on his lap. If only they'd been honest. But no. *I* wasn't being honest. Nothing would have stopped me from falling for Lance and the dream he represented.

Norm offered me a shot of bourbon, but I declined and went to the kitchen to get another beer. Who would have thought some fancy bottle of booze and a mutual disapproval of my taste in men could have bridged the culture gap between my uncle and my boss? When I returned and listened to the three of them bonding over charred-oak barrels and sweet mash, I felt as if I'd entered a parallel universe. Men.

"Can you guys tear yourself away from your trip up whiskey river? I'd like to get back to Buddy's problem."

"What a buzzkill," Hugh said. "But she's right. Did you tell anyone else about going to Darrow's shop?"

Buddy shook his head. "Just Norm and now you all."

"And what about the note?"

He stood, walked to the desk, and removed an embossed notecard. Then he handed it to Hugh.

"What the hell is this?" Hugh asked, pointing to an intricate design on the front of the card.

"It's the Darrow family crest." Buddy put air quotes around *family crest*, then pointed to a shirtless man springing from the head of a knight in armor. "That's supposed to be one of his Scottish ancestors. And that ship is supposed to be the *Mayflower*. As if. Even that jackass's stationery is phony."

Hugh unfolded the card and studied the message before switching topics. "What about surveillance cameras?"

"We keep them in our shop, but half the time the damn things don't work."

"Is there any reason to worry about anything we might see if Darrow's did?"

Buddy stared into his glass and swirled the amber liquid. "Nope. Not a thing."

My bullshit detector went off and from the look on his face, so had Hugh's. But I didn't want to call my uncle a liar. and apparently neither did my boss.

"I'm sure there's nothing to worry about." Norm scooted closer to his partner, who kept his eyes focused on the pattern of the worn Oriental rug.

Hugh glanced at his watch and announced, "It's getting late." He heaved himself out of the chair, leaning heavily on the creaking arm rests. Standing with notes in one hand, drink in the other, he turned to Buddy.

"I'm going to need a list of your customers."

"Sure. But it might take a while to put it together."

"Not since we got that new accounting program," Norm said. "I can run off a copy right now or email it first thing in the morning."

"Morning's fine." Hugh moved toward the entrance to the shop. "Enjoyed the bourbon, boys."

"Let me take you out the back. It's easier." We passed through the kitchen and the porch. "So, what do you think?"

"I think your uncle knows more than he's telling us. If it was anybody else, I'd say forget about it. I hate screwing around with people who lie to me."

One of the few things Hugh and I shared was our allegiance to honesty, so I understood his frustration with Buddy's half-truths. But whatever he was hiding, I knew my uncle wasn't capable of murder, and I needed help to prove it.

"I know, but—"

"I said if it was anybody else. Flushing out a murderer requires specific skills, skills I don't have. There is a guy I used to work with who's got the expertise we need. You realize, though, that bringing in someone else means we'll have to live with the consequences. Can you do that?"

I swallowed hard and nodded.

"Okay."

"Thanks, Hugh. You can't imagine how much this—"

"Yeah, yeah. You might want to hold off on the gratitude. Meet me at the office."

CHAPTER 5

Hugh picked up the flashlight and shined it in my face. "Why don't you shoot up a flare and tell the bastard we're out here rummaging through the trash so we can send him to jail?"

"Okay, okay," I muttered, batting his hand away. Heavy strands of curls escaped from underneath my black cap and clung in sweaty tendrils to my cheeks. "I'm not used to handling other people's discarded body hair, thank you very much."

"Sorry, Princess. But if you keep getting off track, we'll never get through all this mess."

My head was still spinning from trying to make sense of how I transitioned from Buddy's kitchen to the garbage can of Dr. Andrew Johnston. Wrinkling my nose, I attempted to transfer the contents of the doctor's flimsy bags into the extra strength plastic one Hugh gave me. In the process a mustard-stained hamburger wrapper with a grease-soaked piece of paper stuck to it slipped out and fell to the ground. Thankful for the rubber gloves he had provided, I picked it up and offered it to him.

"This looks interesting."

He squinted at it, then raised his right hand in triumph. "Yes!"

Instinctively, I responded to the high five. The impact spewed globs of goo into the air. I squealed and stepped back in disgust. A dog began barking. Hugh eased our finding into an evidence baggie at the same time a light came on inside the upper story of the brick house behind us.

"Shit!" He dumped the rest of the trash into the big, black bag, grabbed my arm and pulled me toward the curb. Wide beams flooded the doctor's front yard, and the howling grew louder. We sprinted around the corner where his Range Rover waited. While I scurried onto the passenger seat, he tossed the garbage in the back and jumped behind the wheel.

I removed the filthy gloves, rolled them into a tight, little ball, and surreptitiously dropped them on the floor where they blended in with an assortment of empty fast-food containers and newspapers. As the car lurched into gear and catapulted forward, I fastened my seatbelt and focused on the street ahead. In normal circumstances, Hugh treated traffic signs as suggestions. Now, late at night hurtling down the road, he was a heat-seeking missile.

"Oh, dear Lord," I whispered in supplication as he narrowly missed sideswiping a parked pickup.

"Son of a bitch," he murmured, glancing in the rearview mirror. "The bastard's tailing us."

He accelerated and made a sharp turn, slamming me into the door. I righted myself and checked the back window and saw headlights approach. I clenched my hands into fists as we raced up the I-75 ramp, sending the other car skidding sideways. He corrected the swerve and sped onward.

"Oh, my God, oh, my God," I repeated. "Looks like he's gaining on us."

Tires squealed as the dark sedan overshot the entrance.

"We lost him," Hugh announced.

Despite his alarming speed, traveling on the expressway with him was less terrifying than hurtling through narrow suburban streets. Plus, the rest of the way was a straight shot, and traffic was light.

After one final stomach wrenching turn, he skidded into a parking spot in front of Idleman's Insurance Brokerage. A sharp pain in my right hand alerted me that I'd been digging my nails into my palms for most of the ride. Unclenching my fists, I removed my black knit cap, and shook out my hair, then sat quietly, enjoying the blessed stillness.

Hugh turned to me with what I had come to recognize as a look of satisfaction. It strongly resembled his expression of irritation, but when he was happy with the results of our efforts, his bottom lip ticked upward.

"The son of a bitch is ours," he said, reaching to the back seat for the evidence. "Good old Doc Johnston finally got sloppy." He held the small plastic bag with the document I found closer to my face. Through the clear wrapper, I detected what appeared to be a bank statement, registered to a Janice Holloway.

"It looks like records of deposits, but what does it have to do with Johnston?"

"Holloway is the maiden name of the good doctor's mother-in-law. Since she croaked last year, it's a safe bet she hasn't been making deposits to her account. If I'm right, we're closing in on the asshole."

Several months ago, he discovered the record number of appendectomies performed over the past five years by Dr. Andrew Johnston. Most of the recipients had names like Nguyen or Phan. Coincidentally, the majority of his patients' policies had been issued shortly before the surgeries.

An avenging angel determined to free the world from insurance fraud, Hugh devoted himself to building a case against Johnston. But tonight—by the light of the dashboard, eyes shining, brow crinkled in response to the rare smile on his broad face— he looked less angelic and more oversized kid with a new bike.

He shut off the engine, signaling the shared moment of triumph was over. Hugh moved fast for a man his size, and I had to scramble to catch up. By the time I reached the office, he'd already unlocked the door and entered the building. The room was dark, lit only by the soft glow of the exit sign.

"Where the hell is that goddamn light?" He stood in the middle of the reception area, staring into space.

I sighed. What kind of detective couldn't remember the switch was behind the potted plant a few feet from the door? I flicked it on and walked past him to the corner of the room.

After removing my lightweight jacket, I held it as far away as possible before giving it the sniff test.

"Yuck!" I turned the offending article of clothing inside out before tossing it onto a chair, then took a bottle of hand sanitizer off the receptionist's desk. "Field work is disgusting." I squirted once, then twice, before slathering my hands and arms with the lavender-scented gel.

He merely grunted. Most likely he'd forgotten I was there. But he surprised me.

"You didn't totally suck tonight. A little wimpy, but still, not bad." He took off his cap, revealing thick, almost completely white hair and glanced at his watch.

"Damn, it's late. Time does fly when you're having fun, right?" Waving his hand at me, he said, "You go on home. I'll sift through the rest of the garbage and start on the paperwork, so I can file it first thing in the morning. I'm listing you as lead investigator."

"Me? But you always take the lead."

"You found the evidence. And it's better for the agency if it looks like we have a staff of investigators instead of a one-man show. Unless you don't want to sign off."

"No, no. I want to."

"So, go already."

I took my keys from my pocket, grabbed my jacket, and headed for the door. "See you tomorrow morning—late."

I hurried out before he could respond.

. . .

While Buddy's problem and my foray into field work had taken my mind off Lance's visit, the drive home gave me time to replay his words. I absolutely was not considering forgiving him yet couldn't help but wonder how he planned to win me back.

"Stop it." I smacked the steering wheel in frustration. Wondering about his plan to reconcile would only bring trouble. It would be too easy to revert to my passive approach to life, where I let things happen to me instead of taking charge.

That's definitely what Bethany would say, what she had said many times.

We met in the ninth grade and became instant friends. Almost immediately, she zeroed in on my inability to stand up for myself. She urged me to stop letting my mother pick out my clothes, to go after Ryan Jessup, the cutest boy on the tennis team. She tried to persuade me to forget my parents' plan for me to attend a local college instead of my dream school. She encouraged me to quit my job at the insurance company and pursue something I was more passionate about. When I started dating Lance, she warned me to make sure I didn't let him dominate me. I hadn't followed any of her advice and now I'd allowed Uncle Buddy to pull me into a situation that was way beyond my area of expertise. Thanks to my passivity, I really had no specialization in anything.

When I reached home, I was so caught up in giving myself a mental and emotional beating, I almost missed the object on the doormat. At first, I mistook it for a crooked stick. When I bent to pick it up, I saw it was a strange rose. It was solid black from the tip of its ebony petals to the end of its sable stem. I shuffled backward, as if touching it with my shoe might conjure up something nasty.

"Don't be ridiculous," I said to no one. "It's just a stupid dead flower." Despite my confident declaration, I took a tissue from my purse to shield my flesh from it. Under the bright porch lamp, I was exposed to anyone who could be lurking in the shadows, waiting to see my reaction. I fumbled with the key, stepped quickly inside, and turned the bolt lock.

In the kitchen, I unrolled a paper towel, laid it on the table, and dropped the flower onto it. I rarely drew the thin wooden blinds in front of the sink. Privacy had never been an issue, as the space behind my apartment faced a natural wooded area that separated the owner's property from the closest neighbor. Tonight, I closed them tight before examining the oddly menacing object.

No note accompanied the disturbing gift, and I couldn't imagine anyone who would have sent it. Certainly, Lance didn't think the gesture would help get him back in my good graces. Upon closer examination, I found that once you got past its unnaturalness, it was sort of, well, striking. But not something my ex would choose.

So, who? And even more important, why? I transferred the bizarre blossom to a freezer bag, still avoiding direct contact with it. I doubted that fingerprints would show up on petals. But, as Hugh would say, you can't be too careful when handling evidence. Not that putting a dead flower on my front porch was a crime.

Too exhausted to consider it any longer, I washed my face and brushed my teeth. It was almost two in the morning when I crawled into bed. As tired as I was, I couldn't help replaying the day's events. I pushed Lance and the rose to the back of my mind and forced myself to concentrate on Buddy and the much more explicitly dangerous nature of his situation.

When I finally fell asleep, images of the black blossom slipped into my dreams. Despite my intention to sleep in, a little after 7:00, I woke from one in which my uncle and I were wandering through a garden. Only instead of roses, photographs of Elsie and Alistair Darrow bloomed from the bushes.

Groaning, I shuffled into the shower. While getting dressed, I considered showing Hugh my unwanted present, but in the reassuring light of day, it seemed far less ominous.

Even though traffic was sluggish, I made it to the office before my boss. I ignored Elsie's file on the corner of my desk and began checking emails. The first few were business related and easily dispatched. A few were junk. Then I saw it. If I hadn't noticed the word 'rose' in the subject line, I probably would have dismissed the message. The sender's name was Suitor.

Did you like my gift? It's the rarest of roses, found only in the Anatolian Peninsula in Turkey. I spared no expense procuring it for you since it so clearly represents the nature of your own dark heart. Enjoy it while you can, my sweet.

I rolled away from the computer, unable to turn from the hateful words. No longer convinced the rose was someone's idea of a joke, I wished I'd brought it with me to ask for Hugh's take. If I mentioned it now, he'd view leaving the evidence at home as a sign of total incompetence. Facing his scorn was almost worse than fear of the email. Before I had a chance to consider the matter further, he barged into the room.

"You look like you caught your folks doing the dirty deed," he announced loud enough for any passersby to hear.

I shut the program. Eventually, I'd share the message with him, but not until I had time to conduct my own research. When I faced him, I saw he wasn't alone.

A dark-haired man wearing a tan cowboy hat with the brim pulled low over his brow sauntered in behind him. He was over six feet tall and his faded jeans and green-plaid flannel shirt were well worn. His boots were a different story. They were deep brown with fine-tooled artwork in gold and leather that looked soft, but solid. At the country western bar Bethany frequently took me to, I learned far more than I ever wanted to about line-dancing attire. These were excellent quality and obviously expensive. They were also quite large which, according to my friend, reflected nicely on the rest of a prospective lover.

While I had been assessing the outfit and possible attributes of the stranger, Hugh seemed to have been saying something.

"Sorry." I shifted my gaze from the boots to Hugh's leathery face.

"I said this is Mateo Sullivan. We worked together a few years ago. He's into all that computer and internet stuff. He might be able to shed some light on your uncle's, uh, his, well, his situation."

Seldom at a loss for words, his hesitancy naming Buddy's problem made me nervous. And even though I agreed to it the night before, today, the idea of bringing in an unknown third party who didn't understand my uncle caused me to fidget.

"I see. Mr. Sullivan, please sit down." I came from behind the desk. "Would you mind waiting just a few minutes? I have some questions for Mr. Farewell."

"It's Mateo." His voice, like his thickly lashed brown eyes, reminded me of dark chocolate sauce melting over vanilla ice cream. He took off his hat and ran his hand over the wavy tracks it left in his jet-black hair. A strand fell across his forehead, creating a striking contrast with his olive skin. I resisted the urge to reach across and push the lock back in place.

"Right," I exhaled. "Mateo."

He sat in the chair in front of the desk and stretched one long, lean leg over the other, his plus-sized boot resting on a knee. With his profile to me, I took note of his firm, square jawline and strong chin. His crooked nose was the only thing that kept him from being too beautiful. I wondered if it had been broken in a fight defending his girlfriend's honor. More importantly, I wondered if he had a girlfriend.

I gave myself a mental shake to remind me that my reaction fell into the rebound category. Yes, he was handsome in a macho way, but my attraction was an attempt to reaffirm myself. I stood and motioned Hugh to join me, then closed the door, leaving Mateo looking like a wild animal cornered in my office.

"What's up, Princess? Other than your blood pressure."

"Is it really a good idea to involve someone else? I realize I said it would be okay, but I don't want to cause Uncle Buddy more trouble. I mean if..." I inclined my head toward Mateo. "If your guy finds out something, um, illegal, won't he have to report it to the police?"

"*If* my guy finds something illegal?" Hugh repeated. "Sometimes I wonder about you, kid. Murder and its associated activities are almost always illegal. But Sullivan isn't a cop. He's not interested in collecting a reward or being a Boy Scout. He owes me a favor, that's all. So, go in there and talk to him. Then we can straighten out this mess and get back to our real jobs."

He gave me one last look of disgust before stalking off. I shook my head. Why in the world had I involved him in the first place? That was easy. My boss was a professional when it came to uncovering the truth, while I'd barely achieved amateur status. The problem was would unearthing my uncle's secret make things better or worse for him.

But I had no real choice. A question had been asked and had to be answered, so I returned to the man waiting in my office.

"Everything okay?"

"I guess. I mean yes, everything is good. So, how can I help? But I don't have a lot to add to what Hugh told you."

"Sometimes people are surprised at the things they remember. Tell me about your uncle's background. Easy stuff like where he grew up and went to school, who his friends are."

I didn't understand why he needed so much information about my uncle's past, but Mateo's velvety baritone had a hypnotic quality. Captivated by its gentle depth, I found myself rambling on about my uncle being born and raised in a small Tennessee town. I'd heard a little about his childhood, just the few stories Mom told me, but I spilled everything from the way his brothers bullied him to his interest in acting. I shared that Buddy had attended the state university and dropped out after his sophomore year. He started dabbling in antiques while trying to make it in the theater, and then he met Norm.

"So, what kind of theater work did your uncle do?"

"What do you mean, what kind?" I could hear my voice scaling upward.

He stopped scribbling on the pad and looked at me. "Was it community theater? Off Broadway? Church plays?"

"Most definitely not church plays. Does it really matter? I mean, theater's theater, right?"

My interrogator held his pen over the notebook, waiting.

"Okay. He did some community theater, but his real talent was more in the line of impersonation."

"You mean stand-up comedy?"

"Not exactly." I sighed and glanced at the ceiling before answering. "Uncle Buddy was a female impersonator." I waited for a snarky comment, but he kept writing. "Early on, he did the usual celebrities, like Dolly Parton and Cher."

Memories of trying on wigs and feather boas from his closet and watching him transform himself into the most glamorous of creatures made me smile. I blinked away my father's reaction when he discovered how my uncle and I spent our time together.

"Eventually, he developed his own persona, Lady Lola, a feisty redhead with a Spanish accent." As always, something close to reverence came over me when I pictured Buddy's transformation. "She was the most beautiful woman I'd ever seen. But he started gaining weight, and there was a disagreement with the club's owner where he performed. The whole thing broke his heart."

"Do you remember any details? The name of the club or his boss there."

Pleased I detected no hint of shock or judgment in his tone, I continued. "The club was called Belles. It went out of business a few years ago. I can't say why Buddy stopped being Lady Lola. It happened about the time I started college, and I was pretty much into my own thing by then."

He asked a few more background questions I couldn't answer. Were there other men in Buddy's life, additional feuds with past acquaintances or on-stage rivals, family disputes? Then he turned to his antique business. Did I know of any financial problems or plans for expansion? Concerns with neighboring stores or landlords? I had nothing but the realization I'd been a self-absorbed jerk. All those dinners and lunches had obviously centered on me, and what little my uncle had shared, I forgot.

"See," he said, "you knew a lot more than you thought you did." He closed his notebook. "This is a great start."

When he smiled, I felt a warm tingling sensation travel from my chest to my face.

He stood and thanked me for my time.

"If you think of anything else or if you need me, call anytime." He handed me a business card: *Mateo Sullivan, Licensed Private Investigator,* with phone number and email address listed at the bottom.

He seemed so genuinely caring and concerned I almost told him about the rose and the disturbing message, but I didn't. Someone was probably just messing around. Or maybe Lance's new, now supposed ex-girlfriend Janelle was acting out. Whatever it was, it had nothing to do with my uncle. Besides, I couldn't put my trust in every gorgeous man I met. That's how I ended up crying in my pillow over Lance. No. I would handle my own problems.

I took the card and watched as Mateo walked out the door.

I returned to the nasty email, googled "black rose" and "Anatolian Peninsula" and found several articles about Turkish Halfeti roses. My sources claimed the roses, which represented mystery and death, were in danger of extinction. In the pictures, the flowers were ebony. However, the article admitted they were a crimson so dark they just looked black. Snopes debunked the whole concept of black roses growing naturally in Turkey or any place else, leaving me wondering why someone would center the message around a hoax.

Whoever sent it must have known I would verify the information. Maybe that was the point, to remind me that refusing to take anything at face value can have unpleasant effects. For example, by checking out the validity of the unwanted gift, I discovered Suitor most likely knew more about me than where I lived.

CHAPTER 6

I spent the rest of the morning reviewing Elsie's case, determined to find something to convince Hugh to go easy on her. Other than her frequent partying, the woman lived modestly. Yes, she received impressive payouts, but she didn't throw her money around. She drove an eleven-year-old Buick sedan, limited her travel to the locations where she staged her fall, and was still in the house she and her husband bought over forty years ago.

By 11:30, I was no closer to discovering mitigating circumstances for Elsie than when I started. Normally, I had a sandwich at my desk, but the appearance of the rose left me so rattled I forgot to pack a lunch. I've never been one of those women who hates to eat out alone, but it wasn't my first choice. Darla might have been a possibility, but her new boyfriend and their sex life were all she ever talked about. Nobody's ever called me a prude but hearing her go on and on about her lover's techniques reminded of my nonexistent sex life. So, she was out. Even if I wanted to ask Hugh, he never ate with any of us, and since my promotion, the underwriters had stopped asking me to join them. Just as I decided to pick up something and bring it back, the phone rang.

"Don't tell me you're too busy because I'm not taking no for an answer. You and I are having lunch together, my treat," Bethany said in her throaty alto.

Thirty minutes later, I was sitting near the bar at a fancy hamburger joint with my best friend. Even with her auburn hair pulled back into a high ponytail and no make-up, she was a head-turner. Three men in business suits ogled her on the way to our table, and the bartender personally delivered our water. Bethany seemed oblivious to the attention. She held a fry in her long slender fingers, swirled it in ketchup, and bit off the end. The barback dropped a glass, and an older gentleman almost fell off his chair. She chewed contentedly.

I filled her in on the rose and the email but not Buddy's problem. Bethany adored him, but it didn't seem right to share a story that wasn't mine to tell. Besides, one family member in trouble was drama enough. Two would have been tastelessly excessive.

She finished her fries and the last bite of her burger, then pushed her plate to the side.

"If I had to guess, I'd say it was that slut Lance was banging. But from what you've told me about her, she's not the subtle type. And can she even spell Anatolian?"

While I appreciated her loyal effort to portray my rival as a bimbo, I was compelled to set the record straight. "Actually, she's pretty smart, one of the firm's brightest associates, or so Lance says. But it doesn't make sense for her to be mad at me. He and I aren't together, and according to him, they're broken up anyway."

"What if she thinks you're the reason he dumped her? If he really did break it off. And I bet he expects you to take him back when you get over the whole *catching him with his pants down* thing." She held up a dainty digit, and the waiter appeared instantly. She asked him for a dessert menu and gave him her 100-watt smile. The poor boy turned scarlet before stumbling away.

"Well, I have no intention of ever letting him back into my life."

The waiter returned, and Bethany ordered bread pudding. I tried hard not to hold my friend's incredible metabolism against her, but it wasn't easy. No matter how much the girl ate, she never seemed to gain a pound. If I hadn't loved her, I would have hated her.

"Okay, okay. But I think you should clue your boss in. Better yet, why don't you tell your potential Latin lover?"

I made the mistake of describing Mateo Sullivan too enthusiastically.

"He's not my potential anything," I asserted. "I am swearing off men. It's obvious I have no judgment in that department, so I'm opting out."

"Mmm," she murmured. I was unsure if she was reacting to my vow of celibacy or the thick, gooey caramel concoction in front of her. "That settles it. If you're out of the dating game, you are most definitely coming to my Sensual Secrets party this Friday night."

I groaned inwardly. For over a year Bethany had been moonlighting from her real estate job, hosting what she referred to as "parties for independent, modern women." I called them sex toy extravaganzas and had avoided attending, claiming I was in a very satisfying relationship. The truth was it hadn't been as fulfilling as I implied, but the thought of sitting around with a bunch of horny ladies examining glow-in-the-dark dildos terrified me.

Before I came up with an excuse for skipping Friday's erotic escapade, the waiter brought the check. Bethany insisted on paying.

Outside, we handed the valet our vouchers and waited. Bethany's car arrived first.

"No excuses about the party. You need to loosen up a little. I'll send you the details." She gave me a hug, seeming not to notice the awestruck youth holding the door to her dark green Volvo. "I'm serious about telling someone about that creepy flower and the email. Probably somebody messing with you, but I'm afraid some weirdo wants to do a lot more than scare you."

. . .

On the way to my office, Darla handed me a message. It was from Dr. Johnston's attorney, requesting I give him a call. Hugh wasted no time filing the paperwork. I agreed to sign off as lead-investigator but had no intention of getting back to him. He might ask questions about how we came across the incriminating evidence against the doctor. Even if going through someone's trash wasn't illegal, it was patently undignified. And I had first-hand knowledge of how easily attorneys twisted things around to get what they wanted.

I had no good reason not to return to Elsie's case, so I dragged out her file. My investigation had found no criminal record outside her lively career in insurance fraud. She didn't even have an unpaid parking ticket. Meticulously punctual in submitting her bills, she had an excellent credit rating. Of course, most of her fiscal respectability was financed by profits from fraudulent claims, but at least she spent her ill-gotten gains responsibly.

I logged into Facebook and scrolled through the pages of Elsie's friends. If the woman had her own account, I hadn't been able to find it. And for some reason, this was especially frustrating. I needed more personal information on the elderly citizen I was about to send to jail. I located her address and discovered she lived about thirty-five minutes away.

I had the irresistible urge to see the woman in person. If I looked directly into those crinkly eyes and heard her speak, I could tell if I should continue my pleas for leniency. Of course, a face-to-face encounter wasn't the most efficient use of time and might not even be particularly sensible. But hadn't Hugh once said sometimes a good investigator has to go with her gut? If not, he should have. I grabbed my purse and headed out the door.

On the way, I realized I had a problem. I couldn't identify myself as the person investigating the fake injury claims. I would have to pretend to be someone a little old lady would invite into her home. That reminded me of Mom's story about being accosted by a woman asking for signatures on a petition to form a neighborhood watch. My mother considered the idea part of the suburban paranoia sweeping the country but signed anyway to get rid of the pesky visitor.

A few blocks from Elsie's, I pulled over and took a legal pad from my briefcase. I printed Edgewood Falls, the name of the subdivision, on top, then scribbled the names of five people, making each signature different from the others and all of them illegible. Satisfied with my work, I restarted the car.

The house was a seventies-style brick split-level. One of the shutters needed straightening, but the dark green trim was freshly painted, and the colorful stones on the pathway looked expensive, without being extravagant. Pots of bright red geraniums flanked the entrance way, and two white rocking chairs on the porch reminded me of Grandma Taylor. The sudden memory of my grandmother sent a flash of guilt through me. Was lying to Elsie to find out the truth any better than cheating insurance companies? Before I could reconsider, the door cracked a few inches.

"Were you planning on ringing the bell, young lady?" The woman peered at me while keeping the chain latch on. I recognized the pale blue eyes and strong chin. Rather than shrill with the irritation her words conveyed, they were crisp and precise.

With no backup plan, I put aside my guilty feelings and pasted on what I hoped was a confident, non-threatening smile.

"Yes, ma'am, I was." I held up my makeshift petition and introduced myself as Lucy Taylor, explaining I was helping to organize a neighborhood watch.

"First I've heard of it." She kept the latch in place. "Where's your house in the subdivision?"

Damn! I hadn't thought to make up an address. "Actually, I don't live here. I'm with a group that helps neighbors come together to ensure greater safety for everyone." I stopped myself from further elaboration, remembering something Hugh said about how expert liars keep things simple, avoiding going into details that might trip them up later.

Elsie unlatched the door and stood on the threshold, hand on hip. After a few seconds, she pronounced, "You don't look too dangerous."

I hesitated, unsure if the statement was an invitation or a judgment.

"Well, come on. We're letting the flies in." She stepped to the side, then led me through a small living room where the drapes were drawn. The dim lighting made it difficult to determine the condition of the furniture or the taste of the owner. We stopped in a surprisingly modern eat-in kitchen.

A full-size quilt in vibrant shades of blue—turquoise, teal, and cornflower—interwoven with pale peach and coral squares dominated the wall behind the dining table. I recognized it from Grandma Taylor's collection as a giant vintage star flower.

"That's amazing. My grandmother made one like it in, but it was yellow. I used to love to watch her turn those little scraps of fabric into works of art. She tried to teach me, but the needlework was too detailed for me. My uncle has several of hers in his store."

"That was a gift from an old friend."

"It's so beautiful. Does she ever sell her work?"

"No. Have a seat, dear. I'm brewing some tea. Would you like a cup?"

Despite the quick shift, I detected an undertone in her curt response to my question about selling the quilts. Instead of obsessing over what might be behind her tone, I took a moment to pat myself on the back for my well-executed deception. Then I remembered my belief in the sanctity of absolute truth, and elation morphed into shame.

"Tea would be lovely if it's not too much trouble."

"None at all."

Sunshine fell across the older woman's gently creased face. With her silvery-white hair pulled back in a low bun, her high cheekbones and firm jawline suggested the still attractive woman had been beautiful in her youth.

She set down the cups, then brought cream and sugar. "So, dear," she said while pouring our tea. "Why don't you tell me why you're really here?"

I dropped my spoon and watched it fall to the floor. "Sorry." I fumbled, reaching for the utensil while trying to process the implications of her question. "I'm here about the neighborhood watch petition." Hadn't history revealed that repeating a lie with conviction would eventually convince people it was the truth? I hoped so, as it was the only tactic I could think of.

She shook her head and smiled. "You seem like a sweet girl, but you are a terrible liar."

I pushed my chair back. "I'm sorry I bothered you. It's obvious you're not interested in my petition, so I'll just be—"

"I didn't say that." She held out her hand. "Why don't you let me see it while you finish your tea?"

Right. The paper with fake signatures I'd expected this cagey old woman to sign without inspecting for authenticity. I sighed and handed it over.

She pulled out a pair of jewel-encrusted reading glasses and scrutinized the list.

"The only name I recognize here is George Reynolds. Lovely man, wouldn't you agree?"

"Well, I, uh, actually," I stammered, trying to recall the made-up names I'd listed. "I have to confess. I didn't collect those signatures. One of my associates originally had this territory, but she came down with a stomach flu, so I stepped in." I had no idea where the inspiration for that story originated, but it sounded pretty good.

"Oh, my. That's awful. Intestinal viruses are the worst." She spoke in a sympathetic tone. At least, I hoped it was sympathy.

"It was terrible." I was on a roll now. "Fever, vomiting, diarrhea. Really nasty."

"Not much worse than a bad stomach virus, except possibly a drop-dead heart attack." Elsie looked at me over her glasses.

"I'm sorry. I don't understand."

She took a sip of tea before answering. "A coronary, dear. That's what killed poor George Reynolds last February. Tragic, but it seems he's made a remarkable recovery."

I considered making a run for the back door, but with my luck the dead bolt would be on, and I'd be cornered. Before I could decide whether to chance it, she began laughing.

"So back to that petition, Miss Taylor. That's right isn't, Taylor?" For a second, I forgot my newly acquired pseudonym and started to correct my hostess, but she didn't give me time. "Or was it Howard? Lucy Howard?"

A cooler liar might have been able to pull it off, but I was done. "I'm really sorry, Mrs. Erickson. I, uh ..." What had I been trying to do? There was no doubt the woman was guilty, so what had been the point in this ridiculous subterfuge?

"It's Elsie, dear." She took another sip of tea.

I swallowed hard. "Right. So, how did you, I, uh..."

"You mean how did I know you entered my house under false pretenses?"

Shit! Was that illegal? Probably wouldn't be a good idea to admit to anything. I reached for the petition on the tablet. If there was no evidence I'd been here, there was no crime.

She grabbed the incriminating document before I could snatch it. "No need to worry. I'm hardly in a position to be turning people in to the authorities. Don't trust them much anyway." She stood and picked up my cup. "Your tea's cold."

Elsie added hot tea from the pot. "We've established who you are, dear, but I don't understand why you're here." She nudged the sugar bowl closer to me and waited.

I took my time sifting the fine granules into the cup, trying to think of an answer. "I've asked myself the same question," I admitted. "Honestly, I have no idea. But how did you know who I was?"

"I saw your name on an insurance form in my lawyer's office. Apparently, you're the one who cracked my case."

I fought the desire to apologize.

"Don't feel bad, dear. It was excellent work, especially for someone so new to the investigative side of the business."

"But how could you tell I was her, I mean me?"

"I googled you. Also, LinkedIn is a reliable resource for discovering career information. I mean the whole idea is to expand that network, isn't it? And everyone wants to be congratulated on promotions and job changes. Then I stalked you a bit on Facebook. I'm your old college dorm mate, Emily Brown. You really should be more careful about accepting friend requests from people you don't remember."

I had no memory of adding Emily Brown to an ever-expanding list of strangers who, with the click of a button, were magically transformed into friends.

"You should be the investigator," I said.

"Interesting idea, but it's all an illusion. I mean, yes, I could identify you in a line up and I'm aware of your work and relationship status. Sorry about the breakup, dear. He sounds like a total ass. But I don't have a clue who the real Lucy is. I thought I did, but when you showed up here today, you threw me for a loop."

"You're definitely not the only one who got thrown for a loop." I smiled. "And, honestly, I'm clueless about the real Lucy, too. But that's not why I'm here. Mrs. Erickson, Elsie, what made you do it? Faking all those claims? Did you need the money because it doesn't look like you're living above your means? I didn't mean that like it sounds." I stopped, unsure how to continue.

"No offense taken. I've been doing some thinking about the same thing myself. Why I started my acting career, that is." She stared out the window for a few seconds before continuing.

"The first time, I really did slip and fall. It was a few months after Frank, my husband, died in the produce department at the grocery store. He didn't die in the produce department. That's where I fell. But that man did love searching for bargains. Anyway, I went down hard and landed on my tailbone, extremely embarrassing."

She twirled a strand of silver hair.

"All these people ran to help me. The stock boy was especially kind, saying over and over how there had been a malfunction in the fruit and vegetable mister and that he'd been on his way to get the mop when I fell. Then the manager came and insisted I sit still until the paramedics arrived. It's difficult to put into words, but I guess I felt significant, as if folks really saw me, cared about me."

I pictured Elsie as a recent widow, trying to get used to shopping for one.

"I know it sounds silly, pitiful really, but when those sweet boys with the stretcher showed up, I became Cleopatra borne by slaves. The ER people were delightful. I was a bit banged up, but they prescribed some excellent pain meds, and the whole thing was just so, well, exciting and somehow comforting. Like making a connection with people outside my own small world, even if it was only for a while."

A high-pitched mewling interrupted her story. I jumped at the sudden pressure against my legs.

"Doctor Jekyll," she greeted the fluffy gray cat nuzzling my ankles. "It must be lunchtime. Sorry, but if I don't feed him, he becomes Mr. Hyde, and, believe me, you do not want to see that."

I watched as she retrieved a can of Fancy Pants Feline food from the pantry. She apologized for the smell as she dished it into a mouse-shaped bowl. Then she returned to her seat.

"When I came home, the house seemed so empty, even with my little physician here." She reached down to pet Jekyll, who was devouring his meal. "The next day, I got this call from the insurance company. They assured me they would cover my emergency room expenses and wanted to discuss my claim."

The cat leaped into her lap, where she stroked his fur. "And the rest, I suppose you could say, is history. You see, it's never been about the money. Not at first, anyway. It was the delusion that I mattered. Of course, it wasn't real, nor did it last, but that didn't make it any less powerful. I must seem like such a foolish old woman to someone so young and pretty and smart."

After several long seconds of listening to nothing but the furry doctor's resonating purr, I said, "It doesn't sound foolish at all. I'm so sorry."

"Please, dear. It's not your fault." She reached over the cat to pat my hand. "You were only doing your job. I've got no one to blame but myself. Besides, if I go to jail, I won't have to worry about getting stuck in a nursing home. I will have to find someone to take care of Dr. Jekyll."

I winced. This charming old crook was most likely going to do time, and no matter what the woman said, it was my fault. My face seemed to reflect my concern.

"Don't look so glum, dear. My attorney's hopeful. Since I operated on my own, I seem to have avoided being part of a conspiracy which is a whole other level of unpleasantness. And I'm such a pitiful old lady." Her steady voice quivered as she shrank back into her chair. It was an impressive transformation.

She straightened her spine and stared at the quilt with a strange intensity. "I've managed to get my affairs in order except for a few loose ends I have to tie up before I hit the slammer." She turned to me with a cheerful smile. "Let's not dwell on me and my many felonies. I wouldn't want you to have to testify against me."

"They wouldn't ask me to do that, would they?" My distress must have been visible.

"Don't be sad, dear. I was only kidding. I doubt if we'll go to court. Now what about you? Tell me about that change in relationship status."

Something about Elsie, maybe it was her grandmotherly air or her nonjudgmental attitude, made it easy to tell her all about Lance: how we'd met, how I fell for him, and how he broke my heart. When I finally said goodbye, it occurred to me that I learned almost nothing new, not a thing that would help exonerate her. Instead, I'd revealed all my secrets and insecurities.

CHAPTER 7

It was late when I reached my car. It didn't make sense to fight traffic back to the office, so I checked in with Darla to tell her I'd be working from home.

The receptionist put me on hold, then told me Johnston's attorney had called again.

"And some woman claiming to work for the doctor insisted on leaving you a voice message. She was a first-class bitch. But I saved the best for last." After a dramatic pause, she added. "Hugh's super-stud friend Mateo Sullivan wants you to call him back. I think he likes you." She drew out *likes* into two syllables.

"Thank you," I said in my most professional tone. "Would you pass the attorney off to Hugh?"

"What about the lonesome cowboy? It'd be a shame making a hunk like that wait too long."

"Text me the number and put me through to voicemail, please." No need to explain to Darla that my relationship with Mateo Sullivan was strictly business.

The opening notes were shrill and nasal. "I'm leaving this message for Lucy Howard. This is Roberta Garrison, Dr. Johnston's nurse." Paper rattled in the background, as if she were reading from a prepared script. "The doctor is an honest, hardworking man who is completely innocent of any wrongdoing or medical malfeasance. I suggest you re-examine your so-called evidence and reconsider pursuing this matter." Definitely a canned speech. The rest, however, didn't sound rehearsed. "If I were you, Lucy Howard, I'd forget about what you think you found while trespassing on private property, and keep your damn mouth shut."

Hostility oozed through the phone. While the language was relatively mild, her sharp change in tone disturbed me. From stiff to snarling in a split-second, she conveyed a bitterness bordering on malice.

Shake it off, I told myself. But it wasn't easy for someone like me, who tried very hard never to offend anyone, to understand such direct hostility. Should I call the woman back and explain I didn't mean to cause trouble, that I was only doing my job?

Seriously? No. I would ignore her.

Remembering how bare the pantry was, I made a quick stop at the store. It wasn't until I pulled into the drive that I thought of the black rose. After examining the area around my front door for other unwanted gifts, I unloaded the groceries and checked the dead bolt. Finally, I nuked a lasagna-for-one entrée and muted the evening news while I ate.

The image of Elsie staring at the beautiful quilt on her wall haunted me. I'd sensed an undertone of sadness when she mentioned the person who'd given it to her. And maybe something more than melancholy.

"Now you're being ridiculous," I told myself. "She is a lonely old woman caught in a very bad situation."

And I was completely in the dark as to how to help her stay out of jail. For a moment, I considered checking for countries that didn't extradite.

"Jeeze, Lucy. Are you suggesting she break more laws?" I asked myself out loud and answered, "Of course not."

Besides, my new friend—that's how I thought of her— was far better at planning and executing criminal activities than I'd ever be.

Discouraged, I poured myself a glass of wine and took a long, hot bath. Afterward, I slipped into cotton pajamas, crawled into bed, and turned on the TV. I flipped through the channels before settling on a rerun of *Law & Order*. There was something comforting about the way my favorite detectives wrapped up difficult crimes in less than an hour. And, because I'd seen almost every episode at least twice, it didn't matter if I fell asleep before the bad guys got what was coming to them.

I woke to a different set of criminals and struggled up in bed, where I realized a sound had wakened me. At first, I thought it was the deep da-dong that signaled the beginning of a new program. I searched for the remote, then glanced at the clock. At 11:15 it wasn't the start of the show that disturbed my sleep.

I left the TV running, slid off the bed, and ran to the closet to get the baseball bat Dad insisted I keep close by. Moonlight from my bedroom window spilled into the hallway. Cheerful human humming streamed from the kitchen.

What kind of burglar does that? Hopefully, the slow and stupid kind.

I stayed inside my room, back against the wall, waiting for the intruder to come my way. My heart was beating so loudly I wasn't sure what the clanging sounds were. Then I recognized them as the rattling of pots and pans. My robber or rapist or murderer or all three seemed to be fixing a late-night snack before launching an attack on me.

The idea of some fiend chowing down at my table, ax or machete or knife at his side, pissed me off. By God, I would not be a doomed starlet rushing directly into the path of the crazed psychopath. No, I was going to get the hell out of Dodge. All I had to do was sneak into the living room, unlock the—oh, shit. The key to the bolt lock was in my purse, which was sitting on the kitchen counter.

Before I conjured up another plan, footsteps sounded on the hardwood and began thudding toward me, closer and closer. I assumed a batting stance and held my breath until the interloper was almost to my room. Then I leaped into the hall, swinging the bat as I landed. The weapon connected with a satisfying thud. When I looked at what I'd hit, I found myself standing over a figure, crumpled on the floor, clutching what appeared to be a large duffle bag.

Still brandishing my all-American weapon, I flipped on the hall light, stood over the stranger, and shouted, "Don't move!"

He crouched in front of me, covering his head with his arms. "Take whatever you want, but please don't hit me again."

Confused, I asked, "What the hell are you talking about? Take what *I* want?" The man on the floor wore a leather jacket and torn jeans. He curled up in a fetal position, making it impossible to determine anything else about him.

He sputtered, "I don't have much cash in my wallet, but my Visa's good for a couple of thousand."

"Why would I want your credit card? You're the one who broke in on me."

The man unfolded and scooted toward the wall, keeping the bag on his lap. He faced me, and I judged him to be in his late twenties. Something about his slender bearded face looked vaguely familiar, but I couldn't place it.

"I didn't break in. I live here. Not me exactly. It's my grandparents' property. They stay in the big house. I hang out here when they're gone."

"Oh, my God!" The picture on my landlord's mantle. I searched my memory for the name and finally came up with it. "You're Connor, Mr. and Mrs. Reynold's grandson." I reached toward him to help him up, but he scrambled sideways.

"Take it easy," I spoke to him the way I did to my uncle's Chihuahuas when trying to calm them. "I promise I won't hurt you."

"You already knocked the crap out of me. For a minute there, I couldn't even breathe. If you'd hit me instead of my bag, you might have broken a rib. Who are you anyway?"

"I didn't mean to hurt you. Well, I did, but I didn't know it was you."

He ran his fingers through his dirty-blonde hair and stared at me.

"What I meant to say is you don't live here anymore. I do." I extended my arm again. This time he took it. A little under six feet, my surprise guest had a hard-muscled runner's body and a ragged beard.

"I rent this apartment from your grandparents. Since they're usually in Florida, they wanted somebody on the premises. If they were expecting you to come back from Colorado, they didn't tell me."

"Yeah, well, I didn't expect to be coming back either, but it's like they say: shit happens." He shrugged, then winced. "You hit hard for a girl." Grinning, he held out his hand.

"Connor Reynolds at your service. Can we sit down and sort out what we're going to do?"

I detected no sinister or suspicious vibes, but I wasn't about to sit down for a chat. He had already begun walking to the living room.

"Wow," he said, flopping down on the sofa. "Everything's different." He leaned his head back, then grimaced. "This is one hard couch."

"It's a fainting sofa." I corrected him, feeling strangely defensive of my furniture. I sat in the chair across from him and hugged my chest, suddenly self-conscious about being in pajamas.

"Well, no offense, but it's not very comfortable. The place looks good, though. I'm not so good at decorating."

According to his grandparents, the only thing he was good at was partying.

He propped his feet on the ottoman Buddy had re-upholstered.

"Look, I'm sorry about the confusion, but I have a signed lease for another year, so you're going to have to find some other place to stay. What about spending the night at your grandparents' house?"

"They didn't exactly give me a key." He shook his head. "I had one, but they changed the locks after, uh, well, let's just leave it at that."

"Can't you stay with a friend?"

"I guess, but it's kind of late to call anyone. And I don't have a car."

"Wait. If you don't have a car, how did you get here?"

"I took a bus from Colorado—not my recommended mode of transportation—and hitched a ride here. Couldn't I just crash here for tonight? I'd ask to use your couch, I mean fainting couch, but I might never walk again after a night on this baby." He pounded the sofa with his fist.

"No worries," he said, apparently mistaking my look of irritation as concern over where he would sleep. "I have my sleeping bag. Is it okay if I take a quick shower?"

"No, it won't be okay." I stood for emphasis. "I'm not comfortable having a perfect stranger pile up on my floor. I sure as hell don't want you in my shower."

"I'm far from perfect," he said with what I imagined he considered a charming smile. "Hey, you know my grandparents. Isn't that almost as good as knowing me? And I promise you'll forget I'm here."

I seriously doubted that, but the Reynolds had been kind to me, and Connor seemed harmless, sort of like an outdoorsy Artful Dodger urging me to consider myself part of the family. Despite my misgivings, or maybe because I was too exhausted to carry on the debate, I agreed to let him stay one night as long as he promised to turn in his key and be gone the next morning.

"This is turning out a lot better than it started, right?"

I ignored him and walked to the kitchen. He followed, apologizing for leaving the eggs and milk sitting on the counter.

"I was getting ready to scramble up some breakfast when I saw your bag over there and realized I wasn't alone."

"You didn't think it was strange there was all this food around?" I put the ingredients away.

"I kind of hoped Grandma was keeping the place stocked for me in case I came back." He shrugged, then sighed as I closed the refrigerator.

"Whatever. I have to be at work early. You can wash up in the powder room. It's at the other end of the hall, but I guess you know that. Anyway, I'm going to bed." I turned off the lights, leaving him in the dark.

"Wait," he called. "I didn't even get your name."

"That's right," I said. "You didn't."

I closed and locked the door, then dragged the hope chest from the foot of the bed as a barricade. I didn't think Connor provided any genuine threat, but it didn't hurt to be cautious. Right, how cautious was it to let a stranger sleep in my home? But his grandparents were such nice people. Surely, I would be safe with their only grandson.

Still, I slept better keeping the baseball bat within reach.

· · ·

I awoke at 6:15 to the sound of clattering dishes and sat up in a panic before remembering my unwanted guest. Leaning back on the pillow, I puzzled over the fact I'd slept surprisingly well, considering I had allowed a possible ax-murderer to spend the night. Was my decision to permit Connor to stay another example of my stupid passivity or the first step to becoming a bolder, more assertive person? Either way, I needed to do something about the strange man rattling around in my kitchen, so I got out of bed, put on my robe, and shoved the chest aside.

The nutty smell of brewing coffee wafted over me.

"Hope I didn't wake you." Connor stood behind the counter. He'd combed back his wild hair and shaved off the scraggly beard, making it easier to see his dimples when he smiled. "Let me pour you a cup."

I should have been annoyed at the ease with which he had established himself in my kitchen, but he had a disarming air about him. I understood how hard it had been for his grandparents to ban him from their home.

"Thanks." I added milk and sugar and took a sip.

"I don't want to freak you out or anything, but I noticed something kind of strange when I brought in the paper." He pointed to the *Atlanta Journal* neatly folded on the table. My landlords had a subscription, and I was surprised at how much I enjoyed the feel of the thin, slightly grainy texture of the printed copy.

"Strange?" Had my sinister admirer returned?

"Yeah. Let me show you."

We walked to the side of the house where an aging willow tree's roots rippled the pavement. It was beginning to shed its leaves, but the tree was still full enough to provide a brilliant splash of gold in the early morning sun. I normally avoided parking too close to it, but last night I'd been distracted and ended up almost completely under its slender limbs.

"There." He pointed toward my car.

At first, all I saw were fairy-like dust motes dancing in the beam of light coming through the spotty foliage. Then I noticed a rope hanging from one of the branches. Struggling against my growing sense of unease, I forced myself to take a closer look and immediately recoiled. The end had been fashioned into a noose, and an object dangled from it. My throat constricted as I considered the dreadful possibilities, but when I narrowed my eyes, I surmised it was, and thankfully had always been, inanimate. It was only a doll.

I walked closer and discovered it was a brown-haired Barbie dressed in a navy-blue suit with a miniature briefcase attached to her skinny little fingers: Business Barbie. But instead of heading to an important meeting, this career woman was at the end of a thin rope with her head twisted at a frightening angle.

"My God," I whispered, staring into the vacant green eyes of the plastic victim. Someone had placed a tiny, silver-duct tape X over Barbie's full-lipped smile.

"I know," Connor said. "Weird, right?"

Weird didn't begin to describe it. Not only had they gone to the trouble of placing poor Barbie directly over my car, but that person had managed to find a doll which, except for the unnaturally small waist and ridiculously inflated chest, strongly resembled me, down to the one suit I owned.

"Have you pissed somebody off lately?"

In the not-so-distant past, the answer to that question would have been a quick no because I wasn't the kind of person who made enemies. I was not the least bit threatening or hadn't been until I threw Chinese food in Lance's face. But there had been no lasting damage, and my ex had never struck me as the doll-for-revenge type. And, if he'd been serious about getting back together, he didn't consider me an enemy. But maybe Janelle did. If she knew Lance had approached me about reconciling, it was possible she'd lashed out.

That wouldn't, however, explain the significance of the tape over Barbie's lips. That seemed to invoke a warning for me to keep my mouth shut, which suggested another group of potential enemies: clients who were unhappy about how I had handled their claims. Elsie came to mind, but I dismissed her immediately. The older woman accepted the blame for her current situation, and regardless of how spry she was, I couldn't imagine her standing on my car or scaling the willow. I remembered the phone calls from Dr. Johnston's lawyer and wondered if the greedy physician could be behind both the rose and the doll.

And there was my uncle's problem. I didn't accept for a single minute that Buddy had shot Al Darrow, but somebody had and that person might not appreciate me investigating the murder.

"You okay?" Connor asked.

"I'm fine. As for enemies, not really. It's probably some kids playing a prank." That wouldn't explain the black rose or the creepy email, but there was no reason to share my suspicions with this affable stranger.

A gusty breeze sent Barbie swaying, her fluffy-haired head still cocked at that hideously unnatural angle, cone-shaped breasts jutting up to the sky.

"You might want to reconsider that." He stared at the tragic figure and sighed. "Should we call the police or something?"

"I'm not sure what they'd do. I mean, it's not exactly a crime to hang a doll."

"I guess you're right, but, man, this isn't any old doll. It's Barbie. She's an American icon."

The sincerity of his tone surprised me. Obviously, Connor was taking this act as a personal affront.

"Icon or not, this is getting on my last nerve." The idea of someone creeping around my house as I lay inside sleeping horrified me. Thankfully, my professional instincts kicked in, and I asked him to wait while I got my camera.

When I returned, he stood in the exact spot where I'd left him, staring mournfully at the defaced figure. I took several shots from different angles, and we raided the caretaker's shed in search of something to use to free poor Barbie. We found a ladder and a pair of pruning shears. I instructed Connor to clip close enough to keep the rope intact in case it revealed something about the person who used it. I steadied the ladder while he climbed it and snipped, keeping the noose attached, bringing the branch crashing onto the hood of my car.

"Uh oh!" he exclaimed. "Hope that didn't scratch the paint." He removed the tangled mess and began working to separate doll from nature.

"Wait. I've got an old sheet. Let's wrap the whole thing up and stick it in my trunk, so I can show it to my boss."

Once again, he waited until I returned. Then he followed my instructions, and we went back inside. I finished my coffee and declined his offer of scrambled eggs but gave him permission to make some for himself. The notion of transporting the twisted little mannequin in my trunk had taken away my appetite. The incident also made me less adamant about evicting my guest so quickly. It wouldn't hurt to have someone else around during the day in case the prankster came back—unless Connor was the one who'd executed the doll. But he didn't seem capable of complex thinking. He could have been a very good actor, but there was something about his voice, a rhythmic serenity, that gave me the impression he was genuine. Plus, it was Barbie.

"About those friends you called," I began, considering asking him to stay another night.

"No worries," he said. "I'll be out of here before lunch." He poured more coffee for himself. "Dinner at the latest."

As I was leaving the kitchen, I remembered the rose and decided I would show it to Hugh along with the doll. I removed it from the refrigerator and put it in my briefcase before heading to my room to shower and dress. In less than forty-five minutes, I was out the door.

Connor followed. "You know, it might not be a bad idea for you to ask Grandpa to install a security system. Or get a dog. Yeah, that's it. A big dog. There are some pretty crazy people out there."

His words echoed Bethany's sentiments, and I felt a surge of anger as I sat behind the wheel. It seemed I was undergoing a forced transformation from my previously easy-going, non-confrontational self into a different person. The kind somebody considered enough of a threat to send messages intended not only to frighten me but to shut me up. I only wished I knew what it was I shouldn't be saying.

CHAPTER 8

By the time I reached the office, I was in an increasing state of confusion. Clearly, I had stepped into something, but what? I parked in my usual spot, grabbed my things, and hopped from the car immediately stumbling into Mateo's broad chest.

"Didn't mean to scare you," he said, holding onto my arm until I regained my balance.

When I backed away from him, the contrast between the cool air and his warm body made me dizzy. The morning sunlight formed a hazy halo around the cowboy hat partially obscuring his face.

"Oh, crap!" I exclaimed, then put my hand over my mouth. "I forgot all about you."

"You sure know how to make a guy feel special."

"I didn't mean I forgot about *you*. I forgot about calling you. Yesterday was so crazy. I tried to fool this little old lady, and she totally saw right through me. And I fell asleep watching TV. Then this man showed up at my house in the middle of the night, and I couldn't get rid of him. And this morning—"

"Whoa," he said. "No worries. I only wanted to see if you were free for lunch today."

Breathless from the frantic account of the previous day and by my proximity to him, I leaned against the car door.

"I have some information about your uncle, but we can make an appointment any time. Bring that guy you couldn't get rid of last night if you want."

"Him? He's practically a stranger who I let stay over." *Oh God.* "That didn't come out right. He used to live in my apartment, but not when it was *my* apartment." I sighed. "It's a long story, but no. Not no for lunch, but no I won't be bringing him with me." *What the hell was wrong with me?* "What I meant to say is lunch works."

"Good." He moved out of the direct light of the sun, and I noticed a tiny cut on his chin. "Why don't I pick you up around one?"

"Yes. One o'clock. I'll be here. Well, not here exactly. Just have the receptionist buzz me if I'm not already there. But I should be there, at the reception area, that is." *Shut up, Lucy. Shut. Up.*

"Got it," he said, tipping his hat. "You'll be there or somewhere."

As he walked away, I stole a quick glance at him before checking my watch. Only 8:05, a very long time until 1:00.

Inside the empty office building, I flipped on the lights and locked the door behind me. Alone in a space filled with shadowy corners and dark places made me realize how vulnerable I was. The cargo in my trunk contributed to my growing paranoia and the implied threat. According to the adage, however, it wasn't paranoia if someone really was out to get you.

I sprinted to the breakroom and started a pot of coffee. While I waited for it to brew, I picked a doughnut from yesterday's box, scraped the chocolate icing off with my teeth, and tossed the rest in the trash.

The familiar echo of dangerously high heels clicking on the hardwood floors announced Darla's arrival.

"You would not believe the night I had." She headed straight for the coffee. "I am so exhausted I can barely hold my head up." She took a cup from the counter before adding, "But it was totally worth it. If you know what I mean."

Thanks to numerous narratives on the insatiability of her latest boyfriend, I was painfully aware of what she was talking about and didn't plan to stick around for details. I grabbed my coffee, murmured something about having to check email, and fled to my office.

I sat behind my desk and stared at the blank computer screen. Although I hadn't received any additional communication from Suitor, the idea of seeing his name pop up made me reluctant to continue.

Determined not to let the actions of some nut make mundane chores frightening, I entered my password, scrolled through the inbox, and answered the most pressing messages. I reached for a client file just as my phone buzzed: a text from Bethany.

Don't forget tonight. Time of your sexual liberation is 6:30, no excuses.

My friend included a winking smiley face and an eggplant emoji.

Crap! Bethany's Sensual Secrets party. It looked as if there was no way to get out of attending the event. On the bright side, maybe looking at sex toys would take my mind off all the weird things that had been going on in my life. It would also give Connor more time to clear out of my place before I got home. And, although I hated to admit it, I was more than a little curious about parties for "independent women."

What exactly does an independent woman look like, I wondered, and would I ever be one? Until my break-up with Lance, the concept of being my own person was alien to me and probably would have continued to be if I hadn't had literally come face-to-face with his infidelity.

I set my phone aside and focused on clearing up a few pending claims, then picked up Elsie's file. Was it possible the sweet little old woman might go to prison? The image of her in an ill-fitting orange jumpsuit facing off with a tattoo-laden inmate with biceps like grapefruit turned my stomach. There was nothing left to do other than advocate for leniency, and, so far, I hadn't seen Hugh's lenient side.

The phone buzzed. It was Darla saying there was a woman on the line demanding to speak to Lucy Howard.

"She won't tell me who she is. Just keeps insisting she has to talk to you right away."

Normally, I would have told her to get rid of the anonymous caller. But today I welcomed the distraction and agreed to take the call.

"Lucy Howard," I began. "How may I help you?"

"It's not how you can help me." The voice was low and husky, not shrill like Roberta's. Possibly a heavy smoker or a hay fever victim. "It's how I can help you."

"Okay, but first, please tell me who's calling."

"Who I am isn't important. What's important is what you're missing."

"What am I missing where?"

"Johnston's more than a small-time crook trying to make a quick buck. Much more."

She hung up.

"Who are you, lady? And what the hell are you talking about?" I asked the dial tone.

I rang Hugh's office, but there was no answer. So, I turned to my computer and pulled up Johnston's information. The bank statement had been scanned, mustard stain and all. I ran my finger down the list of deposits. Most aligned exactly with checks issued from various insurance firms including Idleman's. But there were four entries for $8,200, four more for $4,999, and ten for $2,500. The forensic accountant made a notation questioning these payments, but since they didn't directly involve the agency's investigation, no one followed up on them.

I printed a copy of the ledger sheet and highlighted the numbers in question, trying to decide what the repetition of these odd amounts meant.

I was still looking over the information when Darla called to announce Mateo Sullivan was in the lobby. I grabbed my purse and sweater, then stopped by the ladies' room to check myself out in the mirror. My curls were out of control. I removed a clip from my bag and pulled my hair away from my face. Other than dabbing on concealer, there wasn't much I could do about my dark circles. A touch of blush and lipstick made me look less washed out.

"What's the big deal?" I spoke to my reflection. "You swore off men, so what difference does it make, anyway?" Despite my total lack of concern regarding his impression of me, I fluffed my hair and undid my top button before exiting the restroom.

Mateo sat on the edge of a fake leather chair. Yesterday in my office I'd been too upset about the strangely threatening email to completely appreciate my visitor. And this morning, my view had been partially obscured by the sun. Now, even the unforgiving fluorescent lights failed to highlight any noticeable flaws. He had left his hat behind and brushed back his ebony hair. When I entered the reception area, he stood and gave me a wide smile.

"I appreciate your coming to pick me up. I hope it wasn't out of your way. I mean, I could have met you. Actually, I can still follow you in my car if that's easier." *For God's sake, stop babbling.*

Thankfully, he interrupted me. "It's no problem. I'm not in any kind of hurry."

"Well, uh, okay then." I could feel myself blushing for absolutely no reason, unless maybe it was the sudden image of what an unhurried Mateo might be like in a very different setting.

I turned to tell Darla I was leaving for lunch. The receptionist wiggled her eyebrows and winked before saying, "Hugh called. His car's in the shop. The dealer's dropping him off. He needs to borrow yours."

Although I bristled at the man's high-handedness, it seemed petty to refuse, so I dug out my keys from my purse and handed them to Darla.

Mateo led me to a late model black Honda Accord and held the passenger door for me.

"At the risk of being a walking stereotype, are you up for Mexican?" He pulled away from the curb and eased onto the highway. "I know a great place not too far from here. They have burgers and salads, too, if you're not into burritos."

"I love Mexican."

"Me, too, but I was raised on a combination of tortillas and corned beef and cabbage. Dad's fourth generation O'Sullivan from the Old Country. Somehow, the O got dropped. My dear sweet Granny's still pissed about it, but not as much as she is about my father marrying a Mexican. She's almost ninety now and can't remember where she put her glasses. But she never forgets how he contaminated the family line."

The car in front of us stopped short, and Mateo hit his brakes and muttered something under his breath in Spanish.

"Sorry about that."

"Don't worry about it. I studied French. Was your mother born here?"

"No, she came to the States when she was a baby. Her grandfather was from central Mexico. He got out before the drug lords took over and sent for his family as soon as he could. None of Mom's side was too thrilled about her marrying a Mick from Boston, either. Equal opportunity immigrant bias." He eased into traffic before adding, "Makes for some pretty awkward holiday dinners."

I shuddered at the memory of the last Thanksgiving we'd spent at Grandma Howard's. Dad's ultra-conservative mother sat across from Buddy and Norm and refused to pass the turkey and mashed potatoes. Yes, I was no stranger to difficult family matters but imagined his were even more complicated.

Bob Seger's gravelly voice drifted from the radio, distracting me from thoughts of narrow-minded relatives.

Nothing left to burn and nothing left to prove.

I went for the volume button at the same time he did. His fingers lingered briefly on mine.

"This is one of my dad's favorites," I said. "He passed on his love of classic rock to me."

"Same here, only it was my Uncle Paddy. He took me to my first concert; it was Seger. He told me Bob's Irish ancestry puts the melancholy in his ballads. I saw him the last time he was in town."

"At the Arena? Oh my god. I was there, too. He was fantastic." I wanted to ask if he'd taken his girlfriend to the show. Instead, I asked, "How long have you known Hugh?"

"He was a partner in the firm I worked for after I left the Army. I stayed there about three years until I decided to go out on my own. That's been a little over two years. We keep in touch, get together for a drink every now and then."

He turned into a partially deserted strip mall. "Here it is. Not much to look at, but the food's authentic."

The restaurant, El Encanto, The Charm, was tucked in the corner with only a few cars parked nearby.

"We're missing most of the lunch crowd," he explained, shutting off the engine. "Otherwise, it would be packed."

He was at my side before I could undo the seat belt. I slipped into my sweater and stepped from the car,

We walked through the entrance with its inlay of colorful tiles bordered in a bright blue. I breathed in the warm burst of spices. A petite young woman with golden brown skin and dark shoulder-length hair ran out from behind the register to Mateo and wrapped her arms around him.

I couldn't judge the level of intimacy between the pair and waited impatiently for the embrace to end. When it did, he gave her a kiss on the cheek.

"Lucy, this is my cousin Sofia."

"So glad to meet you," the young woman said.

She offered me the same enthusiastic greeting she'd given Mateo. I returned her hug and pretended my surge of relief from learning they were related meant nothing. After all, hadn't I vowed to avoid getting back into a relationship since I had such crappy judgment regarding men?

She led us to a booth near the back. "I reserved your favorite table," she said. She gave me a menu, then held up her hand to Mateo. "I've got it; guacamole first, questions later."

He nodded, and she walked away.

"Your cousin's very sweet."

"She's a good kid." He smiled. "Real smart, too. She had a couple of scholarship offers for out-of-state schools, but she stayed local to help my aunt and uncle with the restaurant."

I thought of my own decision to remain at home instead of going up north to my dream school. But my motivation had been more about lack of commitment than selflessness.

"Any recommendations?"

"I always order number fifteen, the burrito combo. That's why she didn't bother giving me a menu. But you can't go wrong here."

I tried to decide if I should get what I wanted, the giant quesadilla platter, or go with a more "first date" choice, something like the avocado salad. How many times had I gone home hungry after dinner with some guy I didn't even care about impressing? My companion this afternoon wasn't exactly in the first date category. But he didn't fall into the *uninterested in impressing* bracket either.

When she returned with water, chips, and dip, I decided he didn't seem to be the type of guy who would judge me for having a healthy appetite and ordered the quesadilla. The young woman nodded her approval. I felt vindicated and asked for a Dos Equis. Mateo raised his eyebrows and followed suit.

"If you like guacamole, this is about as good as it gets." He slid the bowl closer to me. "Careful, though. It has a little kick."

I scooped up a generous helping. The combination of fresh avocado, tomatoes, and onion blended with seasoning spicy enough to get my attention, but not so hot it made my nose run, was the best I'd tasted.

"It's perfect," I said, reaching for another chip. "Sorry, it's your turn."

He grinned before digging in. "Don't apologize. I like a woman who goes after what she wants."

My cheeks grew warmer. At that moment, Sofia appeared with our beer. "Food's coming soon."

He held up his glass and said, "Let's drink to Hugh for introducing us."

I clinked the heavy mug against his and repeated, "To Hugh," wondering if Mateo was being polite or really was grateful to my boss. Then I remembered the reason for the meeting.

"I'm guessing you found out something not so great about my uncle."

"Not exactly."

Sofia came with a steaming platter of food. "Enjoy," she said and walked away.

I cut a piece of quesadilla and took a bite. "Oh. My. God."

After stuffing our faces for a few minutes, Mateo put his fork down.

"A friend of mine who's on the force said Darrow died from a single shot to the chest. Then I did some digging in his past. The only thing that came up on Alistair involved a case of fraud. Seems some poor old lady had a Confederate uniform her great, great something or other had worn in the *War of Northern Aggression*, her exact words from the complaint. Darrow told her it was fake and offered to donate it to a local theater group for her. He turned around and sold it for over $20,000. One of her grandkids found out and came after him, but the old woman passed before they settled, and the family dropped the matter. There were a few more incidents of claims against Darrow but nothing bad enough for someone to want to kill him."

"I can't see how any of that involves Uncle Buddy."

"I didn't think so either, but then I got a hit on Darrow's nephew. It seems the Feds are involved. They're looking at Virgil for passing off fake antiques." He washed down his food with the rest of his beer and motioned for a refill. I shook my head when she asked if I wanted another.

"Why would they care?"

"Because he's been using the internet and the mail to advertise and ship the fakes with the specific intent to commit fraud. That makes it a federal crime."

Uncle Buddy had once explained how passionate some Civil War re-enactors were about their hobby. More like a vocation, he said. They were easy prey for unscrupulous dealers. He showed me the Centennial Anniversary of the Civil War 1961 website and told me that lots of crooked sellers passed off the swag as original artifacts. Others were involved in manufacturing outright fakes. He explained they even created legends around pieces to draw in unsuspecting buyers.

Sofia returned with the beer, and he asked for the check.

"Seriously?" she responded, then turned to me. "He knows my parents would kill me if I let family pay for food. Of course, that doesn't apply to tipping." She took his plate, then looked at mine with a concerned expression. "You didn't like it?"

"I liked it very much. I just sort of lost my appetite."

"My cousin does that to women. I'll box it up for you."

"I'll remember that remark when I leave the tip," he called after her.

While he finished his beer, I shredded my napkin, wrestling with the idea that Buddy, whom I'd always considered one of the most honest, dependable people I knew, might be connected to some kind of conspiracy with the sleazy Darrow men. The thought sickened me, but I had to ask, "Do you think my uncle is involved?"

He shook his head. "I didn't find anything directly linking Buddy to Virgil or Al. But I managed to get a list of some of Darrow's clients. When I compared it to the one Norm gave me, one name stood out: Burton Prescott. He must be obsessed with Civil War collectibles because he's bought everything from sabers to buttons from Darrow and a gold coin from Buddy. The coin was authentic. The other stuff, not so much. Prescott filed complaints with anybody who'd listen. When he mentioned the online advertising, that got the attention of the Feds."

"But Buddy's not involved, right? The gold coin checked out, so there's no complaint against him."

"That's where it gets a little fuzzy. Prescott thought your uncle might know something about the fake merchandise but didn't get specific."

Sofia returned with my boxed-up quesadilla, and Mateo put a twenty-dollar bill on the table before the cousins exchanged a good-bye embrace.

"I hope I'll see you again soon," she said to me as we left.

"Me, too," he interjected and smiled.

On the way back to the office, neither of us spoke for several minutes. I was having trouble understanding the implications of the report. Why would Prescott think Buddy was involved?

"I saw the police file. There were cameras all over the place, but none of them were on. They're looking at some of the neighboring businesses, hoping something shows up, which means they'll probably find video of your uncle coming into the store. But there's no way for them to know what went on inside. It might be a good idea for him to go in voluntarily and tell his side of the story before they identify him."

The thought of poor Buddy sweating under hot, bright lights while some burly officer gave him the third degree made me cringe.

"I know you're right, but my uncle's not going to be happy when I bring up the cops. For some reason, he's always been uncomfortable around authority figures. It might have something to do with how he got bullied as a kid and how his teachers and parents either ignored it or told him to man up."

"Even if he wasn't reluctant, it would be better for him not to go alone," he said. "He should get a lawyer and let him do most of the talking."

"An attorney?" Weren't they for guilty people? It certainly seemed like it on almost every crime show I watched. And the only one I knew was Lance. No way in hell would I ask for his help.

Mateo turned off the main road and parked next to my Jetta, where Hugh was standing, staring into the trunk. When he saw us, he reached in and pulled out the branch with poor Barbie dangling by her long neck.

In an unusually soft voice that worried me more than his regular gruff one, he asked, "What in the name of God is this?"

CHAPTER 9

My lunch with Mateo and his unsettling revelations about Darrow made me forget about the rose and doll. It never occurred to me Hugh might pop my trunk.

"I was going to tell you about it." I pushed the small tree limb aside. "You're the one who was late to work and demanded to use my car. Why were you snooping around in the first place?" My boss enjoyed keeping me on the defensive, but this time he wouldn't be in control. "We need to talk."

I turned to Mateo. "Would you mind coming, too?"

Hugh carried the branch in front of him like a divining rod as we walked past Darla, who squinted at us over her glasses. He put Barbie on the table in my office while I removed the rose from my briefcase.

"Jesus," he growled. "What kind of flower from hell is that?" He picked up the baggie and lifted it to the light. Mateo joined him, and together they studied the unnatural blossom while I printed out the email from Suitor.

Hugh sat across from me while I explained how the rose ended up on my doorstep. Then I handed him the printout. Still standing, Mateo examined the branch from different angles. I told them about the online hoax and wrapped up with the picture of Business-Woman Barbie at the wrong end of the rope. I skipped Connor's appearance to avoid the inevitable lecture from Hugh.

Mateo stared at the photo, and Hugh read Suitor's message aloud. Then Mateo spoke.

"This could be related to your uncle's predicament. Someone's trying to scare you away from finding out what's going on."

"I suppose it's possible, but whoever delivered the rose did it while I was at Buddy's. There's no way he could know what he told me."

"Possibly, they saw your uncle when he stopped by the office," Hugh suggested. "If he's involved in something shady, it makes sense he would go to you for help. We should check to see if somebody's been following Buddy."

I remembered the phone call urging me to reexamine Johnston's file. My role in the doctor's case was minor, but it was possible there might be a direct connection between the bizarre threats and him. I explained about my mystery caller and the discrepancies I discovered.

"It sounds as if he was making more money than a few low-end surgeries would pay," my boss said. "But who would gain from tipping you off? I'll check with accounting and get back to you."

"Whoever's behind this stuff doesn't seem too dangerous. I mean, seriously, a flower and a doll? Pretty lame." *And a little twisted.*

"Lame or not, if some shit-for-brains is hanging around your place leaving these calling cards, it won't hurt to keep an eye out. Can you handle the follow-up?"

He looked at Mateo, who nodded. "No problem."

"I'm going to get someone to dig deeper into Johnston's mystery deposits and spend some time tailing your uncle." Hugh pushed himself to his feet and left.

Buddy would be furious if he knew my boss was keeping tabs on him, but it gave me comfort.

Mateo stood. "I'll follow some leads to see if I can find out if there's a connection to Prescott. And I want to run by your place to make sure there are no more surprises. Are you going straight home after work?"

Was he asking me out or just planning a drive-by? It didn't matter since I would be attending a Sensual Secrets party, something that would remain my secret.

"I promised a girlfriend I'd stop by, but I shouldn't be too late."

"It might be a good idea if I watched your place tonight. Could you stay at your friend's, you know, in case there's trouble at your apartment?"

So, not asking me out.

I tried to picture the aftermath of a sex toy party at Bethany's and it wasn't pretty. According to my friend, heavy drinking played a key role in loosening up her guests to increase both the volume and naughtiness levels of their orders. The over-imbibing often resulted in wanton dancing and drunken sexting.

"Don't worry about me. If I see or hear anything strange, I can call 911."

"It's up to you, but I'm still going to come by later. I'll text when I'm in the area."

My sense of relief surprised me.

"Thanks for lunch and everything. I understand you're returning a favor, but I wish you'd let me pay you something."

"That's right. I do owe your boss, so I couldn't take your money even if I wanted to, which I don't. Be careful, okay?"

He touched my shoulder and was gone.

The rest of the day was uneventful, giving me plenty of time to wonder how his hands might feel on the rest of my body.

. . .

It was almost six when I wrapped up. The support staff left at five, and Hugh hadn't returned from his meeting with the forensic accountant but had left a voicemail saying he might be on to what the doctor was hiding. The reception area lights were off, and the dusky fall twilight spewed shadows on the pavement, encouraging me to quicken my pace.

I walked the short distance to my car underneath a light that wouldn't reach full capacity for another ten or fifteen minutes. When I reached for the handle, a gloved hand descended on mine. A thick fragrance—heavy vanilla with a touch of musk—permeated the air. I pivoted and found myself face to face with the woman I'd last seen attempting to cover her breasts. Janelle.

"We have to talk," she said, sandwiching me between her and the car.

I shook off her hand. "I have no interest in discussing anything with you."

She stared at me through dark, thick lashes. "Well, you should because there are things I have to tell you about Lance." She spoke with a curious lack of inflection.

"Are you kidding me? Why would I be interested in anything you have to say about my former boyfriend?"

She tossed her wild mane over her shoulder. "Lance Crawford isn't the man you thought he was. And he may be a lot worse than a two-timing asshole."

More spirited this time, but I couldn't decipher her meaning. Was my ex's ex-girlfriend trying to say Lance had cheated on her, too? Would this make him a two-timer or a three-timer? Math had never been my subject. And as much as I might enjoy Janelle discovering she wasn't the only filly in the stable, I didn't want to talk to the woman. But my former rival showed no sign of leaving.

"Just listen to me for a minute, please."

I sighed. "Okay, but sixty seconds is all I've got. I'm due at a friend's house at 6:30."

"Great," she said, surveying the area as she spoke. "But can we sit in your car? I don't want anyone to see us together."

I glanced around the near-empty lot, a little nervous at her implication someone might be watching. I shook it off and motioned for her to go to the passenger side, where I faced the woman who had upturned my life.

"I imagine you think I'm a terrible person, but if I'd had any idea he was in a serious relationship, I would have never gotten involved with the creep."

"Stop right there. You're saying you were unaware we were a couple? We were together for almost a year." I hesitated. Yes, we had been dating for at least eleven months, but other than the Christmas party and one client dinner, when had I been around any of his associates at the firm? I had to show the security guard my id, and the first time I met Janelle was when I caught her sliding off my boyfriend's lap.

"Please believe me. It wasn't until I saw the look on your face that night in the office that I realized what was going on. That's why I dumped that miserable, lying bastard as soon as he stepped back into the room wearing all that lo mein. Nice job, by the way." She snorted a chuckle that sounded genuine.

But her revelation about being the one to end the relationship cut our moment of shared amusement short.

"*You* ended it with Lance?"

"Yes. Oh." She paused and cleared her throat softly. "Did he tell you he broke up with me?"

So, his pitch to get back together wasn't part of his desire to be some sort of better man, the kind who wouldn't cheat on the woman who loved him. It was more his deceitful attempt to save face, to show the world what a great catch he was, especially for someone like me.

She touched my arm, and I shrugged off her perfectly manicured hand. The only thing worse than being a pathetic loser was having the other woman pity you for being one. But she seemed sincere, not condescending. Had she been just as taken in by Lance as I had? We were smart, attractive women who didn't deserve to be pitted against one another in competition for a lowlife like him. But he was a prime, masculine specimen with money and charm, who also happened to be a first-class manipulator and jerk.

"Of course, he told you that," Janelle asserted. "He'd never admit he got dumped. Technically, twice, I guess, since I'm pretty sure covering his head with hot noodles wasn't your way of saying you wanted him back."

The image of my ex, standing in front of me with slippery strands of pasta framing his handsome face came to me, and I laughed. My shift in mood startled Janelle at first, but she quickly caught on. We shared in one of Lance's most humiliating moments and deserved to enjoy it.

After a few seconds of mirth, I took a deep breath.

"I guess we're both better off with the cheating bastard out of our lives. At least I am, but wait. Didn't you say you had something important to share with me?"

No longer smiling, she nodded. "Right, but you have to promise you won't tell. I could lose my job if it came out I said something to you."

I couldn't imagine how any of the firm's business might concern me but promised to keep her secret.

She scrunched down in her seat. "Usually, Lance and are on the same cases. Since he's a partner, I got most of the grunt work, but I didn't mind so much. Not while we were, uh, together."

I winced at the image of the type of grunt work she performed for her boss.

"I was up on everything he was working on, or thought I was. But I kept getting these bad vibes from him, like he was hiding something from me. And then—"

A car horn sounded in the distance, and she jolted upright.

"Let's go someplace less public." She fidgeted with the strap of her purse.

The lot was still empty except for two cars parked by the coffee shop, but Janelle's nervousness was contagious. Then I remembered the Sensual Secrets party and checked my watch: 6:28.

"Crap! I'm supposed to be at a friend's house by 6:30."

Bethany was going to be super pissed at me for being late, but I had to hear what Janelle had to say. Maybe I could bring her with me. The delight of an additional customer would temper her anger, and I would have time to continue the discussion about my ex.

"Why don't you come with me? It's a kind of, uh, a girl thing, and I know my friend wouldn't mind. We can talk there. That way if anyone is watching, it'll look like we're just hanging out." With a bunch of sex-starved women who most likely have no boundaries, but I didn't mention that.

She agreed, almost too quickly. I gave her the address, and we left in separate cars. On the short drive to Bethany's, I tried to make sense of the way my life had gone from being dependably dull to downright dramatic: Buddy's involvement in a murder investigation, that anonymous tip, the ominous email, and sinister gifts. All while I was recovering from the loss of my one true love and avoiding falling in lust with a sexy, Irish-Latino PI. And now I was headed to a sex toy party with the woman who'd stolen my boyfriend.

. . .

"We'll start the same way most of us prefer in the bedroom, slow and easy." Bethany held up a hot pink tube of Get Glowing warming gel. My cheeks burned.

Sitting beside Janelle, who had taken to the group like a duck in heat—mixed metaphor, but it suited the situation—I squirmed every time our hostess squirted a blob of goo into the waiting hands of a fellow party goer.

When she squeezed it into my palm, I stared at the wriggling pink substance and forgot what I was supposed to do with it.

"Lucy, don't make a fist." Bethany raised her arched eyebrows and commanded, "For God's sake, relax." Her normally sultry voice turned shrill. I loosened my grip, and she smiled her approval. "That's right. All warm and tingly, isn't it?"

To me, it was more a slimy puddle, but I wasn't about to risk sending her into a tizzy. "It's definitely warm, and, oh yeah, extremely tingly."

She rolled her eyes and returned to her spot in the circle to address the group. "Now, imagine that warmth spreading all over your body." She grinned and looked at me.

Please, God, no. Don't let her call on—

"You can imagine that, can't you, Lucy?"

Bethany, still acting miffed at me for springing Janelle on her, speared me with the direct question. It wasn't bringing Lance's hussy to the party that irked her. She just hated it when I managed to shock her. Shocking people was Bethany's thing.

I picked at a loose thread on my sweater and nodded. I must have looked miserable because she took pity on me and moved to the next item: a purple, palm-size massage device with a ten-speed button.

Oval-shaped vibrator in one hand and the cord in the other, Bethany said, "Now this is perfect for the woman who's ready to take charge."

Hilarity broke out in the audience, fueled by the massive quantity of frozen margaritas our hostess had provided.

Beads of perspiration dotted my forehead as Janelle passed the gadget to me. Someone had revved the control all the way to ten, and the object took on a life of its own. I tossed it to the woman next to me, then picked up my margarita and fled from the room into the bedroom, where I stepped onto the balcony. Janelle appeared before I slid the door shut.

"That friend of yours is hysterical," she said.

"Yeah, she's a real riot." I breathed in the cool autumn air and took a sip of the tart tequila and lime mixture.

"I appreciate your bringing me tonight." She joined me at the railing. "I haven't made a lot of new friends since I moved here and started with the firm. Between work and screwing up my love life, there's not much time to get to know nice people. This is an incredible view."

As we stood together, the skyline glittering in front of us, I struggled to determine her level of sincerity.

"I'd like to stay, but I have an early appointment with my trainer tomorrow, and don't tell your friend, but I have a full line of personal satisfaction products at home already. I did order a tube of that Get Glowing stuff, though, just to be polite."

I laughed at how bizarre it was to be standing next to my former rival chatting about sex toys she'd used with our shared ex.

"Anyway," she continued. "I didn't want to leave without telling you what I came to see you about in the first place. About a month ago, I overheard Lance on the phone talking to someone about pickups and deliveries. When I asked him about it, he acted clueless. Later, I was thumbing through his files for a copy of a contract we were supposed to be reviewing and ended up knocking a bunch of papers off the desk. When I picked them up, these fell out." She slid her bag off her shoulder and removed a legal-size manilla folder.

"There was nothing else with them. I returned the originals and made copies for you." She handed over the packet. "Here's my number if you need to talk." She pressed her business card into my hand and slipped through the patio door.

"Wait a minute." But she disappeared. I sat on the bed with its bright floral comforter and artfully arranged pillows, then carefully unsealed the envelope, where I found a small stack of four-by-six photos. I separated one and held it under the light. It was me in my black cap and jacket, holding the greasy bank statement I pulled from Johnston's trash. The next shot showed me on my front porch picking up the rose, the angle suggesting the photographer had been close by. The third picture had me standing beside Bethany as the restaurant valet brought her car. In the fourth I stood at Elsie's door. In the background, a silver van hugged the curb. I couldn't remember if it had been there when I arrived.

Something about the vehicle looked familiar. I flipped back to the shot with Bethany. There it was, parked on the street across from the restaurant lot. There was no way to be sure it was the same van.

Under different circumstances, I would have dismissed it as a coincidence. Hugh said there were no coincidences; you just had to know where to look for the connection. The final picture was of me and Connor walking out of my apartment. At the picture's top right corner, probably only recognizable if you already knew what it was, Barbie was swinging on the tree branch.

I dropped the photo and watched it float to the floor, where it lay for a few seconds before I reached for it, spilling the rest of my drink. I fished a tissue from my purse and blotted up the liquid. When I heard footsteps in the hallway, I stuffed the pictures back in the envelope.

"There you are," Bethany said, her voice barely audible above the high-pitched giggles from the other room. "Your new best friend just left. For a minute, I was afraid you'd gone with her without placing an order." She stood, hands on hips. "You don't look right. I was kidding about making you buy the Galloping Stallion. Better to start small and work up to your total fulfillment." She chortled. "Get it? *Fulfillment?* Seriously, nothing?"

Still shaken from discovering my life was being chronicled by a shadow figure, I forced a smile. "Sorry. I guess I am a little off. Guess I'm just tired. It's time for Cinderella to leave the ball."

"But you haven't even seen the new line."

I held up my hand. "I know, but since I never saw the old one, I'm going to trust you. Go ahead and pick out something for me. But nothing gigantic, please. Make it small and tasteful. Something that says *Yes, I'm a modern woman. But no, I don't want to do permanent damage to myself.* And be sure it's affordable. I need a new vacuum cleaner."

She shrieked in delight before beginning a congratulatory speech about how thrilled she was that I was finally joining the 21st century. I smiled and nodded as my happy friend escorted me out.

"You are so not going to be sorry. I am worried about you, though. Promise you'll get a good night's rest and call me tomorrow, okay?"

I agreed, but after seeing those candid shots of me, I didn't expect to sleep too soundly.

I kept my keys in hand, providing easy access to the bright yellow rape whistle attached to the fob. The idea someone might be watching now set me on high alert, and I ran the rest of the way. Behind the wheel, I double-checked the lock, turned the ignition, and, tires squealing, sped out of the parking garage. Every few minutes, I glanced in the rearview mirror, expecting some ghostly silver vehicle to appear and force me off the road.

CHAPTER 10

It was after nine when I made it home and found three unknown cars parked on the grass. Bright light spewed from within, and a booming bass beat throbbed through me. It seemed I had traded one party for another. Hopefully, the music would be the only thing vibrating at this one.

The door was unlocked, and heavy metal blasted throughout the house. The skunky, sweet odor of marijuana hit me, pungent and strong. Inside, I passed a couple making out on my antique loveseat. I fought the impulse to pour cold water on them and rushed to the kitchen, where Connor leaned against the counter. Two of his companions sat at the table laughing uncontrollably. One was a long-haired male, his skinny arms covered in tattoos, and the other was a female with a nose ring and a partially shaved head. They were passing around a joint and a bag of Cheesy Doodle-doos.

"Lucy!" Connor shouted over the music, smoke swirling from the crooked grin on his face. "Hey, guys, it's my friend Lucy."

He stood, a little unsteady. I stormed past him to the small, cylinder-shaped box on the counter, the source of the deafening sound, and searched frantically for the off button. When I couldn't find it, I yanked the cord from the wall and threw the device into the yard.

"Whoa," Tattoo Guy said. "That was harsh." Nose Ring echoed the sentiment.

"You were supposed to be gone." I snatched the joint from his hand and tossed it into the sink. He lunged for it, stumbled over my foot, and fell back into an empty chair.

"What'd you do that for?" he asked, gazing sadly toward the dwindling smoke.

"If you and your friends don't get out of my house right now, I will call the police."

He seemed unfazed by the threat, so I upped the ante. "And I'll tell your grandparents. I'm pretty sure your grandmother doesn't know you're still a pain-in-the-ass stoner. They just might write you out of the will this time." I had no idea how my landlord and his wife would react but suspected he didn't either.

He snapped to attention at the mention of the word *will*.

"Okay, okay." He held out his arms, palms up in what I took as a gesture of defeat. "Come on, guys. Lucy's not in the mood to party."

He grabbed his duffel from the hallway and herded his two companions to the front door. The couple on the sofa were still wrapped around each other. They jolted apart when Connor shouted for them to get their asses up and out. The girl, who looked about fifteen, adjusted her T-shirt and pulled her partner to his feet. She scowled at me on the way out and muttered something about somebody being a major bitch. I resisted the urge to return the insult and slammed the door behind them, hard enough to jostle the oval table holding my purse.

The corner of Janelle's envelope stuck out of the top. I removed it from the bag, took it to the writing desk in my bedroom, and placed it in a drawer.

Fearful of the damage I might find, I walked back into the living room and examined the fainting sofa and throw pillows for signs of contamination, finding only a smear of black lipstick I hoped would come off with a little hairspray. Other than a thin layer of Cheesy Doodle-doos dust and a thick haze of drug-laden smoke, the kitchen wasn't too bad. After wiping down everything with an antiseptic cloth, I saw the joint I tossed into the sink. It landed on top of a saucer and, while it was no longer lit, had somehow managed to stay relatively dry.

My first and last attempt at smoking pot was my freshman year in college. It had taken several attempts for me to manage a deep inhale. Even after drawing in a lungful, I insisted it hadn't fazed me. But then I began fixating on the ridges in my potato chip, running my tongue along the salty grooves, amazed at the beguiling texture. After my fascination with food ended, the evening took a dark turn when I burst into tears at the thought of letting my parents down by taking drugs when they'd given up everything to make sure I got a good education.

My mom and dad were solid middle-class citizens who had started a college fund for me at birth and had experienced no financial hardships that I knew of. In my pot-induced state, however, they were characters in a Dickens novel, staving off tuberculosis and the devastating effects of having an ungrateful daughter. I quickly established a reputation as a major buzzkill and never tried marijuana again.

Now that I was older and had probably disappointed my parents in everything from my choice of majors to my preference in men, there was less at stake. So why not give it another try? Maybe getting stoned would serve as a mystical connection to the universe. Or if not the entire universe, perhaps entering a blissfully altered state might unlock some of my own mysteries. Possibly, being out of focus would help bring my fuzzy mental picture of a perfect life into focus. It would pinpoint exactly how I could stop allowing other people to superimpose their ideas of perfection over mine.

Whatever. The past few days had been mentally and physically exhausting. Instead of being worn out, I was edgy and irritated. Possibly the drug would mellow me out. It certainly served that purpose with my unwanted houseguests.

I found a coiled cobra shaped lighter on the counter, a gift from one of Connor's friends, and retrieved the joint from the sink. With a flick of the snake's head, I lit up and took a few light puffs before inhaling deeply, surprised I remembered the technique. Must be just like riding a bike. The harsh smoke burned its way down my throat, sparking a coughing fit. I held onto the edge of the sink with one hand and set the glowing stick back on the saucer with the other, then filled a glass with water and drank most of it in one long gulp. Not quite as easy as riding a bike after all.

Determined to follow through, I sat at the table, and took another hit. The burning sensation was much less severe, and I held the smoke longer, the way my college boyfriend had instructed. I waited for euphoria to envelop me but experienced only a little light-headedness. Didn't everyone say the stuff out today was more powerful? Or didn't that apply to Connor's Colorado pot? Was it possible the legal stuff lacked the potency of forbidden fruit? Could bringing it across the country weaken it? Or perhaps over the years I'd gotten cooler and my tolerance had increased.

I took a drag, then another and continued until there wasn't enough left to hold between my fingers without burning myself. I put it in the sink and watched it sizzle and die. My parched throat cried out, but not for water. No, I wanted beer, cold beer. When I stood, my legs wobbled, but there were no other noticeable effects. I was the same Lucy, and that was disappointing. Worse than the recognition marijuana hadn't transformed me into a more interesting person, however, was the possibility I had no beer.

I stared into my refrigerator: eggs, leftover hot and sour soup, wilted lettuce, and a shrunken apple. Then I hit the jackpot. Wedged below the jug of milk was a six-pack of amber-colored cans Connor must have left behind. I removed one and almost dropped it when I found myself face to face with a skeleton head. Momentarily hypnotized by concentric circles of orange and black eyes that danced a little whenever I moved, I read the label: Laughing Skull. What a funny name for a beer.

And suddenly it was one of the funniest things I'd ever heard. Absolutely hilarious. So much so, it took several attempts before I popped the cap because I was giggling so hard the opener kept slipping out of my grasp. By the time I took my first sip, my insane laughter had dissolved into a few wet chortles.

"Oh, my, God. This is totally fricking amazing. Thank you, Connor or Nose Ring or Tattoo Guy or Horny Couple." The memory of the partygoers brought an attack of snickering, and beer spewed out my nose, sending a tickling burn into my nostrils. I ignored it, wiped my face with my sleeve, and drained the can in several long swallows. The cool elixir felt so good going down, I cracked another and took it to the front room where I kicked off my shoes and lay back on the fainting sofa.

Still sipping beer, I became entranced with my nail polish. Was it Too Hot to Handle Pink or Peach Petal Potion? And had my little finger always been bent like that? When the doorbell rang, I bolted upright, sloshing beer into my lap.

"Oh, my God, oh, my God!" I rushed to the door and looked through the peephole. It was Mateo. My heartbeat quickened and filled my ears with a hammering sound like jungle drums from an old Tarzan movie.

"Just a minute." I stopped at the hall mirror.

My wild hair and pallid complexion shocked me. Mascara had drifted south in dark smudges. I wiped them with my index finger and pinched my cheeks, then ran my hands through my curls. The results were minimal, and there was nothing to do about the red lines streaking the whites of my eyes.

"Hey, I wasn't expecting to see you tonight," I said as I let him in.

"I texted. When you didn't answer, I tried calling. Then I got worried and thought I'd stop by. Hope you don't mind."

I was so enthralled by the movement of his lips, I couldn't form an immediate response. Instead, I stood and stared, my heartbeat gradually slowing to almost normal.

"Are you okay?"

I realized it was my turn to speak. "Sure, I'm fine." *And getting better and better.* "Sorry. Please, come in."

I closed the door behind him, taking the opportunity to check him out from behind. Oh, my.

He stopped in the foyer. "Smells like my brother's fraternity house."

Once again, my heart began racing, and I was overwhelmed with the need to confess everything from my venture into sex-toy debauchery to my recent drug abuse. Luckily, my phone sounded from inside my purse. I retrieved it and saw Mom's face on the screen.

"Oh, shit. It's Mom. No way I'm talking to her now." I tossed it back into my bag. "She'll know I'm, uh." I leaned toward him and whispered, "I'm stoned." Then I staggered to the living room, giggling so hard I fell onto the sofa.

He followed and sat in the chair across from me.

I regained control and struggled into a more dignified sitting position before finishing the rest of my beer.

"Have you ever tried this stuff?" I held it up to him but didn't wait for an answer. "You have got to try it." I motioned for him to follow me to the kitchen, where I pulled two beers from the refrigerator and popped the tops.

"Go ahead. Taste it. It is freaking incredible." I gulped down a third of it and emitted a hiccuppy burp, which set off another round of uncontrollable snickering.

He took a sip. "It is good, but you might want to be careful. There's a lot of alcohol in it and you, well, you seem to be feeling no pain already. Maybe we could slow down a little."

For a second, it wasn't Mateo at the table. It was Lance with that stupid expression he wore whenever I was just starting to have fun. "Come on, Lucy," he'd say. "Are you sure you want another drink?" Or that piece of cake or to see that movie or go to that party. Whatever parade I wanted to attend he rained it out.

"You can slow down," I said to the man I now recognized as Mateo but still found annoying. "I'm finishing this beer." I downed most of the remaining liquid in several long gulps and set it on the table harder than I intended in a concluding gesture of rebellion.

He shrugged and sipped from his own drink. Irritation forgotten, I returned to my fascination with the shape and texture of his lips. It took every bit of restraint not to reach out and touch them.

"Have I got something on my face?" he asked, swiping the back of his hand across his mouth.

"What? Oh, no." I gazed into his chocolatey eyes. "Are you hungry? I'm starving." Standing too quickly, I swayed before steadying myself and headed to the refrigerator. "I have eggs and cheese and milk and..." I held up what might have been an onion, wrinkled my nose, and tossed the offending object into the trash. "I'll make omelets."

When I attempted to remove a mixing bowl from the cabinet, a wave of dizziness hit and I stumbled, sending it flying. Mateo caught the crockery before it crashed to the floor. I teetered backward, and he wrapped his free arm around my waist.

He held me until I regained my balance. "Why don't you have a seat and let me fix something?"

I noticed the bag of Cheesy Doodle-doos on the counter and began stuffing my mouth with the tasty little twigs. He moved easily in my kitchen as he located my only skillet and a very old stick of butter. Between bites of cheese snacks, I told him about Connor's visit and how I ejected him along with his friends.

"Hope you didn't spoil your appetite," he said, placing a plate of fluffy yellow eggs in front of me.

They were the most beautiful eggs I'd ever seen, little cloudlike puffs flecked generously with tiny dots of pepper, almost too exquisite to eat. But even after polishing off the remaining doodles, I was starving. I took one final admiring glance at his creation and began to demolish it.

"These are so delicious," I mumbled.

"Glad you like them." He grinned, then pushed a glass of ice water toward me. "You might want to hydrate."

I would have preferred another beer but shrugged and washed down the rest of the meal. A bubbling sensation from deep in my core rose, and I dashed for the hall bathroom, barely making it to the toilet before throwing up my late-night breakfast. I slid to the floor, back to the wall, eyes closed, and waited for the nausea to subside.

"Here you go."

Peering through one eye, I groaned at the sight of Mateo standing over me, holding a washcloth.

He kneeled and placed the cool cloth at the base of my pounding skull. I wanted to thank him but was afraid any movement might set off another round of retching.

He sat beside me, patting my knee.

"Are you up to moving? I can help you to the bedroom."

My heartbeat quickened. Even in my sorry state, the idea of having this man close gave me a pleasant tingle.

Right. Because nothing's sexier than a woman sprawled out on the bathroom floor after puking her guts out.

He helped me up, guided me to my room, and eased me into bed. After freshening the cloth, he brought me more water and a plastic wastebasket.

"Why don't you get some rest now? I'll check in with you tomorrow. If you're okay, we can meet up with your uncle to talk to him about going to the police before they come to him."

I couldn't summon the energy to answer. The next second, everything faded to black.

. . .

It was a little after 8:30 when I woke. My tongue felt as if I'd been licking an ashtray, and my head had doubled in size. I pushed myself up and tried to piece together the events of the previous night. As I headed to the bathroom, the image of Mateo standing by the bed returned, and I struggled to recall if he'd ventured any closer. My clothes had been replaced with a short flannel gown, but I had no idea if the exchange had occurred before or after he left.

A quick peek revealed I was wearing bra and panties. Since I never slept in underwear, Mateo must have assisted in trading my soiled outfit for a nightie without getting too personal. In the kitchen, I noticed a pink sticky note on the counter.

Check your welcome mat. M

I discovered a brown grocery bag. Unsteady and hungover, I lost my grip, and a bottle of ginger ale rolled out. Before I could pursue it, a pair of familiar black Ferragamo loafers stopped the soda from rolling down the walkway. The feet belonging to the pricey shoes were my ex's.

"I'm gone, what, a month and you're already screwing around on me?" He scowled at me and waved a sheet of paper in my face. I pushed it away and stumbled back toward the door.

But Lance was too quick. He grabbed my arm, his trademark musky vanilla smell masking a sharp, acrid odor emanating from his pores. With the note in his free hand, he read in a lisping, high-pitched voice.

Would have stayed to make you breakfast, but thought you needed some sleep. Saw your cupboards were bare, so I brought you a survival kit. My mom swears by ginger tea and bananas. Called your uncle. Noon works for him. Pick you up at 11:30—M

He snarled, then wadded up the note and threw it on the ground, dragging me inside.

I fought the impulse to explain myself.

"Let go of my arm." I jerked free and slapped his hand away. "First, you and I are not together, so it's absolutely none of your business who I see or what I do. Second, what gives you the right to come on my property, uninvited, and read my personal mail before forcing your way into my house?"

I stomped my foot. "And third, get the hell out." I grabbed an umbrella from the antique stand and whacked him on the side of his head and shoulder.

He fell back against the doorframe and ducked before snatching the makeshift weapon away from me.

"We're not over until I say we are." His face turned a dark shade of purple, and his voice popped and sputtered like firecrackers on a hot sidewalk. His eyes burned with an intensity that should have frightened me, but I was too stricken with the realization this was the real Lance Crawford. As long as life was going his way, he maintained a façade of glamor and power. Beneath that illusion, he was this nasty creature, incapable of imagining he could be denied anything.

"Believe what you want," I said, remarkably calm in the face of his rage. "But if you don't leave right now, I will call the police." I couldn't think of a time earlier in my life I threatened to summon the authorities. In the past twenty-four hours, I'd done it twice.

His normal color returned, and he switched tactics. "I'm sorry. It's just the thought of you with another man makes me crazy. I didn't come by to fight. Give me a minute and I promise I'll leave."

The creepy pictures Janelle had taken from his desk came to mind, and I backed farther away. I decided to handle him carefully. "I'll give you five minutes, then you're gone."

He was all smiles as he took a step toward the living room.

I grabbed his sleeve. "We can talk right here or not at all. No way am I sitting with someone who's been," I paused, not sure if I should push him, then said "stalking me."

A quick flash of the real Lance crossed his face, then disappeared. "I am not a stalker. It's about Janelle and how dangerous she is. I know you and she hung out last night. I want to make sure she didn't poison you against me. That woman has no concept of the truth. She'll stop at nothing to get what she wants. I want you to be safe."

Despite the seriousness of the situation, his dramatic delivery and soap opera dialogue made me want to laugh, but I thought better of it. "You have a funny way of showing it. Forcing yourself into my home, shoving me around."

But I was curious. What was it he didn't want Janelle to reveal, and how did he even know she and I had been together? Unless he really was stalking me.

I almost confronted him with his inconsistencies but knew if I asked him directly, he'd lie. So, I kept my face neutral and waited for him to go on. And he would because he was Lance, and that was what he did: sling bullshit whenever he had a captive audience.

His next question, however, surprised me. "What exactly did Janelle say? About me, I mean. Because whatever it was, you can't believe her."

"What makes you think we talked about you at all? It doesn't matter. What I really want to know is how you knew we hung out last night?"

"It wasn't because I was stalking you. I drove by your office on my way home and saw her car. I was afraid she might be there to do something crazy. I parked across the street and watched. When you came out together, I was worried. When you left, I noticed she was behind you, so I followed her. You can imagine how shocked I was seeing the two of you at Bethany's."

He paused and arranged his face in what he most likely considered disappointment. But I didn't fall for it. If anything, his expression was disbelief. No way would he understand how his exes had the nerve to have a good time when they should have been too devastated by mutual loss to carry on.

"I could see Janelle didn't intend to hurt you. Physically, that is. But emotionally? I was still worried. The lies she tells destroy people."

While I didn't believe he'd been watching me out of any real concern, something about that last sentence rang true. But was it Janelle or Lance who had the power to destroy me?

"Well, you wasted your time. Your name never came up."

When had I become such a cool liar?

"We were at a Sensual Secrets party test-driving sex toys. Now you need to go."

"Sensual Secrets?" he sputtered. "You're just as cheap and easy as she is." He opened the door and picked up the bottle. "Here's a gift from whatever big spender you've been screwing."

I took it and watched him walk away, then called out, "Wait, Lance."

When he turned, I flung the soda as hard as I could, aiming at his head. He stepped sideways, and the bottle glanced off his shoulder before bouncing onto the pavement, spurting its contents all over his crisp khaki pants.

I slammed the door and locked it, then listened for an angry outburst that never came. I peeked out the front window. He was gone, leaving a battered bottle and a spreading puddle of ginger ale in his wake. There had been no sound of an engine starting. He must have parked at the end of the landlords' long drive. I wondered if he might not have visited that way before and shuddered at the thought of him skulking around.

I wrapped my arms around myself to stop the shaking—the reaction not only to the idea of his stalking but also at my personal transformation. Other than tossing noodles in his face, I had never resorted to physical violence. In the past thirty minutes or so, I had attacked my former boyfriend twice with the intent of doing him serious bodily harm. Last night, I drove a bunch of stoners out of my house after destroying an expensive musical device. And before that, I went after Connor with a baseball bat.

I should have been worried about the direction my life was taking, but I was too impressed with what a badass I'd become.

CHAPTER 11

Lost in thoughts of the new and improved, if slightly crazed Lucy, I tripped over the grocery bag from Mateo. I carried it to the kitchen and emptied the contents on the counter. Ibuprofen and antacid, a packet of ginger tea, a box of saltines, a banana and gel ice packs. How early had he gotten up to put together this array of emergency supplies? And how different he was from Lance.

Stop that. You are not going to be that girl. Someone who moves from devastating heartbreak without a breather.

I heated water for tea and popped two ibuprofens and one antacid while I waited for it to boil. Not quite ready to face the crackers or banana, I took my cup to my room and sat on the bed sipping it. The combination of spicy citrus and medication settled my stomach and calmed the pounding in my head.

But it didn't ease my mind about Lance. The man I thought I knew, had loved, might not just be a shameless philanderer. He could be something much worse. But what? Even if he'd been stalking me, what possible reason could he have for taking those pictures? I couldn't conjure the image of him hiding in the bushes snapping random photos. Of course, his firm had investigators who did that sort of thing, but using company resources to check up on a former girlfriend wasn't part of Lance's MO.

Trying to decipher his actions made my head pound again, so I headed to the shower. My thoughts shifted to what Mateo would say to my uncle. We would have to bring up the subject of the fraudulent antiques possibly in his possession unless he'd sold them, which would be way worse. Either one might give the police a motive for Buddy being involved in Al Darrow's murder.

Although I planned to keep Mateo at a safe distance, I spent extra time on my hair and makeup. I tugged on my favorite jeans and a sweater in a shade of green close to the color of my eyes. The neckline showcased my breasts in a way that said: "Yes, we're perky, but no, she's not slutty."

I ate the banana, then put my laptop in an oversize purse along with a sleeve of crackers.

At exactly 11:58, the doorbell rang. Mateo greeted me with a smile. "Drop something?" he asked, holding up the almost empty bottle of ginger ale.

"It's a long story. I'll tell you about it on the way to Buddy's."

"I wasn't sure you were going to make it today, but I have to say you clean up real nice."

"Sorry about last night. I'm not much of a drinker, and I haven't, uh ..." I lowered my voice. "Smoked pot in years."

"It's okay," he whispered. "I won't rat you out to your mom."

"Good to hear. And thanks for the survival kit. That was one of the sweetest things anyone's ever done for me."

How pathetic did that sound?

"Hope it helped. I hung out until you were through yakking up the fine meal I prepared."

My face must have reflected how miserable the memory made me.

"Hey," he said, patting my shoulder. "It happens to the best of us. And seeing you in that hot nightgown was worth it."

So, he had helped me out of my clothes.

"Don't worry. I was a perfect gentleman. Okay, maybe not perfect, but definitely a gentleman."

I scooted from the room to get my purse. When I returned, he was looking at the picture of me and the handsome Aussie actor I had subbed for Lance. "Didn't take you for the Hollywood type. Looks like I've got some stiff competition."

My stomach did a little butterfly flip. "We're just good friends."

On the way to the car, I told him about the previous evening, beginning with running into Janelle and the two of us going to Bethany's. I saw no reason to include a description of the party itself but did tell him about the pictures and concluded with Lance's unwelcome appearance.

I didn't mention the part about him accusing me of sleeping with Mateo or the frightening intensity of his anger. I also skipped both the umbrella incident and bottle launching. Instead, I said Lance had left in a snit, knocking over the groceries and accidentally sending the ginger ale flying.

I finished just as we pulled in front of the Past Perfect. He shut off the engine but made no move to exit the vehicle. He stared over the steering wheel for several seconds before speaking.

"You're telling me that son of a bitch forced himself into your house and threatened you?" Muscles twitched in his jaw.

"He didn't exactly threaten me. He was just pissed he wasn't getting his way and that Janelle and I were somehow managing to get on with our lives."

"But he came in without your permission, right?" He faced me, the expression on his face hard to read.

"Well, yes, but I took care of it."

"You shouldn't underestimate a guy like that. Just because you got him to go away doesn't mean he won't come back. I don't suppose you own a gun."

Of course, I didn't own a gun. But the way he assumed I wasn't the kind of person who was proficient in the use of firearms irritated me. "Not one of my own, but my dad taught me to shoot."

If you counted the time I went with him to the firing range. He handed me an angular little pistol, a Glock something or other, and instructed me on how to stand and where to aim. I shut my eyes when I pulled the trigger, never getting anywhere near the target, and, after multiple attempts, Dad snatched the gun out of my hands and told me to wait for him in the car.

I led Mateo to the front of the shop. The closed sign hung crookedly on the window.

"This doesn't make sense," I said, peering into the darkened interior. "Saturday's their busiest day, and didn't you call to say we were coming?" Without waiting for an answer, I headed to the back entrance.

We walked past the toilet and the tub and the flamingoes to the screen porch door. It was locked, but there was a piece of notebook paper folded in half, stuck between the hinge and the frame. I removed and read it, then offered it to Mateo, my hand trembling.

The cops came for Buddy. Don't know when we'll be back. Norm

. . .

Mateo insisted on driving. On the way, I checked my voicemail: three from Mom, each a bit more frantic. The first two pleaded for me to call her immediately. The last demanded I meet her at the station as soon as possible.

The Roswell police headquarters was off the main highway close to the downtown. That small commercial area consisted primarily of trendy restaurants and shops. Most of these businesses were housed in converted homes, creating an atmosphere of chic nostalgia. The government complex on the other side of the four-lane road was a combination of stately plantation-style buildings and no-nonsense institutional structures. The law enforcement building was the latter.

My idea of what to expect when we entered came from my favorite crime dramas. Instead of harried plainclothes detectives sitting at cluttered desks, I found myself in a well-lit waiting room with backless benches against brick walls.

A raised reception desk in the center housed two uniformed officers, both on the phone. A larger room with snack machines and scattered chairs stretched behind a wall of glass. I spotted Norm at the soda machine on the other side and propelled through the entrance.

"Is Uncle Buddy okay?"

"He's all right. Your momma's a hot mess, though. But your daddy made sure he didn't talk to anyone until his lawyer arrived."

"Dad's here?" Things must have been bad if Mom had gotten him to come with her. My parents were one of the happiest married couples I'd ever seen. But when it came to dealing with her brother, she left Dad out of the picture. Buddy was a little too much for him. Too enthusiastic, too colorful, too many Chihuahuas.

I introduced Norm to Mateo, and we stepped into a room that reminded me of a hospital waiting area, where family gathered to learn if the patient had made it. My parents were sitting on a small sofa. Crumpled against Dad's shoulder, Mom was a cartoon version of herself. I rarely saw her when her light brown hair wasn't arranged in a smooth, wavy bob. Today, thick coils of it sprang out in all directions, and she had missed a button on her crisp cotton blouse.

Clad in his favorite UGA sweatshirt and dad jeans, my father nudged her. She leaped from the bench.

"Thank God you're here!" She pulled me into a quick hug, released me, and turned to Mateo. Instead of her usual husband-material appraisal, she barely glanced at him.

Dad joined us and I introduced everyone. "Mateo's looking into Uncle Buddy's connection with Al Darrow's death."

"We appreciate your help, but I expect you're wasting your time. My brother-in-law might be a lot of things–"

"Ted," Mom interrupted, her voice sharp.

"What I'm trying to say is Buddy has an interesting, uh, background, but he's a good guy. He's no killer."

I struggled to remember when my father had taken up for my uncle. He never said anything bad about him, but his disapproval had been obvious. Or had I only thought it was disapproval because

I didn't understand the truth? Dad and Buddy were so different it was hard for them to relate.

"I agree, Mr. Howard. From what I've learned, I don't see a connection between Lucy's uncle and Darrow's murder. But the fact he was present around the time of the shooting gives the police a pretty good reason to question him. You were smart to send a lawyer with him."

Dad nodded his own approval at how well he'd dealt with the situation. I was impressed with how Mateo handled my father. Before they continued the conversation, someone opened a door at the end of the hallway. Buddy and a tall, gray-haired man in an expensive looking pin-striped suit came out. A heavy-set woman in tan pants and matching jacket followed them.

"Thank you for your cooperation," she said. While her words were pleasant enough, I caught an underlying stridency. "I'm sure you understand we may have additional questions at a later date." She turned and walked away.

"Of course, Detective," the man in the suit addressed her back. "We're eager to put this matter to rest." He placed his hand on Buddy's shoulder, and they headed toward us.

Norm didn't wait for Buddy to reach him. He closed the distance between them in several long strides. Then he grabbed my uncle in his signature hug. In a gesture that reminded me of Mom, Buddy laid his head on Norm's broad chest and shut his eyes before easing away.

"Well, that was a little slice of heaven," he said turning to his other companion. "Jimmy, I sure do appreciate you being in there with me. That big gal was a real piece of work."

"Glad I was able to be of assistance." He walked over to Mom and kissed her on the cheek. "Your sister and I go way back, don't we, Anne-Marie? This woman was the prettiest girl at Chandler High. Broke a lot of hearts. And she hasn't changed a bit."

His compliments oozed like molasses, and my mother giggled, then blushed. Dad put his arm around her and pulled her close.

Who are these people? Mom was not a giggler and Dad, well, he considered public handholding was over the top.

If Jimmy detected any hostility in my father's possessive move, he didn't let on. Instead, he chuckled before introducing himself as James Galloway. He explained he'd had a little experience in criminal law and, while he hadn't known Buddy when they were in high school, he thought the world of Anne-Marie Taylor.

"Anne-Marie *Howard*," Dad, arm still wrapped around Mom's waist, inserted. "It's Howard now."

"Right, of course." Jimmy directed a smile at Mom before continuing. "I've advised Buddy not to discuss what we talked about in private, but I have some general information for you. The good news is the video camera in Darrow's store wasn't working. The bad news is the business next door has a surveillance system. It shows him going around back at 1:43 and leaving at 3:39. Buddy told them about Al standing him up. We didn't offer any additional information, so it would be best if no one speculated on why he waited so long. After all, none of you can be certain about anything that might or might not have happened."

He moved toward Mom, his lips puckered in what looked like preparation for a goodbye kiss, but Dad intercepted him. Jimmy hesitated a second before shaking Dad's hand and assuring everyone they shouldn't worry because he had everything under control.

I watched the attorney walk away and wondered why he didn't want anyone to mention Buddy's narcoleptic episode at Darrow's shop. Was he worried people wouldn't understand his illness, that the police might think he was faking, using the disease as an alibi for murder?

On the way out, I introduced Buddy to Mateo, who then took me aside while Mom and Buddy talked.

"I know your uncle's not supposed to say anything about his conversation with the cops, but we should ask him about Darrow's fake antique business. The police may not have connected him with it yet, but it's just a matter of time before they start asking questions about his involvement, and if he has anything incriminating in his shop, well, it could be bad."

It sounded as if he were telling me they needed to make sure Buddy didn't have anything in his store that might connect him to Darrow. The former Lucy, who insisted on the truth, the whole truth and nothing but the truth and who went after the Dr. Johnstons of the world with a vengeance and even persecuted old ladies like Elsie, would have been appalled at the mere suggestion of deceiving the authorities. New Lucy, the one who experienced a pleasant jolt of adrenaline every time I revisited my memories of attacking Lance, knew Mateo was right. If I was going to help my uncle, I had to be willing to bend the truth. Hell, I might have to smash it into tiny little pieces.

I nodded to Mateo as Mom called out. "We're going to follow Buddy and Norm home to sort things out. I'll call you later. Please, don't send me to voicemail again."

I suspected she would pump Buddy for details about what had gone on during his interrogation. If things got tricky, say her baby brother needed an alibi or a get-away plan, Mom wouldn't want an outsider present, even if that outsider was an incredibly handsome potential prospect for her aging daughter. I understood why she would ban Mateo from the meeting, but why hadn't she invited me to the family pow-wow?

Before I could give the matter more thought, she summoned me. "Honey, could you come here for just a second?"

I obeyed and Mom whispered, "Your new friend seems very nice, and I don't see a ring on his finger. What's the story with you two?"

"Seriously? You want to talk about my love life now when poor Uncle Buddy might be in big trouble?" Relief that my mother was back to her old match-making self outweighed annoyance that she was back to her old match-making self.

"Love life?" Mom lit up. "You know, I never liked Lance. He had shifty eyes. Not like Mr. Dreamboat here."

"For God's sake," I glanced over my shoulder at Mateo, who was examining a plaque on the wall. "He'll hear you. And, no, he is definitely not part of my nonexistent love life. He's just returning a favor to Hugh. Frankly, I expect him to bail at any minute."

"I wouldn't be too sure about that, dear. The way he's been looking at you, I don't think he's done nearly enough yet."

"Mom!" I felt a blush burning my chest.

"You two go on *investigating*. I certainly wouldn't want to interrupt in case things heat up, so I won't call until tomorrow morning, not too early, of course."

Dad joined us before I had time to set her straight about my situation with Mateo.

"What's the hold-up, girls?"

"Lucy's not coming. She and her new friend have other fish to fry."

How could the woman make frying food sound like code for an unnamed sex act?

· · ·

We picked up takeout before Mateo took me home.

"Your uncle and his partner seem devoted to each other."

I enjoyed the sound of his casual acceptance of Buddy and Norm's relationship. Since Mom's innuendoes, whenever I looked at him for more than a few seconds, a picture of him standing half-clad in front of a sizzling frying pan popped into my head.

"They really are good together." I mentally traced the contours of his naked chest.

Stop it. You are not ready for this. Oh, God! Had I said that out loud?

A sideways glance in his direction assured me I hadn't. Because he was watching the road with a slight smile on his face, not tensing up at the prospect he might be riding with a mildly unhinged female who whisper-shouted warnings to herself.

"Your parents seem into each other, too. The way your dad got all territorial when Galloway moved in on her."

I was a little impressed myself. "Dad's not usually the jealous type, but he did get intense for a moment there."

I smiled at the memory of my laid-back father staking his claim on my mother and realized I wanted what they had, a contentment that didn't preclude passion. I needed it so badly, I talked myself into believing Lance was capable of the kind of devotion Dad had for Mom and almost settled for my delusion. Probably would have if not for his betrayal. I supposed I should be grateful to Janelle for that reality check.

He turned into the drive, parked next to my car, and shut off the engine.

"My pop's intense most of the time. Flies off the handle a lot, but my mother doesn't take any crap. It can get pretty loud at my house, but it works for them." He leaned closer. "How about you? It's clear you and your lawyer are on the outs, but are you really done with him?"

If he'd asked the question before this morning, my answer might not have been a definitive one. When Lance dropped by to say he wasn't giving up on us, a part of me wanted to think we had a chance. Even after Janelle's revelation about breaking up with him, I had doubts. And the ferocity of our earlier encounter touched me in an excitingly perverse way, both stimulating and frightening.

But now I recognized the heat from that altercation for what it was: false fire.

"I am totally finished with Lance Crawford."

"Good," Mateo said, "because I don't want to fall for someone who's still in love with her ex." He took my hand and held it.

I caught my breath and moved closer to face him. He tilted my chin and kissed me gently before tracing my lips with his tongue. I gasped. He kept up his tender exploration until I couldn't stand it any longer. I pressed against him, and he trailed kisses down my throat, my neck, the top of my breasts. I arched my back. If not for the gearshift between us, we would have been lost.

"Do you think we should take this inside? Unless you want to hop into the backseat."

"Inside would be good."

He sat for a moment before joining me, holding the sack of burgers in front of him.

When I went to insert the key, I discovered the door wasn't locked.

"That's strange. I always lock my door."

He stepped ahead of me and set the food down. "Wait here."

I ignored him and went inside, where I stopped in confusion. Instead of my orderly little cottage, I stared at what could have been the aftermath of a tornado touchdown. Overturned furniture, pillows and books scattered everywhere, and drawers emptied onto the floor.

CHAPTER 12

"Stay put," Mateo commanded. He lifted his right pants leg, revealing what looked like a nylon ankle brace. When he stood, he was holding a small pistol.

"Dial 911 and tell them you've had a break-in, and the intruder might still be here."

I was almost as shocked at the knowledge I'd been about to fall into bed with a man wearing a holster as I was at the idea of someone ransacking my home. I dialed the emergency number and explained the situation. He returned and eased the phone from my hand, then told the operator there was no intruder on the premises, and he would report the incident to the police.

"I don't understand. Of all the houses in the neighborhood, why would someone pick mine? I've got nothing valuable enough to steal."

"Your TV and microwave are here. And you had your laptop with you, right?"

I nodded, glad I followed my impulse about taking it. Then I remembered the envelope from Janelle. I rushed past him and ran directly to my room, dodging upturned tables and chairs. The bedroom was in worse shape than the front of the house, with sheets and blankets thrown everywhere and clothes dumped from drawers and closets.

The intruder brutalized my little desk, flipped it over and left empty drawers dangling. Their contents were shredded and tossed on the floor like confetti.

Mateo joined me. "Are you okay?" He put his arm around my shoulder.

"They're gone. Somebody took the pictures."

The rest of the afternoon was a combination of the surreal and the terrifying. He stayed beside me while I followed two uniformed officers as they picked through the wreckage. I imagined myself as a shell-shocked person on the news after a fire destroyed the family home, or a flood carried it away. Of course, I hadn't lost everything. I just had a gigantic mess to clean up.

But living with the knowledge some stranger was able to enter my place anytime he wanted frightened me the most. I might think I was ferocious and powerful, but I was at the mercy of whatever unknown force was stalking me.

The taller officer nodded toward the sheets and articles of clothing scattered across the room.

"I probably don't have to say it but be careful sorting through your things." When he pointed to the dishevelment, his hand brushed against a pair of black lace panties dangling from a lamp and he blushed. "Sometimes these guys like to, well, you know, *handle* people's personal stuff. We caught this one couple who liked to break in to have sex in strange beds. If you find anything suspicious, bag it up and bring it in."

My stomach lurched at the idea of some perverted Goldilocks and friend rolling around on my bed. Someone's greasy head might have rested on the pillow I paid almost fifty dollars for. A hairy-handed goon could have touched my expensive lingerie or, even worse, seen my assortment of granny panties.

After searching through the debris, I concluded the envelope containing the photos was the only thing missing. When I shared that information with the officers, they were skeptical and urged me to continue looking.

"So, I'm supposed to look for missing stuff? Isn't that an oxymoron or irony?" I asked, before bursting into tears of frustration and anger.

The two men exchanged glances while Mateo held me and spoke to them over my head. "Give us a minute."

I sobbed into his chest while they waited. Finally, I pulled away, took a deep breath, and said, "I'm sorry. I'll keep looking and let you know if anything else is gone."

While I wandered throughout the apartment looking for what wasn't there, Mateo called Hugh. After a few minutes, I repeated my original claim: the photos were the only thing taken. One of the policemen handed me a report to sign and suggested I change the locks. Then they left.

"Do you have anything stronger than Laughing Skull?" Mateo asked.

I remembered the Jack Daniels in a cabinet above the sink. My secret Santa gave it to me the previous Christmas. Since bourbon still reminded me of the worst hang-over of my life, I planned to re-gift the bottle but forgot about it. I led him to the kitchen, the least-trashed room in the house, and brought out the booze. My burglar must have gotten bored by the time he made it this far. He tossed sugar and flour everywhere and broke a few dishes but didn't venture into the pantry or the refrigerator.

Mateo filled our glasses.

"Everything's a mess, but most of the damage is superficial. Like they ransacked it to distract from the real reason for the break-in. Hugh agrees with me."

"You believe me about the pictures?"

"Of course, but what I don't get is why anyone would steal them. If Lance either took them or had someone do it for him, I would say he left the flower and the doll and took the photos to enjoy your reaction, but that doesn't make any sense. Whatever his reason, I can't understand why he would want them after you saw them. What's the point?"

An image hit me at the same time the bourbon did, and I choked. He rose to pat me on the back, but I waved him away.

"The van!" I exclaimed between coughs. "There was a silver van in two of the pictures, and I'm pretty sure it was the same one. It could belong to the person who took the pictures. Could be someone's afraid I'd recognize it and connect it to Lance."

"That's possible, especially if your ex was in on it. But if your boyfriend, ex-boyfriend, wanted to get you back, why would he try to scare you? And what's the point in trashing your apartment?"

"He might have thought I'd be too scared to stay by myself and would beg him to come back. Or he could have done it out of spite because he didn't like knowing he couldn't control me anymore."

"Would that stoner character have any reason to be interested in the pictures?"

It was hard to imagine Connor having enough energy to demolish my home in such a spirited manner. I thought about the sheets and blankets flung on the floor, and a wave of nausea hit as I visualized him rolling around on my bed with Miss Nose Ring.

A strange calm came over me as I swirled my glass before lifting it to my lips. Despite the disgusting image of unwashed bodies frolicking on my comforter and the chaos surrounding me, I wasn't panic stricken. I was glad Mateo was here, but knew I'd be fine if he weren't.

I had become an active participant in my life. No more waiting for someone to tell me what to do or how to feel. I was the one making things happen. Yes, Buddy pulled me into his drama, but once in, I decided on the best way to help him. Throwing out Connor and his pot-smoking cronies emboldened me. And physically ejecting Lance made me feel like a genuine badass.

Mateo downed his remaining bourbon. "Whoever did all this," he glanced around the room, "was pissed. And that kind of anger doesn't usually just go away." He reached across the table and covered my hand with his. "Now might be a good time to reconsider getting a gun."

I liked the weight and warmth of his hand on mine but was determined not to fall into a relationship that might turn me into the same compliant person I'd been with Lance. I didn't want to set aside my thoughts and values to please another person. So, despite the tingle I felt when he touched me, I was glad we hadn't finished what we started in the car.

I slipped my hand out from under his. "I'm better off sticking with my baseball bat."

"If you change your mind—"

"I won't."

"Got it." He stood and nodded toward the bag sitting on the counter. Sometime during the confusion, he must have retrieved it from the front porch. "I'm starving. Are you up for soggy burgers and cold fries?"

Whether from the emotional upheaval, or the adrenaline high and following let down, I was hungry. The burgers were dry, and the fries were rubbery, but we ate them anyway and washed them down with the last of Connor's beer. It was after five when we finished.

"We should check in with Buddy, but let's not tell him about all this." I looked around the room and sighed. "Why don't you go ahead without me? I can't leave until I clear away some of this mess. I'll tell him you're coming and join you after I clean up the worst of it."

"No way am I walking into the lion's den without you. Where do you keep your broom?"

I insisted I could handle it, but he paid no attention. While he swept up the kitchen, I went to the bedroom and picked up the sheets by the corner, dropped them into the washing machine, and set it on extra hot. I collected the scattered clothing and put it in a basket to wash later. Finally, I salvaged as many of my household records as I could. Hearing Mateo moving furniture in the living room made me glad he ignored my protests.

. . .

"I guess you noticed Uncle Buddy's somewhat of a character," I said as we pulled onto the highway.

After we cleaned up the mess, Mateo and I discovered that damage had been superficial. But nothing would erase the feeling of violation.

"I got the impression he's pretty colorful."

Colorful didn't begin to cover it.

After arriving at the antique store, we walked to the back. Mateo took in the clutter without comment until he came to the statue of Venus. "Is it me or are her eyes following us?"

"It's you," I responded. The screened-in porch wasn't locked, so I stepped inside and knocked. Frenzied high-pitched yelping ensued. "Did I tell you about the Chihuahuas?" The desperate shrieks fell to a lower pitch, interspersed with frantic whining.

"Settle down, guys." Norm's admonition had almost no effect on the canine cacophony.

"Norm's not as colorful as Buddy. But he is in a band."

The yapping died down enough for us to hear the skitter of toenails across tile. Norm opened the door, holding Doris, the rotund pack leader. She snarled a warning, while the other two pups pranced at their master's feet.

Norm managed a shadow of his usual smile. "Hey, sweetheart. Come on in." Doris growled and he scooted her farther under his arm. "Don't try to pet her. She's a little nervous after your mom's visit."

Doris and my mother detested each other from the moment they met. The poor little animal had to be locked in the back room whenever Mom came by. I thought the place wasn't large enough to house two alpha egos but kept this opinion to myself.

"Buddy's lying down right now," Norm continued. "But he said to wake him when you got here."

I suspected the dog wasn't the only one recovering from an afternoon with my mother. We sat on the sofa and waited while he went to get Buddy.

"So, what kind of band?" Mateo asked, as the boys frolicked around his feet.

"Bluegrass. He plays banjo and fiddle."

A pup hopped up and wriggled to the back of the couch, attacking Mateo's ear with lusty kisses. He covered his head with his hands, ducking low, and the little dog fell forward. I scooped him up before he landed. His companion yipped and jumped up to join us, licking indiscriminately.

I scrambled to get control of the squirming little creatures before placing each one on the floor.

"That's Pepe." I pointed to the dog on the right. "And this is Paco."

"You got it basakward," Buddy said, rounding the corner. "The one with the black spot on his ear is Paco." Norm followed, minus Doris, whose indignant wailing could be heard in the background.

"Let's get a treat, boys," Norm called and the dogs raced him to the kitchen.

Sitting across from us, Buddy's usually rosy cheeks were pale. The circles under his heavy-lidded eyes had grown darker, and I wondered how his erratic sleep patterns affected his health and how much this murder investigation might hurt him.

Buddy had never had an easy time. Growing up he didn't fit in, but instead of withdrawing from a world that didn't understand him, he jumped in headfirst and created his own world. He danced and sang and became whoever he wanted to be. He made a good life for himself, one filled with love and antiques and Chihuahuas.

Al Darrow's death put everything in jeopardy. To be fair, the murder had been harder on Al than it had on Buddy, but Al was the kind of man who brought trouble on himself. Since placing blame on a deceased person offered little comfort, I transferred most of my anger to his surviving surrogate, Virgil. I didn't have to know the man to recognize the damage he could do to my uncle. I determined not to let that happen.

"Your lawyer recommended you keep your conversation with the police confidential," Mateo began, "but we have to ask a few questions."

He nodded.

"Are you familiar with the name Burton Prescott?"

I watched Buddy grow even paler before he answered. "I've done some business with him. Nutso Civil War reenactor, likes to call himself a 'living historian.' What a crock of shit. He's just looking for an excuse to dress up and play soldier. He is willing to pay big bucks, though. I sold him an old coin for a pretty fair price, but he was more interested in weapons: muskets, knives, sabers. Had his heart set on picking up a Merrill Carbine. Not really my area of expertise."

Norm returned, minus the canines, and asked if he could get anybody anything. We requested coffee. Buddy asked for water.

"Caffeine this late in the day messes with my new medication," he explained. "Anyway, I told Prescott I didn't have much to do with war relics. They're usually all banged up, pardon the pun, with too many fakes in the mix. Since Prescott is a huge pain in the ass, I sent him to Al." Buddy grinned. "Perfect match."

Maybe not so perfect.

"Do you know if the two of them are connected?" Mateo asked.

Buddy shook his head. "I never heard back from Prescott, so I figured he got what he wanted. At least that's what I thought until last week. That's when Al called and asked me to stop by the shop. Said he and Prescott had a deal I might be interested in."

"How come you didn't mention all this when you talked to Hugh and me?" I asked.

"I was embarrassed, honey." Buddy hung his head, then continued, "I didn't even tell Norm about it. I mean, it doesn't say much for me that I was willing to do business with a crook, does it?"

He didn't wait for a response, which was good since I didn't have one.

"But I've told him now. I like to think I would have opted out if Al was planning on passing off fakes, but I can't be sure. Things have been slow, and a deal like that could be hard to pass up. I never got the chance to find out."

The idea Uncle Buddy would do something dishonest was hard to accept. The thought of him in cahoots with someone like Al Darrow was beyond belief.

"Other than your reason for the meeting, is there anything else you haven't told us?" I kept my tone as neutral as possible.

"No," he said. "Well, I did snoop around the store more than I let on. But other than that, I told you the whole truth."

"Did you tell the police about Prescott?" Mateo asked.

"Jimmy said to answer only the questions they asked and not to volunteer anything else, so no. They didn't mention Prescott, and neither did I."

"How about your lawyer? Did you say anything to him?" Mateo scribbled on his little spiral notepad.

"I hoped nobody would find out I'd even consider working with that old snake. Should I have said something?"

Slumped low in his chair, he looked as miserable as I felt. What right did I have to expect others to be transparent when I planned to take liberties with the truth if it meant helping the people I loved? Or in Elsie's case, someone I liked a lot and didn't want to send to jail.

"You were right not to offer information," Mateo offered. "It's better if they come across Prescott on their own, and I'm sure they will. Can you think of anything else that might help establish a motive for someone wanting to kill Darrow?"

Norm came back with Buddy's water and stood behind him, one hand on his shoulder.

"Other than Al Darrow was a miserable human being and there's most likely a long line of folks who wouldn't mind seeing him dead, no," Buddy answered.

"Not a good idea to offer up that theory," Mateo said, closing his notebook and sticking it back in his pocket. "That's about it, unless Lucy has some questions."

I shook my head and walked to where my uncle sat with his head in his hands. "You said you didn't know what you might have done if you'd had the chance to work with Al, but I know." I swallowed the lump in my throat. "You would never have tried to pass off fakes as the real thing, regardless of how much money was at stake, because that's not the kind of person you are."

And I wasn't just saying it. Someone like my uncle, who had always been true to himself no matter what other people thought, would never have sold out.

Buddy sat up straighter, smiled, stood, and embraced me. Norm came from behind, wrapped his arms around us, and kissed the top of my head.

"I hope we gave you something to work with," Buddy said, ending the group hug.

"Definitely. I'm going to do a little digging and see if I can find out more about Prescott and any other customers the Darrows might have swindled. In the meantime, follow your lawyer's advice."

On our way out, Norm stopped us and insisted we take home some leftover lasagna. He filled a picnic basket not only with the pasta but also with salad, bread, and a gigantic slab of lemon pound cake.

"Give me a second," I said to Mateo and popped into the living room to say goodbye to Buddy. But he had slumped sideways and lay with his head on the arm of the sofa, softly snoring. So, I grabbed a quilt from his collection on the console table and draped it over him.

Back at my apartment, Mateo carried the food to the door. "Wait for me here while I go in and check things out."

"You don't think he came back, do you?" I asked.

The picture of a hulking figure waltzing in and out of my home at will threatened to destroy my peace of mind. It also made me angry. This was my place, and I wasn't about to let some weirdo ruin it for me. Still, there was no harm in staying near the man with the gun, near enough to catch the faint, citrusy smell of his aftershave.

The memory of our hot make-out scene reminded me of how close we were to falling into bed. But then what?

Bethany lived by the adage *the best way to get over one man was to get under another*, but casual encounters weren't my thing. Lance was my only experiment in the fast and furious and look how that turned out.

After we checked every room, I was confident nothing had been moved or rifled and invited Mateo to stay for dinner. He set the table while I warmed the lasagna.

"There should be a bottle of red on the top shelf in the pantry. I'm not much of a wine person, but Lance bought it, so it will definitely have a pretentious bouquet."

He laughed, then located and uncorked it while I dished out the food. I watched him as he poured the dark burgundy liquid. When he gave me the glass, his fingertips grazed mine, rekindling the sensation of his hands on my back. I resisted the urge to reach out to touch him.

"We should probably toast something, don't you think?" He raised his glass.

I wanted to suggest "here's to getting to know you better," but what if he didn't want to know me better? What if he just wanted to see me naked? Although I wouldn't mind that at all, it didn't make for much of a toast.

After a few seconds of silence, he said, "Here's to finding answers." When I hesitated, he asked, "That is what you want, isn't it?"

"I guess it depends on the question." But I clinked his glass with mine. "To finding answers."

I kept the conversation first-date light during dinner, searching unsuccessfully for clues as to how he felt about whatever might be developing between the two of us.

It was after nine when we finished eating and cleaning up. The wine was gone, and I was exhausted. Even so, I wasn't ready for him to leave. It was, however, fast approaching the point of no return, the time at the end of the evening when, as Dad would say, "*You've got to fish or cut bait.*" Of course, when my father had given me that piece of folksy wisdom, I was relatively certain he hadn't expected it might apply to anything remotely sexual.

If I asked Mateo to sit with me, I'd most likely find myself waking up next to him in the morning. And while that would probably be completely fantastic, it was what I wanted, but not what I needed. So, I didn't ask him to join me on my fancy Victorian fainting sofa.

"I really appreciate everything you did for me today. Buddy and the police and cleaning up the mess at my apartment. I don't know what Hugh did for you, but I'm sure you've more than paid him back. From now on, I want to pay—"

"Please, forget it. But I am worried about you staying here by yourself."

I flushed with sudden heat.

"Remember," he continued, "whoever got in might have used a key. I called a security guy I know, but he can't stop by until tomorrow afternoon. Is there somebody you could spend the night with?"

Well, yes, someone standing right in front of me.

"What about your parents?" he coaxed.

I shook my head and tried to focus on the idea there was someone out there who might have a key to my place. Both Connor and Lance had returned theirs, but either could have made a copy. And the thought that the intruder could have gotten in without a key was even more disturbing. The fact I hadn't considered these possibilities was a testament to how rattled I'd been.

"My parents go to bed early, but I can stay at Bethany's." I wasn't particularly keen on the prospect. She would ask a million questions that I was too tired to answer.

"Why don't you call her before I leave? Then I'll help you lock up."

I called Bethany, who was out with someone she met on Tinder. She was having a lousy time, though, and was happy to have an excuse to leave.

Mateo's definition of locking up included setting booby traps around the house. He shoved a chair against the front door, then placed pots and pans on the floor near the back.

"Now we'll know if somebody tries to get in," he said after checking the windows. "Give me a call on your way home from work tomorrow, and I'll meet you here with the new keys."

Dodging obstacles, we went out the back. When we reached my car, he promised to report anything he learned about the Darrows.

"Thank you again for everything, and I meant what I said about the money."

"Are you kidding? I should be paying you. I haven't had this much fun in a long time. And text me when you get to Bethany's, okay?"

Then he kissed me on the forehead and walked away.

CHAPTER 13

"Let me get this straight," Bethany said, curling her slender legs underneath her while sipping a cup of hot cocoa. "You guys made out in the car like crazy teenagers, and nothing else happened?"

"How many times have I told you I'm not ready for a relationship? And seriously. Connor Reynolds invaded my home in the middle of the night and had a pot party there the next day. Someone ransacked my place and stole pictures some stalker took of me—pictures that were given to me by my ex's ex—and all you want to talk about is me *not* having sex."

"That pretty much covers it." Bethany nodded, foam forming a mustache on her upper lip. Even with no make-up and the suggestion of facial hair, she was gorgeous.

"Don't kid yourself; this Latin hunk is not just another guy. The way you sounded on the phone. Oh, my, God. 'I'm at Bethany's, Mateo. Thanks again for everything.' And what is *everything*, I'd like to know. But the expression on your face whenever you say his name is exactly like the one you had over that stupid soccer player freshman year in high school."

"Peter Kramer was not stupid," I asserted. "He was dyslexic." Why the hell was I defending the moron who had tried to feel me up while I tutored him in English? "And I do not have a crush on Mateo."

I closed my eyes in frustration. Neither Bethany nor Peter Kramer was the source of my irritation. I was annoyed with myself because I was way beyond the crush stage.

"Hey." She patted my knee. "I'm just kidding around. It scares the shit out of me that some psycho is after you."

"After me?" Hearing my best friend echo Matteo's fear made it more real. Someone was trying, at the very least, to unnerve me, to make me vulnerable. And it was working.

"Yes, Lucy," Bethany spoke as if I were incredibly slow. "What else would you call it? And lunatics who do crazy shit, like sending freak roses and executing dolls and trashing your apartment, don't stop until they get what they want. And this guy wants you."

I had no idea what my intruder, or stalker or whatever he was, wanted, unless he hadn't broken in to steal from me. What if it was more of an attempt to distract and threaten me? But why?

"Hello." Bethany put her empty cup on the coffee table. "Did you hear what I said about taking this seriously?"

"Sorry. I am taking it seriously. If I weren't, I wouldn't be crashing on your couch. And Matteo has a security person coming over to change locks and set up a system. He's very thorough,"

"I bet he is." Bethany's suggestive grin was cut short by a yawn. "Well, if you're not offering any juicy details on your soon-to-be Latin lover, I'm going to bed."

"Thanks again for letting me stay."

I switched off the crystal lamp by the sofa and scrunched under the blanket, wishing I'd brought my own pillow. After the policeman's warning about robbers and sex in strange places, however, I might have to burn it.

At 5:38, after a long night of trying to get comfortable, I gave up, wrote a thank-you note on a scrap of paper, and gathered my things. Then I threw a light-weight jacket over the T-shirt and sweatpants I'd slept in and slipped out the door. I wasn't eager to go home but putting it off would only make it harder later.

I parked close to the front of my apartment and scurried to the back door. Inside, I stepped over the pots and pans, which were thankfully in the exact spots as we'd left them. After making sure the rest of our high-level security precautions were in place, I walked through the bedroom and into the bathroom, locking both doors behind me.

One of my guilty pleasures was taking extra-long showers, enjoying the sensation of the cascading water. This morning, however, the scene from an old black and white movie, where the woman gets slashed repeatedly while standing in her shower, looped through my mind. I was in and out in record time.

I towel-dried my hair, swept it into a high ponytail, applied a little make-up, and dressed—all before seven fifteen. I ran through Starbuck's drive-thru and picked up coffee and a muffin, thinking I would still be the first one in. But when I pulled into the parking lot a few minutes after eight, Hugh's car was already there. Not a good sign.

I went directly to my office where I found him in the chair in front of my desk.

"Why didn't you tell me about those damned pictures?"

Mateo must have told him everything.

"Good morning to you, too."

"Yeah, right, good morning, Sunshine." He bared his teeth in a semblance of a smile. "Now, about those pictures."

I put my breakfast on the desk and sat before describing the photos in as much detail as I could, including the van.

"Let me get this straight. This Janelle chick gives you the pictures without any real explanation and then *poof,* the next day they're gone. Doesn't make sense."

"Believe me. I've been trying to figure it out all night."

"Could be the same person who's been trying to scare you off all along. Only now it's escalating. He's not just sending you creepy messages and gifts. He wants you to know he's following you and can get to you whenever he wants."

"Jesus, Hugh. If you're trying to scare me, it's working."

"I'm trying to get you to take this thing seriously."

"I am taking it seriously." *Why did everyone keep saying that?* I repeated Mateo's plans regarding the locks and alarm system and added, "And I'll be careful. I promise."

He growled something unintelligible under his breath and shook his head, then abruptly shifted subjects. "I talked to the accountant and he couldn't figure out where Johnston's extra money was coming from, so we checked with a guy I know at the bank."

I was constantly amazed at the number of nameless guys who provided Hugh with information.

"He tracked down the deposits and found out they were all in cash and none were over the magic number."

"Magic number?" I echoed.

"Back in the 70s the government passed a law stating that any cash deposit of over $10,000 had to be reported to the FDIC. The idea was to stop money laundering. Obviously, the good doctor is wise to the law."

"You think he was laundering money for someone?"

"That's not what it looks like to me. I think he was conducting a little under the table or, in his case, a little on the table shady business. I think the son of a bitch was brokering organs."

"Brokering what?" I put my cup down harder than I intended, slopping coffee on my hand.

"Selling organs. If I'm right, it's going to be tough to prove, though. His donors are probably the same illegals involved in the fraud cases. No way they'll come forward."

"You mean someone would willingly let a person take out a piece of them for cash?" I had read about people turning up in hotel rooms missing an important internal part, but they were unwilling participants.

"A kidney can fetch as much as $200,000 on the Red Market."

"The Red Market?" I whispered.

"A person can live with one kidney. Some guy in Chicago even advertised a kidney on Craigslist. So, yes, plenty of people are desperate enough to willingly sell their organs." He reached across the desk, broke off a piece of muffin, and stuffed it in his mouth.

Still chewing, he continued. "Usually the donor goes through channels and doesn't see anywhere near the going price. There's the broker, probably a middle-man." He paused, raised his hands, and continued. "Drum roll, please." Using his index fingers as makeshift drumsticks, he rapped them rapidly on the desk. "The surgeon. In Johnston's case I use the term lightly. More like a butcher."

I scooted the remaining muffin across the table to him. The image of the doctor cutting into some person for whom auctioning off a body part was as much an option as selling used furniture sickened me. Then it occurred to me that the doctor couldn't have been standing in that horrible operating theater alone. He would have had help.

"That must be why his nurse didn't want me to keep looking into his finances. And I wouldn't have if it hadn't been for that anonymous caller. Any ideas about who that might be?"

"Don't know, but I'd sure like to. Whoever it was knows what's been going on in that hell-hole office of his. Since state lines are almost always crossed in cases like this, the Feds take the lead. I've got an appointment in an hour with—"

"With a guy you know at the Bureau," I finished for him. He gave me a blank stare.

"Right. I want you to lay low on this thing."

"Lay low?" I had no idea what that might look like. Surely, he didn't expect me to sit around waiting for someone else to discover whether there was a connection between the doctor and my personal safety?

"Yeah, don't do any more digging around. If Johnston's nurse knows you're involved in the investigation, that means the doctor knows, too, and on top of all that other stuff with those damned pictures, the whole thing sets my teeth on edge."

"I don't think handling a surly nurse could be all that dangerous. And Johnston's still locked up, right?"

"That's the problem," he said, heading toward the door. "Johnston's been out on bail for almost a week now."

. . .

The rest of my morning was remarkably unproductive. Hugh's announcement about Johnston being free destroyed my concentration. Even though nothing connected the missing photos and the doctor, I couldn't shake the image of the ghoulish surgeon, skulking behind bushes, spying on me. Every time I tried to focus on completing paperwork or a background check, images of a scalpel-wielding psycho hiding in the shadows kept popping into my mind.

After over two hours of accomplishing next to nothing, I decided to take another look at Johnston's file. I wouldn't do any actual "digging" around in the case, but I needed to know more about the man.

I ran a search and found Johnston listed as the director of Stalwart Medical Consolidation. Apparently, he was the only doctor in the group. The website was a dreadful attempt at sentimentality but came across as crassly commercial. A caricature-like replica of the Norman Rockwell painting of a doctor, holding a stethoscope to a doll's chest while an anxious little girl looks on, dominated the upper right-hand corner. Instead of the original kindly old physician, Johnston had photoshopped his face into the picture. His close-set eyes peered at me, and his thin lips were stretched into a grimace I supposed was intended as a reassuring smile. Rather than eliciting confidence, however, the image seemed more like a warning about child predators.

In addition to the standard information, Johnston referred to himself as a world-renowned gastroenterologist. There was no online booking option. Obviously, the doctor was out. I wondered what they were telling patients, assuming he still had any.

Hugh's warning to "lay low" came to me, and I considered turning away. But what possible harm could come from a phone call, especially one that would most likely be a recording? Instead of an automated message, a real person picked up.

"Dr. Johnston's office. How may I help you?" It was the unmistakable voice of the woman who had left that bizarre blend of a well-rehearsed but slightly unhinged message.

"Uh, well, I, uh." A flash of Hugh's face twisted in an expression of disapproval almost made me hang up. But the woman's imperious tone grated on my nerves.

I took a deep breath and asked, "Is this Roberta Garrison?"

"Yes. This is Dr. Johnston's nurse. How may I..." She stopped mid-sentence, her cool phone voice ratcheting into a ten on the shrillness scale. "Wait a minute. Is this Lucy Howard? I cannot believe you have the nerve to call this office. You know damn good and well Dr. Johnston's practice is closed. And thanks to your meddling, it may never open again. You are a spiteful little bitch who deserves to burn in hell."

Her vitriol slammed each word like a hammer.

"Hmm," I murmured, surprised at how unaffected I was by Nasty Nurse.

"You think I should burn in hell for exposing your boss as a cold-bloodied quack willing to use poor people with no options to defraud insurance companies?" The more I said, the angrier I became. "And don't think I don't know you were right there beside him. How much blood money did you make? Or maybe you didn't do it for the money." I paused for effect. "Maybe you did it for love. Was that it? Did you do it because you love your boss?"

I waited for the obscenity-laced shrieking to die down before continuing.

"Sounds like I struck a nerve." I grinned because that was literally what it had sounded like. It had grown so quiet on Roberta's end I wondered if the other woman was still there, but the sound of deep, ragged breathing confirmed the nurse's presence.

"Look, Roberta," I began. "I don't think you're a bad person." *I think you are despicable.* But now wasn't the time to share my opinion. So, I said, "I think you just got caught up in your emotions and made some bad decisions. It's not too late to help yourself."

I thought of Elsie and how the sweet little old lady would most likely go to jail when people like Johnston and Roberta committed truly heinous crimes and might never have to pay. The idea fueled my desire to lash out at the deplorable woman, but I kept my voice soft and even. "If you come forward with what you know now before things get worse, maybe you won't end up in a cell yourself."

The only response was a quick intake of breath from Roberta, then more silence. Had I gone too far? Had the nurse taken my comment about things getting worse as a reference to Johnston's involvement in the organ business? I hadn't intended to drop that kind of hint. I hadn't even planned on talking to his nurse. But the woman's smug condemnation of me for simply doing my job combined with the memory of Elsie had released something in me, and I'd forgotten about everything: the possible danger I was in, Hugh's warnings, common sense in general.

I waited. Since I hadn't come right out and accused Roberta of handing her boss the scalpel so he could remove a kidney, maybe the damage to the investigation was minor. Maybe the nurse would be rattled enough to blurt out a confession or at least reveal some important details.

After several seconds, Johnston's nurse responded in a cold, steady voice. "I have no idea what you're talking about. But I can tell you this. You're in way over your head. I tried to warn you, but no, you wouldn't listen. Now you're the one who better worry about helping yourself."

She disconnected, leaving me staring at her phone, wondering how in the world I was going to tell Hugh what I had just done. But what had I really done? I'd only wanted to listen to their message explaining why the office was closed. It wasn't my fault the rabid nurse picked up. And when Roberta answered, I had to wing it, but I hadn't said anything specific about organ brokering.

And why had the nurse been the one answering phone calls? Surely, the doctor had other employees, a receptionist or file clerk, who would be a more logical choice for manning the office during the doctor's absence. Maybe Roberta was the only one willing to step up, to take care of patient requests and emergency calls. She didn't seem like the overly conscientious type. If she cared about anything other than financial gain, I would bet it was her boss. The woman's defense of the doctor went beyond employee loyalty, as demonstrated by the way she lost it when I hinted there was something going on between the two of them.

I assumed she was in the office alone, but if Johnston were out on bond, he could be there, too. The police had searched both his home and office and had confiscated his records. But that didn't mean they'd gotten everything. Maybe the doctor and nurse were destroying evidence right this minute. Or possibly they were just using the office to have sex since he couldn't very well take Roberta home to his wife.

His wife! Hugh hadn't mentioned talking to Mrs. Johnston. Thumbing through the file, I couldn't find any mention of her other than the doctor's hidden accounts being listed under the name Janice Holloway, the doctor's mother-in-law.

I turned to my computer and typed in her name. I discovered a five-year-old obituary naming Andrea Holloway Johnston as the only surviving relative. When I Googled Andrea, I found a two-year-old photo of the Johnston couple from the St. Stephen's Hospital Gala.

Unlike my fascination with Elsie, I hadn't been the least bit curious about any personal details concerning the doctor. Yes, we had established a somewhat intimate connection through the contents of his trash, but beyond that, I wouldn't have known him if he were standing in front of me.

I zoomed in on the doctor's face and was shocked at how ordinary he looked. He could have been any slightly balding man in an ill-fitting tuxedo. His eyes were glassy and too close together, but they weren't frightening or soulless. Seemingly at ease as he posed for the camera, he exuded a soft harmlessness, like someone's slightly tedious uncle.

The woman standing next to him in a long-flowing dress, however, looked distinctly uncomfortable. Stiff-shouldered with tendons visible on her long, slender neck, she leaned away from the doctor. His arm was wrapped around her narrow waist, restricting the possibility of escape. Platinum blond hair smoothed back in a sleek, severe fashion emphasized her large dark eyes and high cheekbones. Gazing at the camera, unsmiling, she looked defiant, like a French resistance fighter facing a firing squad. The caption identified them as Dr. and Mrs. Andrew Johnston, bronze sponsors.

I wondered what it would be like to be listed as an "and Mrs." If Andrea Johnston's expression was any indication of what she thought of that status, it wasn't good. And being forever linked with the kind of man her husband was would make it even worse. But there must have been a time when the doctor's wife had wanted to be on her husband's arm, when she'd been proud to be known as Mrs. Dr. Johnston.

I wished I had access to the couple's wedding album. Surely, the blushing bride would have been glowing with the happiness that comes from knowing you've made it. Not only are you safely married, you're that luckiest of all beings: a doctor's wife. I could picture Mom's look of delight if I were to bag a surgeon or even a lowly optometrist.

Suddenly overcome with sadness, I was unsure if my melancholy was the result of the specter of a young Andrea Holloway, a woman so eager to join the ranks of the happily married she was willing to up her individuality.

Most likely, I was projecting. Just because Lance had tricked me into believing in happily-ever-after didn't mean Johnston's wife had been deceived. One grim-faced photo didn't tell the whole story. Andrea could have been having a rough night, or maybe she'd eaten a bad oyster. Instead of some naïve victim, maybe she was the mastermind behind the doctor's criminal activities.

Only I didn't believe that. Something I was beginning to recognize as solid instinct told me Andrea Johnston didn't like her husband at all and would be more than willing to blow the whistle on him if given the chance. And if she were the anonymous caller, maybe she'd already started the process. The only way to be sure was to talk to the woman.

After my encounter with Roberta Garrison, however, I didn't think it would be such a good idea to contact Johnston's wife myself. No, I would follow Hugh's advice and let him handle it. But it was my lead and I would insist on going with him.

I dialed his cell and was more than a little relieved when it went to voicemail. It was much easier summarizing my conversation with the nurse in a recording rather than trying to explain it directly to my boss. Another plus was I ended on a positive note by suggesting we might be able to get Mrs. Dr. Johnston to turn on her husband.

I filled the next few hours tying up loose ends on several outstanding cases before checking to see if there were any updates on Elsie. As far as I could tell from Hugh's scribblings, a court date was pending. I'd hoped it wouldn't come to that. Trials could be so unpredictable, especially in a situation where the presiding judge might need political backing from one of the companies the older woman had swindled.

I started to read through Elsie's case one more time when Darla buzzed. "You've got a visitor," she said. "I explained she needed an appointment, but she insisted you'd want to see her." Darla lowered her voice. "It's Janelle Ragsdale." Then, in a louder, more aggressive tone, she said, "Should I tell her to come back at a more convenient time?"

In a weak moment, I told Darla all about Janelle's role as the other woman. The receptionist had been appropriately indignant, and I was sure Darla was treating Janelle with extreme scorn. I appreciated the loyalty but was no longer sure if my former rival deserved contempt or sympathy.

"Thanks, but it's okay. You can send her back."

I hesitated. What was the proper procedure for greeting the other woman when you were no longer sure she was a slut? If I were European, I could pull off double air kisses without having to touch Janelle. The traditional Southern hug was out of the question. I was still mulling over acceptable etiquette when Lance's former paramour charged into the office and wrapped her arms around me, creating a perfume-infused haze.

I submitted to the enthusiastic welcome for a few seconds before pulling away. "Please, sit down," I said, retreating behind the desk.

Janelle fluffed her thick blonde waves before draping herself across the leather chair in front of my desk. She removed her lightweight jacket, revealing an abundance of creamy white cleavage.

Did she dress like that for court appearances? Probably only for predominantly male juries.

"Is there something I can help you with?" I was completely at a loss as to how I should feel about this woman. If Janelle shared my discomfort, she didn't show it.

"No, honey. I just heard about the break-in at your apartment and wanted to make sure you were okay. It must have been terrible for you."

Today her delivery was as smooth as a synthesizer, except for one off-note when she said *honey.*

"How did you know someone broke into my apartment?"

"Bethany told me when I stopped by to pick up my tube of Get Glowing. You know, the stuff I ordered at the party? She mentioned you stayed at her place because you were so upset."

Picturing my best friend and Lance's former girlfriend chatting away about my misfortune deeply disturbed me.

"Thanks for worrying, but I feel much better now. And it turned out to be not as bad as it looked." I almost told her the intruder hadn't stolen anything other than the photos Janelle had given me. Instead I said, "I needed to change the locks anyway."

"Do the police have any ideas about who it might be?" Janelle touched a finger to the tip of her tongue and smoothed an already perfect eyebrow.

"Not really, but there have been a few break-ins in my area. Hopefully, they'll catch whoever it was soon. Regardless, I'm having an alarm system installed. And I'm thinking about getting a really big dog." I hadn't consciously considered Connor's advice, but some flicker of intuition told me it might not be a bad idea for my visitor to think I planned to do some serious security tightening.

"Did you tell them about Lance?" Janelle crossed her legs.

"About Lance?"

"You know. About your break-up and how angry he can get? I wouldn't put it past him to trash your apartment to get even with you for not taking him back."

I tried to recall my conversation with Janelle when we were sitting in my car. I didn't remember mentioning Lance's desire for reconciliation before going to Bethany's party and was certain it hadn't come up later. Of course, Connor's weed and beer could have dulled my memory of the entire night. Still, sharing something like that with my former rival wasn't the kind of thing I would have done.

"I guess it's possible. But I don't think so. Anyway, if he did do it, he's too smart to get caught."

"Well, I wouldn't put anything past that man." Janelle stood and tossed her jacket over her shoulder. "I'm glad you're feeling better, but I'm still worried about you. A man like Lance can be very unpredictable."

"Thanks for checking on me." I joined Janelle on the other side of the desk, unable to gracefully dodge a parting hug.

"Don't hesitate to call me if you need any help."

"I will. But if Lance is on some crazy rampage, you should be careful, too. You know, since we both rejected him." Once more equable, her voice offered no clue, so I studied Janelle's face, hoping to see a reaction that might give me a hint about the woman's motivation for coming to see me. But like the lawyer she was, she had mastered the art of dissembling.

I watched Janelle walk toward the exit, her shapely hips swaying. Before turning the corner, she turned and smiled before giving me a finger-wave.

Was she concerned or was it something else?

. . .

Back at my desk, I replayed the night of the party, starting with Janelle showing up unexpectedly and ending with the envelope of photos. Nowhere along the way could I recall discussing Lance's request for me to take him back. If my memory was accurate, how had Janelle come up with this information?

And it was awfully convenient that she had found out about the break-in from Bethany. Had Janelle had some sort of sexual emergency that demanded she pick up her order immediately? And what kind of high-powered attorney has the time to stop by to check in on a woman she barely knows in the middle of a workday?

I thought of how the old Lucy might have taken Janelle's concern at face value. The new Lucy, the one I thought I liked so much better, was not so trusting.

CHAPTER 14

After Janelle left, I revisited Elsie's case to see if I'd missed something to convince Hugh to go light on the woman. My best argument was that other than the insurance companies no one had been hurt by her scheme. I would volunteer to talk to them about reaching a settlement that would reimburse them and avoid any bad press arising from sending an elderly citizen to jail.

But I couldn't set aside my questions about her quiet rage when she stared at the quilt her friend had made for her.

The discomfort I experienced from my flashy visitor made it easier to put Elsie on the back burner. I expected Bethany could shed some light on the situation, so gave her a call, and was sent to voicemail. As a real estate agent, my friend was at the mercy of her clients and their schedules. I left a message asking her to call back.

I checked my messages to make sure I hadn't missed one from Hugh. The man was notoriously bad about checking in, so it was not a shock to find no response.

Johnston's file was still lying on the corner of the desk, so I took another look. Possibly, Hugh had listened to my news about the wife and had contacted her on his own. Maybe he was at the doctor's house right now interviewing the woman. The Johnston residence wasn't exactly on my way home, but it was only a quick detour.

I would only drive by to see if Hugh's car was parked there. It wasn't as if I planned to knock on the door if he wasn't there or anything crazy like that.

I buzzed Darla to let her know I was leaving, stopping when Johnny Cash's ragged velvet voice echoed from inside my purse. *I fell into a burning ring of fire.* Norm's ringtone. A wave of guilt washed over me. Poor Buddy was probably a wreck after his encounter with the police, and with the recent chaos in my life, I hadn't thought to see about him. I felt even more guilty ignoring Norm's call but assuaged my conscience with the decision to stop by as soon as I left the Johnston home.

Sprinting to my car, I pushed aside thoughts of Buddy and Norm and concentrated on what I might learn from Andrea Johnston. If someone had asked what seeing the house in daylight might accomplish, I wouldn't have been able to put my concern into words. It was one of those nagging brain tickles when something is trying to surface. You don't know exactly what it is, but you know it's important.

About a block from the doctor's address, I slowed to a crawl. This was the kind of neighborhood where the only vehicles parked on the street belonged to landscaping firms or security-system companies, so I turned onto a side street before shutting off the engine. There were no cars in front of the house, and thick shrubbery obstructed my view of the winding driveway.

Sudden movement near the passenger side startled me, and I hit the auto lock. A determined power walker in a loose-fitting sweat suit breezed past so quickly I couldn't determine the sex of the exercise buff. Watching as the person strode away, I decided he or she wasn't tall enough to be Andrea Johnston nor wide enough to be the doctor.

The passerby gave me an idea. I reached into the backseat where I kept a bag prepared for the rare occasions when I might go to the gym. I exchanged my work shoes for sneakers and slipped on an oversized sweatshirt. I pulled up the hood and examined myself in the rearview mirror. With my head down, it would be almost impossible to recognize me.

I stepped onto the sidewalk and mimicked a runner's stretch. After a few awkward attempts at grabbing my foot from behind with the opposite hand, I gave up and broke into more of a trot than a run.

My plan was to get close enough to the house to see if Hugh's or anyone else's car was in the drive, then pretend to have a cramp and stop. Unfortunately, my competitive nature kicked in and the gentle jog became a brisk run. It turned out I didn't need to fake an injury. At the far edge of the property, near the spot where Hugh and I had rummaged through the trash, I experienced a very real pain in my left ankle and stopped abruptly, leaning against one of the red and gold maple trees lining the way. After flexing and unflexing my foot. I took several tentative steps before hearing an engine behind me.

Instinctively, I turned to see how close the approaching vehicle was and stood completely still when I saw it was a silver van. Dropping to one knee in the pretense of tying my shoe, I kept my back to the street and my head down as the driver rolled past. Only then did I take another look, hoping to see the license plate. But it was smeared with mud and unreadable as it turned up the winding drive and out of my line of vision.

Like Hugh, I believed true coincidences were rare occurrences and was certain this wasn't one of those rarities. The driver of the silver van had to be the person who had been snapping photos of me.

Partially hidden beneath the branches of the maple, I watched the house. But the two-story home with its attached three-car garage blocked all view of whoever had continued up the curving drive to a side entrance and there was no movement in the front.

Although I had established somewhat of a connection between my stalker and the doctor, I returned to the car feeling defeated. I no longer had the photos proving that connection, and I didn't want to think about how many silver vans there were in the metro area alone.

I had no idea how Hugh would react to my discovery. He was definitely going to be pissed about my conversation with Roberta and probably wouldn't be thrilled about my trip to spy on Johnston. But surely he would be impressed by what I had uncovered.

As I inched away from the curb, it occurred to me it might not matter all that much what Hugh thought. Yes, he was my boss, and he was good at what he did, but my own instincts weren't so bad either. For the first time in my career as an investigator, a career Hugh had thrust upon me, I felt a sudden rush of confidence and not just because I discovered several leads in the case. No, it was more than that. It was standing up for myself and facing my fears. It was about actually beginning to understand what I might be capable of.

So, bring it on, Hugh. The new and improved Lucy Howard was ready.

. . .

Still buzzing from my recent self-awareness, I took out my phone and scrolled through a dental appointment reminder and a prescription refill notice before I go to one from an unknown number.

Ms. Howard, this is Elsie. I have some information that could prove helpful to your uncle. Please give me a call.

I planned to get back to her as soon as I got to Buddy's. Seeing Mom's car parked in front of the shop didn't exactly sound an alarm, but it made me uneasy. Walking across the lot, I saw Buddy's Outback wasn't in its regular spot. That wasn't worrisome. He often ran errands after work, but Mom didn't normally hang around unless he was home.

I passed the usual, unusual backyard accessories, noting the addition of a banged-up carousel horse lying on its side next to the goddess with the wandering eyes. The screen door was ajar, so I walked onto the back porch where I could hear Norm and Mom talking from within. I almost tripped over a fake tombstone and knocked it into one of the plastic skeletons.

Norm appeared at the kitchen door with his hair sticking out at strange angles as if he'd been running his hands back and forth through it. Instead of his typically enthusiastic greeting, he merely held the door open and motioned me inside where I found my mother sitting at the table, holding her head, shoulders shaking.

"Mom, what's wrong?" The last time I remembered seeing her cry was at my grandmother's funeral.

"Thank God you're here." Using a bright yellow napkin, I wiped at the snail-like mascara trails lining her face. She waved me away and said, "It's Buddy."

I kneeled beside her.

Norm put his hand on Mom's shoulder. "Now Anne-Marie, you're scaring her." He gently pulled me to my feet. "It's not as bad as your momma's making it seem." He held out a chair and guided me into it. "It's just that we can't find Buddy."

Other than the rhythmic ticking of the Cheshire cat clock and an occasional sniffle from my mother, the room was quiet.

"You can't find him?"

"Nobody's seen him since early this morning. He was gone when I got up at 6:00. And you know the man is not an early riser. I tried his phone, but he didn't answer. We all know how he is about charging that thing, so I still wasn't too concerned. But when I didn't hear from him by 10:30, I got worried. He swears his new medicine makes driving easier, but I don't trust it. I started calling hospitals and checking in with the police. Nothing." His voice broke.

Mom took his hand. "Norm called me a little after 4:00, and I came right over."

Before his diagnosis, Buddy had been known to go missing from time to time. On two of those occasions, the police found him in the car napping alongside a busy highway. Both times they shook him awake to administer a breathalyzer and were puzzled when he passed.

Since there was technically no law against sleeping in your car, they released him with warnings to be more careful. Another time he drifted off at the movie theater and might have spent the night there if not for an observant teenager sweeping the floors. But the film was *The Great Gatsby*, so no one was overly concerned.

His medication improved things. Buddy rarely dozed off for more than ten or fifteen minutes unless he was in a stressful situation. Like, say, being a suspect in a murder case.

As if he were reading my mind, Norm said, "This whole Darrow mess has been sitting heavy on your uncle. He's been talking about visiting Burton Prescott, that creepy Civil War re-enactor, but we agreed we should step back and let the authorities take care of things."

Mom and I exchanged skeptical glances. We both knew patience wasn't one of Buddy's strong suits. And with his love of drama, the odds of him sitting on the sidelines in a murder investigation were low, especially when he was the primary suspect.

"Do you think maybe there's a chance he changed his mind, you know, about stepping back?" I asked, trying to be tactful.

Apparently, Mom felt no such need. "I think we all know what a hard-headed jackass my brother can be. I'm surprised you believed his bullshit about not sticking his nose into things he shouldn't."

I winced and said, "We can't be sure about that. I mean he's never been involved in anything this serious before. Maybe he—"

"No, honey," Norm sighed. "Your momma's right. I just didn't want to go there."

"But this could be a good thing," I offered. "I bet he went to see that re-enactor guy and got into some long, drawn-out discussion about authenticating old stuff and lost track of time. He probably hasn't even realized his phone's dead. Do you have a number for Prescott?"

"I never talked to him, and Buddy keeps his contacts in his phone, but maybe it's on an order form." He left the room to check the shop records.

"Do you really believe what you said about Buddy losing track of the time?"

I shrugged. "It's possible, but he's been gone for hours now, and he might be stubborn, but he wouldn't want everyone worrying about him like this."

Instead of waiting for Norm to return, Mom took out her phone and searched for Prescott. She eliminated a Dr. Prescott, Ph.D. and a Burt Prescott in Dalton. That left her with two in the area. The first number had been disconnected. She was in the process of dialing the second when Norm returned, empty-handed.

"I think this might be our guy," she said, while waiting for an answer. She put the call on speaker and placed the phone on the table. The three of us stared at it while listening to the hollow ringing.

"Oh, I wish I was in the land of cotton!"

The refrain to "Dixie," the song emblematic of the South's propensity for looking backward, filled the air. The lyrics faded, leaving the twangy tune as background to what sounded like an imitation of blustery cartoon character Foghorn Leghorn, the bombastic southern rooster who occasionally shared the stage with Bugs Bunny. The booming voice identified itself as Burton Prescott, historian and Civil War expert, and explained he was away on important business, before instructing callers to leave a message.

I ended the call without recording one.

"What an ass," Mom said.

"Exactly," Norm responded. "The guy's completely full of shit. And Virgil Darrow is even worse. That's why Buddy didn't want anyone to know he'd done business with those guys. Especially you, baby girl."

"Me? Why me?"

"Because you're the real deal when it comes to knowing history. I think Buddy wishes he'd finished his degree, so he could work at a museum or something sophisticated and interesting like that. Not that Past Perfect isn't great, but I'm afraid sometimes selling antiques feels more like something he fell into rather than a career choice."

I could identify.

"And your uncle also considers you one of the best judges of character he knows, except for that asshole Lance. But that guy was slick, kind of a bright, shiny object. Buddy knew you would have recognized Darrow and Prescott right away as the phonies they are."

I didn't share my uncle's assessment of my judgment, but it was reassuring to know everyone didn't think I was a total fool after the Lance fiasco.

"What's next?" Mom had been so quiet I had almost forgotten she was there.

"Norm covered most of the bases when he checked in with the police and hospitals. It's too early to file a missing person's report, but Hugh probably knows somebody who could get the word out about being on the lookout for Buddy's car. I'll give him a call." And I would try Mateo, too, but there was no reason to mention him to my mother. I stepped into the other room.

There were no messages from Hugh, which was odd since the way I handled Roberta gave him the perfect opportunity to berate me for incompetence. Of course, he might be waiting for the chance to yell at me in person. I tried his number and was sent to voicemail and left a message asking him to call me back as soon as possible.

Mateo answered on the second ring. "I was just getting ready to call you in case you forgot about getting your new keys," he said. "Hope you're not locked out."

Crap! Meeting Mateo for the key exchange had completely slipped my mind. I apologized and spent the next few minutes telling him about my missing uncle. He agreed that about all they could do at this point would be to wait but promised to contact a friend who was with the Atlanta police department.

"She might not be able to do too much, but she can keep us up to date on anything new."

She? How good a friend was this *she*?

I knew I should be ashamed for worrying about my non-boyfriend's romantic involvements when God only knows what might have happened to Buddy. But that didn't stop me from picturing Mateo in the arms of some tall brunette, wearing a badge and gun and very little else. I shook away the image and thanked him for his help.

"No problem. Are you hanging at your uncle's or heading home? I can meet you either place. But I do need to show you how to disarm the alarm."

"Alarm?" God, how much would that cost?

"Don't worry. We're billing your landlords. They've got plenty of money and it's their responsibility to make sure your safe."

I started to protest, but he was right. The Reynolds were loaded, and they owed me for not calling the police on their grandson and his stoned friends.

"There's really nothing to do here. Mom said she'd hang with Norm for a while, so I'll meet you at my apartment in about forty-five minutes if that works for you."

He agreed and I returned to the kitchen where Norm was making coffee.

"If you're okay, I'm going home to pick up my new keys." As soon as the words crossed my lips, I knew I had screwed up royally.

"New keys? Why do you need another set of keys? What's wrong with your old one?" Mom's voice steadily rose in both volume and pitch. I heard one of the dogs, whining from the bedroom.

"It's not a big deal." I considered making up a story about accidentally dropping the keys down a storm drain or leaving them in the back of an Uber. But there hadn't been enough rain to sweep away the pollen what's less suck down my giant set of keys complete with rape whistle and mini-pepper spray, gifts from Mom.

That pretty much left telling the truth, which had until a short time ago been my go-to move. I offered the briefest possible explanation of the break-in, making it sound as harmless as possible. Omitting details like the scattered underwear, broken dishes, and general dishevelment, I wrapped up by saying it was most likely neighborhood kids playing a prank. I vaguely attributed that conclusion to the police but assured Mom the authorities were taking the crime seriously and would be driving by with increased frequency. The last part of the story was more wishful thinking than conviction, but I did my best to sell it.

My mother, however, wasn't buying. "I can't believe you didn't call us. We would have come right over. You shouldn't have been alone until the police got there."

"I wasn't alone, Mom." Shit. I had stepped in it again. Had my mother set me up like that intentionally? Had the woman been a covert agent in some previous life?

She and Norm were looking at me expectantly. "I was with a friend."

It was a questionable trade-off, but I had hit on the one topic almost as important to my mother as my safety: the increasingly unlikely possibility I might someday produce a grandchild.

"What friend, dear?" She spoke in a purring hostage-negotiator-voice. "Is it that lovely young man who was with you at the police station? The one with those beautiful eyes."

Trying to establish rapport, smooth. But I was determined not to be drawn in. It wasn't that I didn't want to share. I valued my mother's opinions. It wasn't like Mom was judgmental or even overly intrusive.

No, it wasn't the need for privacy that made me want to keep my growing attraction to Mateo secret. I just didn't want to disappoint her again. I remembered the way Mom's eyes lit up when I told about her Lance. Although she had been supportive when I broke up with him, that light had dimmed. Besides, once I admitted I would very much like to at least explore the relationship, I could never take it back or deny it.

"Please, Mom." Better not to raise her hopes at all than dash them later. "It's not like that with us. He owes Hugh a favor and is paying it back by helping Buddy. And that's it."

A look of what appeared to be skepticism flickered across Norm's face, but it passed quickly, and I didn't think Mom noticed.

"Well, whatever it is, I'm glad he was with you." She added cream to her coffee and blew on it, before returning to her original point. "But I want you to promise me you'll never, ever keep something as serious as thugs breaking into your home from your father and me." She took a sip, then brought in the big gun. "Your poor father is going to be so upset about this."

She knew how much I hated worrying Dad, and momentarily considered an attempt to divert her by mentioning what beautiful children Mateo and I might make. But I stayed strong.

"Tell Dad not to worry. The locks are changed, and I had a security system installed."

"I just hope you didn't pay too much. I'm sure your father could have done it cheaper." I assured her the Reynolds would pick up the expense, vowing never to admit it if they didn't. After a few more reassurances about my commitment to keep the family informed about my life, I escaped.

Driving past the other small businesses in Buddy's neighborhood, I set aside my feelings of guilt about not being completely honest with Mom and turned my thoughts to what Norm had told me concerning Buddy's opinion of me. Of course, he loved me. I was family, so he had no choice. To discover he respected me for my insight and perspective, however, touched me deeply. He must not be able to see the real me, the one who second-guessed and doubted myself.

Was it possible other people saw me differently, too? I felt as if I'd been dropped into a carnival house of mirrors. But instead of watching my reflection morph into an ugly distortion, the woman staring back looked better than the original. Or maybe the person I'd grown used to seeing in the mirror of my mind had changed while I wasn't looking.

I remembered Elsie's message and had a second of unease. Something about it troubled me, but I couldn't figure out what it was. I vowed to return her call as soon as I got home. But when I turned off the tree-lined street, Mateo was already there, by his car, cell phone in one hand and a bag from Moe's in the other. He waved and smiled as I pulled in beside him, then nodded at whatever the person on the other end of the phone was saying.

I took my time getting out of the car and walking to the porch to keep from eavesdropping. But he joined me at the front door, wrapping up the call with a quick thank you.

"That was my friend at the department. I'm afraid she hasn't heard anything about your uncle, but that's not necessarily bad news."

I looked away from him to hide the tears welling in my eyes.

"Hey," he turned my face to him, lifting my chin. "It just means he hasn't been in an accident or arrested. This is one of those times when no news really is good news."

Standing close to him like this made me want to curl into his body and stay there. "I know, and I really appreciate your help. I keep saying that, don't I?"

"And I keep telling you it isn't a big deal." He reached in his pocket and removed a small brown envelope. "Your new keys. I made three." He handed them to me and motioned toward the lock. "You should do the honors."

I inserted the shiny gold key, experiencing a little resistance from the new device, then unlocked and opened the door. Mateo stepped in and pointed to the alarm. He called out numbers as he punched them in and gave me a card with the code and a few instructions written on it. He spent the next few minutes explaining how the system worked and what to do if there was a break-in when I was home.

He led me to the kitchen. "The back door's pretty much the same, but it has sensors in case somebody tries to break the glass." He set down the sack of food and said, "Hope you don't mind, but I didn't have time to eat dinner. I brought tacos."

I hadn't eaten either, but losing Buddy had dulled my appetite. The smell of tacos wafting from the greasy bag sharpened it. "Who doesn't love tacos?" I smiled and started setting the table with paper plates and napkins, then took out a bottle of white wine.

While we ate, I told Mateo about the Johnston case, starting with my conversation with the nurse and ending with seeing the silver van.

He asked if I'd run any of my story by Hugh.

"I left him a message after I spoke to Roberta to let him know I might have screwed up a little."

I suggested we take our drinks to the living room, where I set the bottle on the coffee table. "I didn't get a chance to tell him I saw the van at the Johnstons'. He hasn't called me back."

"Probably got busy. I'm more concerned about your uncle."

I watched him lift the glass to his lips and took a sip myself, unsure if the warmth traveling through me was alcohol or Mateo induced.

"I know. It really isn't like Buddy to stay out of touch this long." The impact of what his absence might mean was sudden and terrifying. "Oh, God. You don't think somebody intentionally hurt him?" I fought back tears.

He moved closer, put his arms around me, and promised everything would be fine. I allowed my body to melt into his, very much wanting to believe his reassurances, wanting even more to get as near to him as possible.

Tiny alarms, like the tinkling chimes on my cell phone, sounded from inside the thinking part of my brain, and I questioned the wisdom of going with the moment. Overwrought about Buddy, still wounded from a bad relationship, and desperately wanting to be part of something bigger than myself. This wasn't the time to abandon logic. I needed to be cool, rational. Then Mateo smoothed my hair and grazed the top of my head with a soft kiss. I was gone.

Within seconds I was lying back on the fancy little sofa with this incredibly handsome man leaning over me, trailing gentle kisses over my throat and neck. By the time he reached my lips, my breath was ragged with eagerness. I wrapped my arms around his neck and placed my lips on his. He ran his hands down my back, stopping just below the curve of my waist. I heard a deep, low moan and realized it came from me.

"We could go to the bedroom," I whispered.

He put his hands on my shoulders and studied my face. "Are you sure? I don't want to rush you."

Please rush me, I thought. "I'm sure." Of course, I wasn't sure. I'd known him less than a week and, except for the business lunch, hadn't even had anything close to an actual date with the man. But what I lacked in longevity with Mateo, I made up in intensity. The man had seen me at my worst. He had met my crazy relatives and helped me through the break-in. He'd gone with me to help keep Buddy out of jail and was with me now when I was so worried about my uncle I couldn't think straight. And he still wanted to be with me.

He stood and pulled me up with him, then led me toward the bedroom. Thanks to the break-in, the room was relatively uncluttered, but I'd put on my third best sheets and couldn't remember the last time I'd cleaned the toilet. I needn't have worried, though, because the chorus of Sam Cooke's "Working on a Chain Gang" drifted up from within my front pocket before we made it through the door.

"It's Hugh." I never ignored a call from him, but now seemed like the perfect time to start. "I'll call him back later."

"I can't believe I'm saying this, but you should answer. It could be important."

I sighed, dug the phone from my pocket, and clicked on speaker for Mateo's benefit. "Hello, Hugh."

There was a sputter, and I smiled despite my irritation at the man's crummy timing. As sharp as he was, the concept of caller ID remained an elusive one for my boss. I always enjoyed his slight look of bewilderment when the person he was calling greeted him by name before he identified himself and could picture that puzzled expression now.

"Right, it's me," he began. "I'm at your uncle's and we need to see you."

"We? Did you find Buddy?"

"I don't have time to talk. Just get over here and bring Sullivan with you, okay?"

He disconnected before I had a chance to repeat the question or to ask how he knew Mateo was with me.

"Guess we better answer the summons." He tucked in his shirt and smiled. "But I want a rain check." He took me in his arms and kissed me. The kiss was, as Bethany would say, one that said, "I'm coming back for more."

The pleasure I felt disappeared when I realized what it was about Elsie's message that troubled me. She said she had news about Buddy, only I had never mentioned I had an uncle.

CHAPTER 15

Elsie's phone went straight to voicemail. I couldn't think of what to record, so I hung up, planning to call later.

When we arrived at Buddy's, one police car, an emergency vehicle, both of my parents' cars, Hugh's SUV, and a sedan I didn't recognize were crowded into the little parking lot of Past Perfect.

"Oh, God," I murmured as Mateo squeezed in between Dad's car and the police cruiser.

He put his hand on my knee. "Hey, there are no flashing lights, right? That means everyone's okay."

Or dead, so there's no hurry.

About fifteen or twenty onlookers were scattered in front of the building. I didn't spot anyone I knew. As Mateo maneuvered us through the crowd, a flash of silver hair from beneath the hoodie of a figure dressed in black set off a brain tickle. But I was in too much of a rush to take a closer look.

The store lights were on, and people were moving around inside. I bolted through the door with Mateo close behind. The jingling bell announced our arrival, but no one noticed.

A tall, muscular man in an EMT uniform leaned over someone sitting in one of the cane-bottom rockers Buddy had recently acquired. Norm insisted they were too damaged to repair, but my uncle had painstakingly restored them to almost as good as new status. A second technician kneeled in front of the chair, holding what looked like tubing. Together, they completely blocked my view.

I stopped, trying to make sense of the tableau in front of me. Then the taller man straightened and walked to the entrance, and I gasped. The man in the chair was my father. With the larger of the EMTs out of the way, I could see Mom behind the rocker, gripping Dad's shoulders. His face had turned an alarming shade of gray. I raced toward him.

"Mom!" I called, but kept my gaze focused on the man in front of her.

The EMT with the tubing stood up and held out her arms to keep me from getting close. A heavy-set woman with a stern expression, said, "Please slow down, Miss. We've got things stabilized, but I'm going to have to ask you to stay back."

"But that's my father," I cried, louder than I intended.

"Lucy! What in the world are you doing here?" Dad said with a loopy grin on his pale face. "Look, Annie." He turned to Mom. "It's Lucybird."

"Your father experienced some shortness of breath and chest pains," the EMT explained. "He doesn't seem to be in distress, but his pulse was erratic. We want to make sure everything's good. Right, Mr. Howard?"

"I'm not going to the hospital," he said, goofy grin still in place.

"Don't pay any attention to him," Mom said. "I thought he was having a panic attack, so I gave him a Xanax, and you know how crazy he can get." She came from behind and got close to Dad's face. "We are going to the hospital, and I don't want to hear another word about it."

The other EMT reappeared with a stretcher and positioned it next to the rocker. I watched as they eased Dad out of the chair and onto the gurney. Mom took hold of his hand.

"He's going to be fine, honey. What with all the excitement and Buddy getting shot, your dad just got over-anxious, but better safe than sorry. Right, dear?" She brushed a lock of hair from his eyes. Her voice was steady, but her hand was shaking.

I took a step toward them, then stopped. "Wait. What did you say about excitement and Buddy being shot?"

"Not shot exactly. I don't have time to get into all that right now. Norm and your boss are waiting for you in the back. I'll ride with your dad and call you after we see the doctor."

"But Mom."

"Your mother's right, baby. I am A-okay," Dad mumbled. "See you later, gator," he added as the paramedics wheeled him through the door.

I tried to follow, but someone grabbed my arm. It was Hugh.

"I promise your mother's telling the truth. Let's get out of everybody's way." He nudged me away from the crowd. "Apparently, she worked herself into a full-on frenzy waiting to hear about Buddy. Norm said she'd had two vodka tonics and one of her pills, but when I brought your uncle home, she lost it. We called your dad to come over and settle her down, but she wasn't having any of it. Kept yelling at me about how I was trying to get her brother killed and wouldn't listen to a damn thing." Hugh took a deep breath before he continued.

"That got your dad riled up, and he started holding his chest and breathing hard. I thought he might just be reacting to your mother's shrieking, but he looked bad. Bad enough that your mom snapped out of it and shoved a Xanax and an aspirin down his throat. Then she called his doctor and an ambulance. By the way, are you aware that your mother is a walking pharmaceutical department?"

I felt light-headed. "Oh, God. I don't care what she says, I need to get to the hospital." I watched the medics load the stretcher onto the ambulance, Mom climbing in behind him.

"Wait." I turned to Hugh. "What do you mean after she saw Buddy? What's wrong with my uncle?" My voice had reached a decibel level like the one Mom frequently hit.

"Take it easy," Hugh said. "Your uncle's fine, just a little banged up, that's all. And your dad's going to be all right, too. Why don't you come on back with me and let me explain what happened? Better yet, we'll let Buddy tell you. Then we'll get you to the hospital to check on your dad."

Mateo and I followed him through the store and into the apartment. Once inside, I heard voices drifting from down the hall where the master bedroom was and pushed past Hugh. I stopped and listened in front of the closed door, fearful of what might be behind it. Before I could knock, low-pitched whining followed and frantic scratching sounded from within.

Someone whistled, then called out, "Doris! Get your fat little butt back on this bed."

I threw open the door, sending poor Doris flying sideways and into the dresser. She scrambled to her feet, growled, and shook herself before hopping up beside Buddy, who was propped up in the bed. Norm scrunched near them with Pepe and Paco perched like sentinels at the foot of the bed, glaring at a strange man in the armchair across from them.

Glassy-eyed with tiny beads of sweat dotting his high forehead, my uncle greeted me with a weak grin. "Hey, sweet girl. I told Hugh he shouldn't bother you this late. But it's good to see you."

I rushed to the bed, stopping when I noticed his arm, resting on a stack of pillows. It was encased in a sling.

"What happened?" I touched him gently on the shoulder. "Mom said you got shot."

Buddy barked out a short laugh before his face twisted into a grimace of pain. Norm checked his watch. "You're about due for another dose." Standing, he reached for the bottle of pills on the bedside table, opened it, removed two tablets, and handed them to Buddy with a bottle of water.

"Just one," Buddy said, and Norm helped him take the medication. Then he eased back and closed his eyes. "These things are great, but too many make me sick to my stomach."

Doris maneuvered closer to her master. She bared her teeth at me before settling down near Buddy's neck.

"I think he's pretty much done in," Norm announced, directly facing the man in the chair. "If you need any more information, you'll have to contact our attorney."

I watched the tall man in an ill-fitting coat and tie unfurl from his seat. He closed his notepad and turned to me. "Detective Allenwood, ma'am." He held out his vein-roped hand and I shook it. "I'm investigating your uncle's involvement in the arrest of—"

"Miss Howard is not connected to the investigation." Hugh stepped between me and the officer. "We appreciate your time, but like the man said: for more information, check with his attorney."

Allenwood shrugged and smiled. "No problem. And you can tell that lawyer to expect a call." He brushed past Hugh and Mateo. "I can see myself out." Hugh still followed him.

Suddenly, the events of the evening spiraled around me and my knees grew weak. I took the seat the policeman had vacated and rested my head against the back of the chair. Mateo stood beside me. Staring at the scene in front of me— the unlikely couple with their three vicious watchdogs, two of whom were dozing while the third was vigorously licking himself—I began shaking with laughter.

Buddy opened his eyes and regarded me with a confused expression. Mateo placed his hand on my shoulder.

"We are a mess, aren't we?" Norm asked adding his own deep-throated chuckle to my semi-hysterical giggling.

"I don't get it," Buddy said. But he started laughing, too, probably more from the kick of his pain pill than the situation.

Tears streamed down my cheeks as I tried to rein in my emotions and avoid full-on sobbing.

Hugh returned from escorting the detective to the door and stood at the foot of the bed looking back and forth from Buddy and Norm to me.

Finally, I managed to gain enough control to speak. "I'm really confused here, guys. Maybe somebody could tell us what happened today and why that grim-faced detective was here."

The two men on the bed sobered up, or at least Norm did. Buddy quit laughing but was clearly high as a kite. With a crooked grin on his face, he began his narrative.

"I had trouble sleeping last night, so I got up before the crack of dawn. My phone was already beeping with a voicemail from that weasel Virgil. He said it was urgent I call him back as soon as I got the message. He had something to show me that would prove to the police I wasn't involved in killing his uncle." He scratched Doris behind her ears, and she groaned with canine contentment.

"I started not to call him back, but I thought maybe he was telling the truth. Or if he wasn't, maybe I could get him to. When I called, he sounded out of it, like he was drunk or something, said he had to see me in person and no one else could find out we were meeting. I know it was stupid. Hell, I knew it then, but I was so sick of just waiting around, doing nothing. I couldn't think of a reason Virgil would want to hurt me. And he's a puny little son of a bitch, so I wasn't scared of him."

"You could have left a note," Norm muttered.

"I should have," Buddy agreed, patting his companion on the hand. "And I'm real sorry." He was starting to slur his words. Speaking more deliberately, he continued. "Even though I wasn't afraid of Virgil, I didn't trust the skunk, so I decided to call good old Hugh." He aimed a goofy grin in my boss's direction, then looked at me. "Good old Hugh and I are best friends now. Did you know that, Sugar? Your boss is a really great guy. I know you said he was kind of an asshole, but—"

"I'm sure that's not what Lucy said," Norm cut him off. "I think you're getting a little confused. Why don't you let Hugh finish the story?"

"Stop saying I'm confushed. And Hugh can't tell the whole story because she ran off before he got inside. Lucy will believe me because she, uh." He drifted off.

"Wait a second." I said before my boss could pick up the story. "Uncle Buddy, did you say someone else was there?"

He fell back on the pillow without answering.

"He keeps insisting there was a woman with Prescott. Neither Hugh nor the police saw anyone else there." Norm patted his leg and nodded toward Hugh.

"He gave me the address for the meet-up, an abandoned warehouse on the west side, and I told him to wait for me there. I called the cops on the way there. My big plan was to let them handle the whole thing."

"It was a really good plan, Hugh, old pal," Buddy chimed in. "The best goddamn plan in the whole world." From the undertone of belligerence, I suspected the pain pills and my uncle's normal medication might not be agreeing. His next words confirmed my suspicions

"And if anybody says it washn't the besht plan in the whole freakin' world, I'll kick the living shit out of . . ." Before he could finish his threat, he closed his eyes and, head lolling to one side, began snoring softly.

"Anyway," Hugh resumed, "when we got there, I planned on stalling Buddy until the police came, but we could hear that crazy-ass moron screaming inside the warehouse."

"You mean Virgil?" I asked.

"Well, he's a crazy-ass moron, too, but I was talking about that braying jackass in a musty old Confederate uniform, Burton Prescott."

"Surely, it wasn't an actual uniform from the Civil War," I said. "I mean, if anyone tried to put one of those on, it would fall apart. Those things are—"

"Who gives a rat's ass if the goddamn uniform was real or not?" Hugh growled.

"Right, sorry. Please, go on."

"As I was saying, we could hear that Prescott character screaming about how Virgil was a traitor to his profession and to the entire Confederacy. Said it was time for him to face the consequences of his cowardice. And a whole bunch of crazy talk like that with the bottom line being he—Captain Burton Ulysses Prescott, he called himself—was sentencing Darrow to death. And if Buddy didn't get there soon, he'd have to do it himself. That's when things got weird."

That's when they got weird, I thought.

"Apparently, Prescott wanted your uncle to join in on the fun. He started ranting about how Darrow had impugned the honor of both the Prescott and Taylor names, and the only way to set things right was for Buddy to take up arms as a member of the firing squad."

"Firing squad!" Mateo and I echoed.

"I told you it was weird," Hugh said. "Anyway, Buddy decided he had to get in there and stall Prescott somehow. I tried to stop him, but he took off."

Hugh explained how he followed Buddy to the back of the warehouse, but the two men slipped into a room off to the side and closed the door. He could hear my uncle trying to calm Prescott down. But the maniac in Civil War garb wouldn't have any of it.

"That nutjob was shouting that Buddy could reclaim his honor or be counted along with Darrow as a traitor to the cause. According to your uncle, Prescott tried to force him to take an ancient rifle, so he could take part in Virgil's execution. He was poking Buddy in the back with the gun when a storage cabinet came crashing down, and all hell broke loose. That's when things got even weirder."

He and Norm exchanged a look.

"All we know for sure is that damned rifle exploded. I kicked in the door and found Buddy under a pile of shelving. It looked like Prescott got knocked down and hit his head hard on the concrete floor. Darrow was hanging from a pipe, trussed up like a Thanksgiving turkey. About that time, the cops came charging in." He chuckled. "Easiest take-down I've ever seen."

"You mean all of this was about Burton Prescott being upset about buying fake Civil War relics?" I asked.

"Not entirely," Hugh responded. "Obviously, Prescott is bat-shit crazy. But he's also a pretty savvy businessman." He scanned the room for a second before finding what he was looking for, a velvet-backed chair in the corner. After dragging it closer to the bed, he eased down into an awkward sitting position.

I noticed how pale and drawn Hugh looked and wondered if maybe the take-down or the actual chase had been as easy as he claimed.

"He invested quite a bit of money with the Darrows. The Feds weren't moving fast enough, so he went over to confront Al and found Virgil there. That's where it gets confusing." He paused to remove an oversized handkerchief from his pocket, then wiped his broad face with it. "My friend at the precinct got tight lipped when I asked if they knew what happened when Prescott found out Virgil was involved. My guess is there was an argument, and Virgil came out the loser."

"Does this mean Buddy's in the clear?" I glanced at my dozing uncle.

"It's not official yet, but I'm sure your uncle will be removed from the suspect list eventually. That cop was just being a jerk."

"What about the woman Buddy says he saw? Could she have something to do with Darrow's death?" I tried to imagine Elsie mowing down the antique dealer like an old-timey gangster but couldn't.

"Probably a figment of his imagination, resulting from the shock of being shot," Hugh offered.

Hearing the pronouncement of Buddy's innocence should have given me a sense of relief, but I couldn't shake the feeling Elsie was somehow involved.

"Thanks for going with Buddy and keeping him from getting killed." I stood, a bit shaky, and walked to the bed where my uncle was sound asleep with his mouth slightly open. Norm rose and hugged me, scooping up Doris to give me room to plant a kiss on Buddy's damp forehead.

"Now I really need to get to the hospital." A wave of panic flooded over me, followed by a wave of guilt. What if something horrible had happened to Dad while I was sitting here asking questions about some stupid antique scam?

"Remember what your Mamma said," Norm began.

"I know what she said, but I'm not letting her sit around the hospital by herself." I turned to Mateo. "I hate to ask, but could you drive me to the hospital?"

"Don't be ridiculous."

Outside, we passed the assortment of plastic fowl. "I didn't think it was possible," Mateo said. "But I think your family might be crazier than mine."

. . .

Mateo stood with me in the long registration line at the ER. A man sitting to our immediate right held a bloody towel on his forehead with one hand; with the other, he patted the thigh of the sobbing woman next to him. An elderly couple huddled together on a bench, while a toddler in a sagging diaper wandered around the room, leaving a wet trail behind him.

I jumped at the sound of violent retching from around the corner, and Mateo put his arm around me. The heavy-set woman directly in front of us was next up and demanded to know what was taking so long for someone to look at her son's abscess. The receptionist assured her it wouldn't be long, and the woman left muttering something under her breath about how much better medical care was in Canada.

I explained I was trying to find my father. After a few minutes of shuffling paper, the receptionist directed us to another waiting room a few doors down, where we found my mother, looking small and alone.

"Mom!" I rushed to her side and sat next to her. "Is Dad . . . is he . . ."

"Your dad's fine. They're going to keep him overnight as a precaution. But his heart's strong." Her voice broke. "Oh, honey, I thought I might have killed him. They didn't come out and say it, but I shouldn't have given him that Xanax. You know how he gets when he isn't in control of things, and I thought if I could help him calm down. . . you know, he'd be okay." She took a tissue from her purse and wiped her eyes.

I put my arm around her, unable to find words of comfort. I thought of all the times she had made me feel better. From scraped knees to a broken heart, Mom had always known what to say to make the hurt more bearable. She made it seem effortless. But now that it was my turn to ease her pain, I felt useless.

I was still holding her when a nurse approached to let us know Dad was stable enough to be moved where, she confirmed, he would be kept overnight for observation. After she assured us everything looked good, she directed us to Dad's room.

Mom gathered her purse and sweater. She reached for the mustard-yellow jacket Dad had been wearing earlier and hesitated. Then she picked it up and clutched it to her chest. "Your father hates this jacket." Her voice broke and she buried her face in the slick rayon material. Inhaling deeply, she gulped back a sob. "He says it's itchy and the color looks like something you'd scrape out of a diaper. I told him he was being crude and ridiculous. But he's right, isn't he? It does look exactly like baby shit. Why would I make him wear it, Lucy? Why would I make a wonderful man like your father go around in a poopy-looking jacket?"

Mom focused her enlarged pupils on me, and I wondered exactly how many little pills she had taken since boarding the ambulance. "The coat's not that bad," I said in a lame attempt to talk her mother off the ledge. "I mean, you'd wear it, wouldn't you?" I turned to Mateo, who was standing behind my mother.

He replied without a second's hesitation. "Absolutely. It's a great jacket. And the color is, uh, breathtaking."

Oh, boy. He'd been doing so well, but *breathtaking?* No, that was going too far. I studied Mom's face, ready to call for help when the hysterics hit.

But she smiled, plucked a tissue from the box and blew her nose. "Thank you, dear," she said. Then she squared her shoulders and strode to the elevator.

. . .

"Your dad looks good. don't you think?" Mateo sat across from me in the all-night coffee shop.

It was almost 2:00. We had helped Mom get situated in the small pull-out bed next to Dad's bed, and she insisted we go home and get some rest. She called her older brother, one of my less favorite uncles, and he agreed to be there by 8:00 when the doctor was supposed to release Dad. I was torn about whether I should stay or not, so Mateo and I stepped out to give me time to think it over.

"Better than I expected." I'd been shocked to see Dad swathed in a hospital gown and connected to monitors. He looked tired and, well, old. Not old really, but so much older than the man who'd taught me to ride a bike and drive a car and speak my mind. I didn't want to think he might be getting older because if I acknowledged that possibility, I had to acknowledge the inevitable next step and no way could I imagine life without Dad.

Mateo seemed to sense my fears. "Hospitals are scary." He reached across the table and took my hands in his. "They make everyone look much worse than they are. I think it has something to do with the power of suggestion. Speaking of looking worse, you look exhausted. Let me take you home. Otherwise, both you and your mother are going to be too worn out to take care of your dad."

"Oh, no," I groaned. "I hadn't thought of that. What if Dad needs therapy or rehab?"

"No, no, no. I only meant keeping him company while he rests. Bringing him iced tea and Jell-O. He's going to be fine."

"Jell-O?" The idea of Dad propped up in bed, slurping Jell-O and washing it down with my mother's ungodly sweet tea was so ridiculous it made me feel better.

I agreed going home wasn't a bad idea. On the way out, we stopped to tell my parents goodbye. Lit by the soft amber glow of the nightlight, the room was quiet. Mom wasn't sitting in the chair by the bed. Thinking she had stepped out while my father was sleeping, I fished pen and paper from my purse, then jotted a note telling her I would check in tomorrow. Mateo waited as I crept inside.

Other than the nightlights, it was dark. I moved closer to the bedside tray, where I planned to leave the note, and was startled to see two heads on Dad's pillow. Still wearing her reading glasses, my mother lay curled around him. Under the gentle lighting, the fine lines around her eyes had softened. Shadows played across Dad's face, and I thought of the many stormy nights as a child when a crack of thunder would send me racing into their room. Most times, Mom would wake up and scoot over to make room for me under the covers before she fell back to sleep. Shivering from the flashes of lightning across the night sky, I would lie there watching them. I took comfort from their peaceful nighttime faces, so different from the ones they wore during the daylight hours.

No longer a child, instead of comfort, I ached with thoughts of their mortality.

CHAPTER 16

On the drive home, I opened the window and inhaled the smokey October air. Dad loved a roaring fire. But the possibility of flying sparks igniting some random item left too close to the hearth and turning the house into a raging inferno terrified Mom, so they rarely used the fireplace. Even though I knew it was irrational and unfair, I felt a twinge of anger at her for denying him this simple pleasure.

I dozed off and the image of sitting with my father in front of a crackling fire drifted over me like the smell of smoke from a stranger's house.

"Wake up, Sleeping Beauty. We're home."

I awoke, and for a moment couldn't remember where I was. Looking into Mateo's deep brown eyes returned me to reality. I yawned and stretched.

He came around to my side and helped me from the car. As I passed the willow, a branch caught in my hair. I stepped back, realizing how close I was to the scene of Barbie's execution and wondering if I would find any more unwelcome surprises. Happily, nothing had been hung from the trees or dropped on the porch. When I unlocked the door, the alarm system was armed and intact.

Even so, after I punched in the code, Mateo insisted I wait in the foyer while he did a quick check of the house. Although watching him move from room to room was reassuring, it was also oddly annoying. Not because I resented it or found it condescending. More because I didn't want to start believing I needed someone else around to ensure my safety, to oversee my well-being, when taking care of myself was my responsibility.

"Looks like the coast is clear," he announced.

Standing beside him, I thought of how we'd been earlier in the evening before Hugh's call and felt a warm familiar feeling. But something had shifted for me. I still wanted this incredible man in my bed, and probably if we hadn't been interrupted that would have been enough. Now, it was different.

Seeming to sense the change, he said, "It's really late, and I should go home and let you rest."

He brushed his lips against mine. "You've been so great, but I am really tired," I admitted.

"I'll call you tomorrow afternoon." He touched my cheek and stepped out the door. I leaned against it until I heard the crunch of his tires as he drove away.

Despite my exhaustion, the short nap had given me a spurt of energy, as if a low-voltage current ran under my skin. I drew a hot bath and slipped into it. I rested my head on the back of the tub and tried to make sense of the direction my life was taking. The painful recollection of the discovery that my relationship with Lance had been a sham had gotten stuck in rewind until Buddy shared his possible involvement in Darrow's death. From then until I left my parents at the hospital, events flew into fast forward, giving me no time to process my emotions. It was as if I were watching a movie featuring Lucy Howard as the star, but the entire production was blurry. The terror I experienced at the idea I might lose Dad had slowed and sharpened the picture.

After seeing Mom keeping watch over him in the hospital, another movie began playing out in my mind, this one in crisp technicolor. It featured slow-motion memories of Dad, touching my mother when he entered a room. Softly lit images of them holding hands while sitting on the sofa watching TV dissolved into sunny shots of Mom making sure the paper was waiting for him on the breakfast table. Close-ups as she straightened his tie. A tight shot of

Dad's face as he bristled at the way Buddy's lawyer looked at Mom. A thousand tender moments that accrued over the days, weeks, and years, creating my parents' ongoing love story.

Would it be possible to create a story of my own with Mateo? Once, I thought Lance would be the lead in my movie. With my ex I was star-struck, not so much with the man, but with what he represented: money, prestige, security. I was willing to overlook the condescending way he spoke about my job and family. Worst of all, the idea someone like him had chosen someone like me pushed me to be swept away by his desire without thinking of my own needs and values.

If I was right about Mateo, he would understand my need to take the time to discover what I wanted.

After my bath, I changed into pajamas, then rechecked the locks on the doors and windows, not completely trusting the new alarm system. Satisfied no one would be surprising me, I crawled into bed. Within minutes, I fell into a deep sleep.

· · ·

In my dream, Mateo held me close while we danced to Clapton singing "You Look Wonderful Tonight." I knew it was a dream because of the ease with which I matched even the most intricate of his moves. According to Lance, I was a difficult partner because I kept trying to lead.

Mateo and I were in the middle of executing an effortless twirl around the floor when an insistent sound caused me to miss a beat and stumble. My ankle twisted and I tumbled toward the ground. Instead of landing, however, I woke to the sound of the doorbell.

Sunlight streaming through the blinds startled me with the realization I had overslept. A glance at the clock confirmed it was almost ten.

The memory of my father in the hospital returned. I rolled out of bed, grabbed my robe, and slipped it on as I raced down the hall.

In the process of throwing open the door without checking to see who it was, I hesitated as I remembered my stalker. It was unlikely whoever had been trying to scare me would show up in broad daylight, but I knew it wouldn't hurt to check before welcoming someone into my home.

Peering through the peephole, I saw the profile of a tall blonde. She looked vaguely familiar. Her beige sweater draped gracefully over light brown slacks, so sharply creased they looked as if they could cut glass. Still drowsy, I wrestled with whether to open the door. Then the visitor turned to face me, and there was no mistaking those enormous eyes, so brown they were almost black. It was Andrea Johnston.

I ran through the pros and cons of inviting her in. In the positive column, I recorded getting more information on the Johnston case. That was the end of the list. On the negative side, there was a litany of reasons not to allow this stranger into my home. First and foremost, she might be involved in the threats I had been receiving. I couldn't be sure the doctor's wife was the one who'd tipped me off to the irregularities on the bank statement and even if she had, what did it mean? Secondly, if she knew nothing about the email and creepy gifts, she still might have hard feelings for anyone wanting to send her husband to prison. Then there was the possibility she was simply crazy after being married to Johnston for so long.

I stopped cataloging the risks and undid the bolt lock but kept the chain on.

"Can I help you?" I asked, peeking from around the door frame.

"I believe we can help each other," the woman responded in a husky voice that was also vaguely familiar. She tucked her platinum hair behind her ears. "Do you think I might come in? I promise I won't take up too much of your time."

How much time would it take for the doctor's wife to pull a gun from her Coach purse and shoot me?

"Could you tell me what this is about? My father's ill and I need to check in on him."

Andrea reached into her purse, and I jumped back, certain I was about to be shot. But instead of a gun, she removed a thumb drive.

"I'm Andrea Johnston and I believe you're interested in information regarding my husband's involvement in some unsavory activities. I may be able to help you with that, but I need to explain a few things first. May I please come in?"

Her perfectly modulated tone and curiosity about what she had to offer convinced me she wasn't dangerous. I undid the chain, stepped back, and waited for her to enter. Walking with the assurance I associated with power and wealth, Andrea stopped in the middle of the foyer and extended her hand.

"It's nice to meet you in person, Lucy," she said. "I mean, I've seen your name on my husband's insurance claims and—I won't be coy— I spoke with you once."

I accepted the woman's cool, firm grip. "Why don't you have a seat in here?" I motioned to the living room. "I have to make a phone call and start the coffee. Can I make a cup for you?"

She shook her head, maintaining the same tensely erect composure I recalled from the photograph of the woman and her husband. Was it knowledge of her husband's side business or being married to a jerk like Johnston responsible for that tension? Would a life with Lance have turned me into a woman like Andrea Johnston? Someone who had to remain in complete control of her emotions to keep from disappearing.

On the way to the kitchen, I punched in Mom's number and switched on the coffee maker. After several rings, she answered in a soft voice.

"Sorry to call so late, Mom. I overslept." Saying it out loud made me feel even more guilty. Of course, so many of my conversations with my mother involved some level of guilt with most of them beginning with the word "sorry." So much so it seemed to have replaced almost all my more conventional greetings. *Sorry to bother you, Mom. Sorry I forgot to call last night. Sorry I'm not married yet.* But this time I really was sorry.

"It's okay, dear. Your Uncle Dennis and I got Dad home about an hour ago. His blood pressure was a little high, but it's fine now. They think it was a panic attack. The cardiologist wants to see him next week just to be safe."

When she uttered the words "panic attack," I detected what could have been a note of glee. She had been vindicated by the experts. Instead of administering what she had feared was a potentially lethal dose of happy pills, she had correctly diagnosed the situation. In the process, I suspected, Mom had now become the family authority on life-threatening situations. Dealing with this self-proclaimed expertise, however, was a small price to pay for having my parents back, safe at home.

"Thank, God! I'll stop by on the way to work. Can I bring anything?" Foolish question since Mom's cabinets were stockpiled with enough supplies to survive both flood and famine.

"Don't worry about us. We'll be fine."

I wasn't about to fall for that line. "I'm still going to stop by."

"Really, honey. I didn't get much rest, and neither did your dad with people coming in and out all night. Stop by after work if you want."

The genuine exhaustion in her voice made me feel even worse about suspecting a guilt set-up. I promised to check in later.

I poured coffee into an oversize mug and joined my guest in the living room.

"Sorry to keep you waiting." I sat in the chair across from Andrea, wondering if all my future conversations would begin with an apologetic note.

"I'm the one who should apologize. I should have called before I came by. More importantly, I should have spoken up much, much sooner. But years of living as an 'and Mrs.' have turned me into a coward."

"As an 'and Mrs.'?"

"You know, 'The party was attended by *Dr. Johnston and Mrs.*' Even when he's not with me, I'm a footnote: *Mrs. Andrea Johnston, wife of Dr. Andrew Johnston*." She picked at a non-existent thread on her sweater. "I'm actually a very bright woman, you know?"

I nodded encouragement although I questioned how a smart woman could end up with a loser like Johnston. Of course, the only difference in our situations was that I had gotten out early. I couldn't, however, take credit for that escape.

"I graduated third in my class from Wellesley, making me vastly overqualified for playing the role of doctor's wife to a second-rate surgeon." She stared out the window before smoothing her already perfect hair. "Please excuse my little pity-party. I knew what I was getting into when I married the man. I just didn't realize how all-inclusive the commitment would be." Holding out the thumb-drive, she continued. "But I'm opting out now."

I held out my hand and she dropped in into my palm.

"I'm not sure exactly what's on it, but I believe it's a second set of books with names of what he refers to as recipients. My husband is both unbearably arrogant and remarkably careless, constantly forgetting to log out of his computer. He seems to have never thought I might one day find out how despicable he is and use it against him. I suppose you might say he lacks imagination."

"If this information is as damaging as you seem to think it is, why not take it to the police?"

"I did mention I'd become quite the coward, didn't I?" She gave me a tight-lipped smile. "No, I'll leave that to you."

"I'm sure they'll want to question you."

"Most likely. But I'm not worried. I've become extremely adept at avoidance." She rose in one fluid motion.

"Please, just one question." I stood beside her. "Does the name Lance Crawford mean anything to you?"

She considered it for a second. "I may have met someone named Crawford at a party at the law firm Andrew uses to handle some of his affairs, but I can't be sure. I'll be going now."

I escorted her to the door.

"One more thing," Andrea said as she stepped off the porch toward the black Mercedes roadster in the drive. "My husband is involved with some very dangerous people. If they suspect he's about to be exposed, there's no telling what they might do. If I were you, I'd be very careful about whom I trusted." She slipped into her car before I had time to ask who these people were.

Watching the shiny car disappear, it occurred to me that Andrea Johnston might be one of those people I should be wary of trusting.

• • •

When I called the office to let Darla know I was running late, the receptionist expressed concern about Dad and assured me no one, including Hugh, expected me to come in.

I touched the pocket of my robe where I had placed the incriminating thumb-drive. "Thanks, but I have something I need to drop off. Please tell Hugh I need to see him in about an hour."

I put on navy slacks and a pale blue sweater, then smeared a bagel with cream cheese and, at a little after eleven thirty, left for work.

On the way, brightly colored displays of pumpkins, skeletons, and ghosts lined both sides of the street, advertising a variety of local businesses. A mother with two small boys dressed in identical denim overalls and red shirts stopped to check out one with a giant dollhouse lying on its side. One of the boys stooped down to examine a pair of tiny feet clad in ruby red slippers sticking out from under the wooden house. The other boy was swinging from the sign in front of the shoes: "House for Sale: Good Witches only need apply. Findley Realty, Inc."

Buddy would love this whimsical combination of both his favorite holiday and one of his favorite movies. Hopefully, he would recover quickly enough to enjoy the season.

Bright sunlight deepened the shades of red and gold on the tree-lined street, and gentle gusts of wind sent the leaves swirling. While I shared my uncle's enthusiasm for Halloween, I wasn't a big fan of fall itself. What was that Frost poem I studied in high school? Not the one with the little horse thinking it queer line—that line had always brought a few homophobic remarks and chuckles from some of my less enlightened classmates. No, the one about spring and decay and impending doom. Nothing gold lasts forever or all gold things fade? No. It was "Nothing Gold Can Stay," and it captured the underlying melancholy I felt every fall. All this brilliance here one day, then faded and brown the next.

Seeing my parents and uncle looking frail and vulnerable the previous night underscored their mortality. But Uncle Buddy had come out of his trouble with minor injuries and was no longer a murder suspect. And while I wouldn't feel easy about my parents' situation until I saw them, they seemed relatively unscarred by Dad's incident. I decided to put aside Frost's gloomy warning about how quickly "dawn goes down to day" and take a more optimistic approach.

Not only had my family survived their ordeals, but I had managed to obtain what was most likely the piece of evidence that would help put Johnston away for a very long time. It might also vindicate me in Hugh's eyes for how badly I botched the phone call with Roberta.

I let the window all the way down. A light breeze brushed across my face and rippled through my hair. Tucking back a loose curl, I cranked up the radio and sang along as the Beach Boys extolled the virtues of California girls.

In less than twenty minutes, I arrived at the office in a much better mood. Darla announced Hugh was in if I wanted to catch him before he went to lunch, so I headed straight to his office.

"What the hell are you doing here?" he growled as he hung up the phone. "I told Darla to tell you to stay home."

"She did, but you'll never guess who came to see me this morning." I paused, then remembered Hugh hated guessing. "Andrea Johnston." Still no reaction. "You know, Dr. Johnston's wife." I produced the thumb drive from my purse with a flourish and placed it directly in front of my boss. "Records from the doctor's laptop. A second set of books."

He glanced at the drive, then said, "I just got a call from a detective I know, and I don't think we'll be needing any more evidence on the doc. He's dead."

"Dead? What do you mean he's dead?"

"I mean he stopped breathing, bought the farm, bit the dust, cashed in his chips, kicked the—"

"Dammit, Hugh! I know what dead is. What happened? How exactly did he die?"

He raised his eyebrows slightly before answering. "The police are being pretty tight-lipped about it, but the word is he hanged himself." He mimed tying a noose around his neck and jerked his head abruptly.

"Oh, my God!" I wasn't sure if I was more upset about the doctor's death or his timing, which made my discovery anticlimactic. Before I had time to reflect on my callousness, the newspaper photo of the condescending smirk on the doctor's face and his confident stance came to mind. I couldn't picture a man with that kind of self-assured entitlement taking his own life. And if his wife was right, the combination of his lack of imagination and his attitude in general made him an even more unlikely candidate for suicide. Dr. Andrew Johnston would never have been able to see himself getting caught and going to prison, so there would have been no reason for him to kill himself. And hanging? That required a specific type of determination, one I didn't think the doctor possessed.

"I'm not seeing it," I said to Hugh, who was now miming being strangled by the rope around his neck. "Cut it out, Hugh. I'm serious. I don't think Johnston killed himself."

"Calm down, Buttercup." He released his imaginary grip on his neck. "It does seem a little too convenient. The doc taking a powder just as we're zeroing in on him and his accomplices." He pushed his chair back and stood. "I can't get anything else from the cops right now, so I'm going to take a run at some of the neighbors. Since you ignored my advice to stay home and rest, you might as well come with me."

"Come with you?" I echoed. He had never included me in an active investigation that didn't involve going through garbage.

"That's what I said. Unless you have something better to do." He brushed past me, turning off the lights on his way out the door. I stood in the darkened office for a few seconds before scurrying after him.

As we exited the reception area, Darla called after us, asking when she could expect our return. Hugh ignored her, and I shrugged apologetically, leaving her mumbling under her breath.

I had to hustle to keep up with Hugh on the way to his SUV. Once inside he focused on the road while I pulled a legal pad from my purse.

"Do you want to make a list of questions?"

Without taking his eyes off the road, he responded, "That's a great idea. How about we start with 'did you see anybody string your neighbor up and leave him dangling over the door frame?'" He spoke in a cheerful falsetto. "Or we could ask 'did you murder the doctor and make it look like a suicide'?"

"You don't have to be nasty about it."

"Just put the damn notebook away," he said as he took the entrance ramp to the expressway. "And let me ask the questions. All you have to do is listen. Got it?"

"Yes," I sighed, shutting my eyes as he jerked the wheel to pass an eighteen- wheeler. "Did Johnston strike you as the suicidal type?" I opened one eye to make sure we'd cleared the truck.

"Not sure if there is a suicide type." He veered back into his lane.

"Who found him?"

"The gardener came by to collect his check and found the back door open. Said he kept ringing the bell and calling the doc's name. He saw Johnston's car in the garage and called the cops. They found our guy hanging over the door in the master bedroom."

"Wait a minute. Did you say over the door?"

"Yep. He probably attached the rope to the doorknob and tossed it over the frame. If you do it right, you pass out fast. Body weight takes care of the rest. I investigated this one case where the guy was, uh you know, *enjoying himself.* Must of slipped and," he paused for a beat and grinned. "And things got out of hand. Get it? Things—"

"I get it. I get it." I waved my hand to stop him from elaborating.

The grin disappeared when he announced in a somber tone, "The cops aren't officially calling it a suicide, though."

He cut off a car in the right lane and exited at well over the recommended speed. Within minutes we were in the doctor's neighborhood. Ours was the only vehicle cruising alongside the strip of neatly manicured grass, bordering the sidewalk. The same multicolored trees I had seen less than twenty-four hours ago greeted me, but even in that short amount of time they seemed to have lost vibrancy.

Hugh pulled in front of the doctor's house. Yesterday, its sprawling design had been awkward but imposing as I had tried to catch a glimpse of its occupants. Today, it loomed on the horizon, turned into a realtor's worst nightmare: a suicide site. Or maybe a murder house.

CHAPTER 17

There were no cars in the drive. I tried to recall if Andrea had mentioned anything about leaving town. She had said something about being good at avoidance. Did that mean she intended to disappear? And if so, did she even know her husband was dead?

Hugh interrupted my reverie.

"I ran a list of addresses and got names of the Johnstons' closest neighbors. A widow named Mabel Gutteridge lives in the house on the right. We'll start with her. And remember, I'll do the talking."

Mabel's brick ranch-style house was smaller than the doctor's but well maintained—fresh paint and beautiful landscaping. Beds of seasonal flowers, strategically placed on the lawn, provided bursts of color. As we made our way along the winding walkway, I heard water bubbling and located the source: a stone fountain where a fairy-like creature hovered over its mushroom-shaped base.

Hugh lumbered up the steps to the porch. He waited a few seconds, then rang again. His thick finger was poised for the third time when someone cracked open the door a few inches, keeping the chain on.

"Yes?" A soft, girlish voice greeted us.

"Mrs. Gutteridge, my name is Hugh Farewell, and this is my associate Lucy Howard. We're here about your neighbor, Dr. Andrew Johnston," he stated in an authoritative voice. "Would you mind answering a few questions?" He removed his wallet from his back pocket and flashed his PI license in her general direction.

Either she was very gullible, or her eyesight was poor. Whichever it was, the woman opened the door. I was startled to see the childlike voice belonged to a tall, thin lady with powdery white hair that sat on top of her head like a flat cinnamon bun.

"It's terrible about the doctor, but I already told the police I didn't see anything, young man," she said.

I shot a glance Hugh's way and decided the woman was definitely near-sighted.

"Yes, ma'am, but there are other ways a person with your knowledge of the neighborhood might be able to help."

"Well, I do think it's important to stay vigilant, especially in today's world." She motioned us in. Near-sighted and gullible.

"Thank you, Mrs. Gutteridge."

"Let's go into the parlor to talk."

The parlor was more of an over-decorated den. A flowery chintz explosion of pillows dominated the room, making it difficult to find a seat. I spotted an empty space on one of the chairs and started to sit.

"Not there, dear," Mrs. Gutteridge warned. "That's Mr. Whiskers's seat. Why don't you join me on the sofa?" She tossed a few pillows onto the floor and patted the spot next to her.

I looked for Mr. Whiskers. Had he merely decided on a better chair or had he abdicated all earthly chairs and left this creepy memorial behind?

"We'll let the gentleman sit in the manly chair." She pointed to the leather recliner and beamed at Hugh. "Now what did you say your name was?"

I could have sworn the woman was batting her eyelashes.

He repeated our names, then said, "Thank you for seeing us, Mrs. Gutteridge."

"Please, it's Maisie," she interrupted. "My given name is Mable, but all my *friends* call me Maisie."

Yep. Giving him the eyelash treatment. He shifted his considerable weight and ran his finger under his collar. This was going to be fun.

"Okay, Maisie," he began. "I was hoping you might be able to tell us if you've noticed anything unusual lately. Anybody at the Johnstons' who didn't look like they belonged there or any strange sounds?"

"Well, I don't like to speak ill of the dead, and I abhor idle gossip, but that man was not very nice. Not friendly at all, really. And his wife wasn't much better." She paused to adjust a pale blue-woolen throw behind her. "Oh, I am so sorry. I don't know where my manners are. Please let me get you something to drink. Tea or coffee?"

He declined for both of us, but she ignored him and excused herself to "prepare a little refreshment for her guests."

When she left the room, I leaned forward and asked, "Who the hell is Mr. Whiskers, and what do you think she did with him?"

He gave her a blank look.

"You know." Switching to a Southern soprano, I said. "*Mr. Whiskers's chair,*" and pointed to the seat I'd almost taken before being warned off.

"Oh, *that* Mr. Whiskers." He shrugged. "Who the hell knows? Maybe it's her pet name for the late Mr. Gutteridge."

"Her husband?" I considered the possibility for a second, then shot him a dour look. "*Pet* name," I repeated. "Very funny."

"Come on," he said. "You have to admit it's a little funny."

It was so dreadful that it was funny, but I didn't want to encourage him. I was still struggling to keep a straight face when Maisie returned with a platter of store-bought cookies which she thrust toward Hugh. He held up his hand, and she placed the plate on the coffee table without offering any to me.

He urged her to continue trying to remember anything odd about her neighbors.

"Now that I think about it, I did hear a commotion over there around dinner time. The two of them were shouting and slamming car doors. I looked out the window and saw that fancy car Mrs. Johnston drives screech away from the curb and tear around the corner. Didn't even slow down at the stop sign." She wrinkled her nose in disgust. "I wish I'd thought to tell the police about that. People drive entirely too fast around here."

"And you're sure it was Mrs. Johnston you heard?"

"One of them was definitely Mrs. Johnston."

"One of them?" he repeated. "You heard more than one woman screaming?"

"Isn't that what I said? Yes, two women and the doctor. Then the wife took off, and I haven't seen her since." She paused and put her hand over her heart. "Oh, my! I forgot all about the racket coming from over there when I talked to the police. Do you think I'm in trouble for, uh, obstructing, uh, what do they call it when you get in the way of...the way of...?"

"Obstructing justice and no, you won't be in trouble. Not if you tell me everything you remember now. For instance, did anyone else leave?"

"If they did, I didn't hear them. And that van blocked the doctor's side of the garage."

"The van? What van?"

"That dirty silver van, dear. I assumed it was the maid, the way it shows up at odd times during the day. The driver normally goes around back, but whoever was driving it yesterday must have been in too big a hurry."

I held my breath. Could Mrs. Johnston have come home unexpectedly and discovered the driver of the van and her husband in a compromising position? If so, was that why she turned over the thumb-drive?

On the day I saw the van at the Johnstons', however, the driver had been careful to pull completely out of sight. Had something changed? Something that made hiding an illicit relationship less important?

"What about later last night? Did you see anyone get in or out of it?" he asked.

Maisie gave him a sorrowful look and shook her head. "I wish I could help, but after the wife left, it got quiet. I went to bed and when I got up, the van was gone."

He asked a few more questions about where Maisie had been when Johnston's body was found, but she had run out of information. She did let him know she was in desperate need of a bridge partner if he played. When he thanked her, but said he'd never taken up the game, she insisted she would be happy to teach him. Face a cardinal shade of red, he stood abruptly, signaling the end of the interview.

I grabbed two cookies and stuck them in my pocket. Hugh stopped at the door to give Maisie his card with instructions to contact him if she thought of anything else pertinent to the investigation. She tucked the card into the front of her blouse and smiled.

Beads of perspiration dotted his forehead and upper lip as Hugh took the porch steps two at a time and dashed toward his car.

"Somebody's got a crush on you," I said, racing to keep up.

He unlocked the car, hopped in, and yelled for me to hurry up. Once I was inside, he hit auto lock.

"What a nut-job," he said, using a left-over napkin from Arby's to wipe his brow.

"I don't know." I fastened my seatbelt and grinned. "I thought she was kind of sweet—on you, that is. Get it? Sweet on—"

"I get it," he growled and started the engine.

After a cursory glance in his rearview mirror, he jerked the wheel and gunned it.

I balled my hands into tight fists and looked straight ahead.

"I'll drop you at the office, then let my guy at the department know about the women fighting and the van. They'll probably want to talk to the old bat again. I know I'm not going back there."

"About that van," I began, then filled him in on the missing pictures with the van in the background and seeing what could have been the same van at the Johnston house the day before.

"Why the hell are you just now telling me this? And what in God's name were you doing wandering around the neighborhood without telling anyone where you were?" He pounded the steering wheel.

I started to explain I hadn't had time to tell him much of anything, but he didn't wait.

"You do know whoever is in that van might have seen you, right? If they had anything to do with Johnston's death, they could be coming for you. And why didn't you tell me you thought a van was following you?"

"If you'll give me a chance—"

"Forget it. It doesn't matter now." He took a deep breath. "What does matter is that you understand this whole Johnston thing is bigger than we thought and much more dangerous. When we get back to the office, I want you to get in your car, go straight to your parents' house, and stay there."

I wanted to protest, to tell him I was perfectly capable of taking care of myself, but since my original plan coincided with his dictate, there was no reason to argue.

Back at the office, he pulled into the spot next to my car. "Do I have to sit here and watch you leave, or can I trust you?"

"Jeez." I opened the door. "You can trust me to go check on my parents, but I won't promise to stay there." I resisted the urge to stomp my foot. Looking down at my boss's solemn face, I added, "But I promise I'll be careful."

"Goddamn it, Lucy," he said softly. "I guess if that's the best you've got, it will have to do."

Watching him slam the car in reverse, then shoot out onto the road, I marveled at his sudden change in tone. It wasn't until I was almost home that it hit me. Despite his gruff exterior and condescending attitude, Hugh's concern for my safety was genuine.

And while I liked the idea I was more to him than an annoying subordinate, his concern worried me. Hugh Farewell wasn't the kind of man who frightened easily. If he was afraid I was in danger, I probably was.

I arrived at my parents' house a little after four and spent less than an hour there. Normally, Mom would have insisted I stay for dinner. After they ate, Dad would ask about the last time I had my oil checked, and no matter what answer I gave, would check it himself. While he was playing mechanic, Mom would find a way to engage me in a conversation, centered around the dangers of late-in-life pregnancies or some friend of a friend who knew a nice young man with a good job. Then Dad would return with dire warnings of the dangers of a flashing engine light, and the three of us would watch one of my parents' favorite sit-coms.

But this afternoon, Mom was listless and preoccupied. She alternated between fussing over Dad, fluffing his pillows and checking his pulse, and straightening up their already impeccably tidy bedroom. My father was uncharacteristically vague. His already succinct responses were reduced to monosyllabic ones, and several times I caught him grinning at my mother in a way that made me feel as if they shared a very private joke.

No one mentioned dinner at all. For the first time in recent memory, my parents didn't try to find ways to delay my departure. In fact, I got the impression they were eager to see me go.

Waiting for the light, I fumed at Mom's total lack of interest in how her daughter's day had gone. And what about my oil and the engine light? Of course, I didn't expect Dad to get out of bed and check them, but he could have at least reminded me instead of ogling at Mom like some...Oh, my God! They wanted me to leave so they could have sex. Was that even safe after what my father had just gone through?

Although I knew it was ridiculous, I felt betrayed. The car behind me blasted its horn, alerting me the light had turned green I hit the gas harder than I intended, coming way too close to the rear bumper of a truck stopped in front of me to make a left turn.

"Son of a bitch!" I shouted. My head was pounding, and I was slightly nauseated. A quick time check revealed that, other than Maisie's stale box-cookies, I hadn't eaten in over six hours. Hopefully, that explained the threat of a melt-down over my parents' renewed interest in each other and abandonment of their only daughter.

At the familiar sight of the Checkers logo, I eased up to the drive-through window and ordered a chicken sandwich, fries, and a chocolate shake. Before I left the lot, I stuffed a handful of fries in my mouth and washed them down with milkshake. By the time I pulled in beside the willow tree, all that remained of my meal was a bite-size piece of bun.

I shut off the engine but remained in the car. No longer fearing I might dissolve into a hot mess of tears and self-pity, I tried to analyze my emotions. I had to face the fact my family dynamics had shifted from a Lucy-centered focus to a more couple-centered one with me watching from the outside. But hadn't that been what I'd been saying I wanted since adolescence? For my parents to acknowledge my independence.

I hadn't expected their recognition of my autonomy might result in a change in their relationship. Or maybe it wasn't a change, so much as a renewal of their pre-Lucy world. I didn't begrudge their rediscovered passion. I just hadn't thought their absorption with each other might mean they wouldn't be so intensely interested in the details of my life. Worse, it seemed to have triggered a separation from me. And that sense of separateness highlighted the fact it was time for me to take charge of my life and possibly find someone else to share it with.

After an examination of the front of my home, I determined there had been no additions to my collection of weird gifts. I unlocked the door and slipped out of my shoes, almost forgetting to disarm that damned new alarm system. My next stop was the bedroom where I changed into sweatpants and a long-sleeve Bonnie Raitt T-shirt.

Now what I needed was a glass of wine and some mindless TV. Two glasses of Riesling and halfway into a Lifetime movie rerun later, I saw the message notifications. Struggling from underneath one of the many knitted throws my grandmother had made for me, I shuffled sock-footed to retrieve my cell from the foyer table.

Bethany had left a text to let me know the new toy had arrived and offered to drop it off on her way home from work. Not in the mood for company, I replied with a brief explanation of Dad's episode and intimated I was tied up being a dutiful daughter. If my parents were going to ditch me for a romantic interlude, the least they could do was provide an excuse to avoid Bethany's enthusiastic instructions on better living through battery-powered sex. The images of Mom and Dad locked in a passionate embrace and Bethany gleefully unwrapping an oversized vibrator collided, and I took a gulp of wine.

Standing by the bed, I discovered two missed calls from an unknown number and a voicemail from Mateo.

"Hey. I wanted to see how your dad's doing and make sure you're okay. Trying to catch up on some work, but I'll call back later." There was a pause while someone in the background said something I couldn't decipher. "Well, uh, okay then. Bye."

I was tempted to replay it just to hear his voice but resisted the urge.

A fourth caller from a number I didn't recognize also left a message. It was Janelle. "I heard about that doctor on the news, and it jogged my memory about," she lowered her voice to a whisper before continuing, "that thing we discussed at your friend's house. What if I pick up a bottle of wine and drop by your place around 9:00 tonight?"

Shit. It was after 8:30 now, and one of the last people I wanted to see was my boyfriend's ex-mistress or whatever the hell she was. I considered turning off the lights and pretending to be asleep, but suspected Janelle was the kind of person who'd keep ringing and pounding on the door until I answered it.

To be honest, I was more than a little curious about Janelle's allusion to that *thing* we'd discussed. Was her conspiratorial tone for effect or had she uncovered incriminating evidence about Lance?

I grabbed a brush and ran it through my hair before sweeping the mass of curls into a high ponytail, then used a tissue to dab at the mascara smudges beneath my eyes. After considering changing into nice jeans, I reminded myself I didn't give a damn what Janelle thought. Technically, I could claim victory over my adversary. Not only had Lance begged me to take him back, but I was the one who literally fired the last blow in our relationship when I flung the soda bottle at his head.

I was too exhausted to feel anything close to victorious. I carried both wine glasses and bottle to the kitchen and left them on the counter.

The doorbell rang at exactly 9:00. Somehow, timeliness didn't jibe with my idea of a wanton woman. It was, however, a characteristic Lance admired. Funny how, even though I had no interest in getting him back, it still stung that he'd found me wanting in some way, so much so he'd turned to another woman.

When I opened the door, a gust of wind sent dust swirling across the porch and carried with it the overwhelming scent of Janelle's perfume. The woman brushed pine needles from her hair before flashing her startlingly white teeth. Lipstick in the same shade as her power-red business suit coated her lips. Her windblown waves framed her face. I flashed on the hot scene I'd interrupted at Lance's office. What might it take to purge that image from my memory? More than the bottle of wine Janelle had brought, but it was a start.

I offered her a seat in the living room, then went to the kitchen to uncork and pour the expensive-looking Merlot. Drinks in hand, I returned and sat across from her.

"Thanks for agreeing to see me," Janelle began.

Technically, I had not agreed to anything, but I smiled and sipped the dark burgundy liquid. I wasn't crazy about reds, but this one wasn't bad. Or maybe the two glasses of white made this one taste the same. No, wait. That was beer. Whatever. I swirled her glass and drank more.

I experienced a twinge of pleasure at the sight of the dark roots snaking through Janelle's highlights and the fake eyelash sliding toward her cheek.

"How have you been?" Her voice had an undertone of an out of tune viola.

"I've been fine." Was this woman seriously asking if I was still heartbroken over a loser like Lance? Jesus. "How about you? It must be hard working with him every day." Two could play at the fake concern game.

Her hand shook slightly, dribbling a few drops of wine directly down her cleavage. She wiped it away with her fingertip, one with a big chip in it.

"Things have been awkward, but not just because we're not together anymore," she said. "Since Lance and I were already working together on cases, we put all that sex stuff aside and stayed professional."

All that sex stuff. Was that all their relationship had been about?

"But I haven't been able to get those pictures out of my mind. Did you come up with any ideas why Lance would want to follow you?"

"Not really." I didn't mention the photos had been stolen. "He's always been a control freak. Most likely he wanted to know if I was dating again. I'm sure he's past all that now."

"I wouldn't be too sure about that. Lately he's been acting weird. Disappearing for hours at a time without telling anyone where he was, missing important meetings. At first, I suspected he'd found some other poor girl to fool around with. I even thought you might have taken him back." She paused for a second, letting the prospect of a reunited Lance and Lucy linger heavy in the air.

"When I saw those pictures," she continued, "I realized he wasn't over you. I told myself I gave them to you because I wanted you to know how creepy he is. But if I'm being completely honest, I have to admit I was jealous he was stalking you, not me. Not that I wanted someone spying on me like that. It was insulting, you know. I mean to find out I wasn't the object of his obsession. Sad, but I really don't like the idea of the two of you getting back together."

Was she annoyed because I was such an inferior choice? Stop it. Who cares what she thinks? I should be concentrating on those pictures. Life had been moving so quickly since the break-in, I hadn't had time to think about them. Like Janelle, I believed Lance had been behind them and was most likely responsible for taking them back. But how would he have known I had them in the first place unless he found out from the person who made the copies? Suddenly, the other woman's declaration of honesty didn't quite ring true.

"You definitely don't have to worry about Lance and me getting back together." *Not after I attempted to kill him with a ginger ale bottle.*

"I know. A woman would have to be crazy to welcome that kind of attention, right? But Lance kept getting more and more secretive. I worried he might be shutting me out to get back at me for dumping him, so I stepped it up."

I cringed when she repeated she was the one who dumped Lance. But my current reaction was more irritation than pain. Progress.

"I went back through his files, but I didn't find any more folders with pictures or any unfamiliar cases. I even went through his email." She ran her finger around the rim of her wine glass.

"You hacked his email?" I didn't know whether to be appalled or impressed.

"Didn't have to." Janelle waved her hand dismissively. "He almost never closes out of it. I just waited until he was out of the office. Sometimes I wonder how he puts his shoes on the right feet." She took a tiny sip from her almost-full glass.

I tilted my glass, but when I compared mine to Janelle's, I set it aside without drinking. I needed to stay sober during this conversation.

"Anyway, I scanned through his mail and almost missed it. It was one of the automatic appointment reminders for the Stalwart Medical Group. I wouldn't have thought much about it except—"

"Except Lance refuses to go to the doctor unless he's afraid he's dying," I finished for her. We had argued over on several occasions when he'd been too sick to sit up but refused to get professional help. He said it was an admission of weakness. I suspected he was afraid of doctors.

"Right. And when I looked up Stalwart online—"

"You found Dr. Johnston listed as the director."

"How did you know?"

"Lucky guess. Please go on."

"I didn't think much about it. I mean, Lance could have gotten past his phobia if he felt bad enough. But I couldn't shake this funny feeling. Then I heard on the news Dr. Andrew Johnston had hanged himself, and they flashed a picture of him with his wife. That's when it hit me. Lance and I sat at their table last year at the symphony fundraiser. He went on and on about how happy it would make the partners if he could land the doctor as a client and told me to be extra nice to the guy."

"Did you say the symphony fundraiser?" I asked.

"Uh," Janelle stammered a little, then blushed.

"The one Lance told me he had to miss because he was out of town on business?" That asshole had been cheating on me for months. "Never mind. Go on."

This time she took a substantial swig of her wine before picking up the story. "I spent most of the night pretending I didn't mind having Johnston's hand on my thigh while Lance chatted up the wife. But it was pretty much for nothing since we didn't get his business. Or maybe I should say the firm didn't do any business with him."

I tried to remember if I ever mentioned Johnston by name in my conversations with Lance. We had already broken up by the time Hugh and I had gone through the doctor's trash, but he'd been on our radar well over six months before that night. I might have said something about looking into medical fraud, but I would have never mentioned names. And since Johnston wasn't Lance's client, would it have mattered if I had? No, I hadn't revealed his identity. But the doctor had access to forms requesting information, forms with my name on them. It wouldn't have taken much for him to discover I was in a relationship with Lance.

All of this, however, was speculation based on Janelle's word. And the feeling I experienced at Bethany's party, the one suggesting maybe Janelle and I could be friends despite our past, had dissipated into something I couldn't quite identify. But it wasn't warm and fuzzy.

"You think there's a connection between Lance and the doctor? That seems like a stretch to me." Of course, if Lance told Johnston he was sleeping with one of the investigators on his case, it wouldn't be too farfetched to think the doctor wanted him to try to find out what the agency knew about his illegal activities. How many times had I left Lance alone in a room with sensitive files? Maybe his desperate attempt to win me back had more to do with wanting access to information than wanting access to me.

"You're probably right. It just gave me a weird feeling when I saw that picture." She smoothed her skirt and rose from her seat. "I hope I didn't keep you from anything special tonight."

"Not a thing," I assured Janelle. When I opened the door, the crisp breeze made me wrap my arms around my chest.

"I meant what I said before about not being able to make good friends since I moved here." Janelle draped her crimson jacket across her shoulders like a cape. "Maybe we can have drinks or dinner sometime."

"Sure," I lied politely, suddenly certain I wanted nothing more to do with the woman. "Give me a call sometime."

Janelle flashed her broad, biting smile and said, "Great. I definitely will." She stopped at the bottom of the steps. "You take care of yourself, okay?" She wiggled a goodbye salute with the tips of her fingers and walked out of the light.

CHAPTER 18

I locked the door behind her and double-checked the alarm. Dressed in her bright red outfit, she should have called up images of Little Red Riding Hood, but her wide grin was more wolf than waif. And there was something else making me feel uneasy. Something she said, but what was it?

On the way to the kitchen, I picked up the wine bottle and glasses. There was a little left in the bottle, but the thought of finishing Janelle's gift made my stomach lurch, so I dumped the rest in the sink. The wind scraped a low hanging tree limb outside the window, creating a shadow against the pane. The angle of the branch reminded me of the willow with its sad little figure hanging from it. That led to an image of Dr. Johnston dangling from a rope.

Jolting back from the counter, I rushed to my phone. It was almost eleven, but this couldn't wait. I punched in Hugh's number and held my breath until he answered a gruff hello.

"Did you happen to hear the news tonight about Johnston?" I asked.

"What? Wait a minute." I could hear paper crinkling in the background. "What the hell are you talking about?"

"Please, Hugh. Just tell me. Did you see the story about Johnston on the news?"

He answered in the affirmative and I continued. "Tell me what they said, as exact as you can."

He cleared his throat and recounted the story of the police discovering the doctor's body and saying an investigation was pending.

"So that's all they said. An investigation was pending. Nothing about how he died?"

"I told you they always keep stuff like that quiet until later. That's why I said not to say anything about it being a possible suicide. You didn't tell anybody, did you?"

"No. I didn't have to tell. She already knew."

. . .

When the alarm sounded at 6:30, I was already awake. I wasn't sure if I ever really fell asleep after recounting my conversation with Janelle to Hugh, who agreed the woman couldn't have known about the circumstances of Johnston's death without inside information. The most likely explanation was that she had somehow seen the body before the police arrived or had heard about it from someone else at the scene. Hugh promised to take the story to the police first thing in the morning and urged me not to meet with her again.

From underneath a warm shower, I tried to understand what Janelle's level of involvement in the doctor's case might be and why she wanted to meet with me in the first place. If her account of Lance's connection to Johnston was accurate, Janelle's intent might have been to warn me away from him. But that wouldn't explain how she'd known about how the doctor had died.

The actual cause of Johnston's death hadn't been decided, but I knew it took a great deal of determination for a person to hang himself. Nothing about the man indicated he had that kind of resolve. If he hadn't taken his own life, did that mean he'd been murdered? It was highly unlikely Janelle could have strangled the doctor and strung him up on her own, which suggested the possibility of an accomplice. Was it possible that the man I once loved was capable of murder? The thought made me shiver despite the heat from the shower.

After drying off and wrapping my hair in a towel, I put on my robe and went to the kitchen for coffee. Sunlight glinted off the wine glasses in the sink from the night before. A perfect outline of Janelle's crimson lips on one of them reminded me of how close I had been to a woman who might be a stone-cold killer. The image of her dazzling smile turned predatory, like a perverted Cheshire cat grin, mocking as it refused to fade away.

If I accepted the theory Janelle had played a part in Johnston's death, I also had to believe Lance was involved. And if there was any truth to Janelle's story, my ex was most likely more than a bit player. After all, he was the one courting the doctor as a prospective client. Unless the whole account of that dinner had been fabricated.

Pursuing this circular line of thought was both frustrating and fruitless. Better to clean up and put away the remnants of the encounter. Holding the lipstick-marked glass by its stem, I stopped just before filling it with warm soapy water. If Janelle had been telling the truth about being new to the area, where had she come from and why had she settled on Atlanta?

Lance's firm set high standards for attorneys on the partner track, but they gave those employees a lot of leeway when it came to hiring their assistants. I imagined my former fiancé bedazzled enough by Janelle's physical charms to accept her resume at face value. From my experience with insurance fraud, I knew it wasn't particularly difficult to manufacture an entire persona. If Janelle Ragsdale was someone other than an ambitious first year attorney, her wine glass might be the key to separating truth from fiction.

All I needed to do was get someone to run the prints on the glass. Hugh was the logical choice, but his phone went straight to voicemail, probably because he was sharing our suspicions about Janelle with the police. That left Mateo, who picked up on the second ring.

"You're up early," he said. "Is everything okay with your dad?"

"What?" Shit. What kind of daughter gets so caught up she forgets about her father's panic attack? A really crappy one. "No. I mean yes. Everything's okay with dad." Unless something had happened during hot sex with my mother.

"Are you okay?"

The genuine concern in his voice warmed me, and I wished I hadn't sent him away. But there was no time for that kind of thinking, so I assured him I was fine and gave him a brief account of my conversation with Janelle, leading to the reason for my call.

"Normally, Hugh would call one of his guys, but I don't know how long he'll be tied up, and I know you have some of the same connections."

"I use a private lab owned by an ex-Army buddy. He used to be with their criminal investigation department." He agreed to meet me at the office to pick up the glass and see if his friend could expedite the process.

After thanking him and hanging up, I returned to the kitchen and put the glass in a freezer bag, which I wrapped in a dishcloth before placing it in my briefcase. Then I threw on clothes and make-up.

On the way to the office, I called home and was relieved when Mom answered in a cheerful tone and told me dad had a good night and was feeling much better. I blinked back thoughts of just how good that night might have been based on those sly looks they had exchanged behind my back before my mother practically pushed me out the door.

"I'm so glad he's better," I said before offering to deliver dinner on my way home from work.

Mom insisted they were fine, countering with an invitation to come the next night. "I'll fix pot roast. And maybe you can bring that lovely young man with you."

"Do what, Mom?" I rolled down the window letting in the sounds of the heavy morning traffic. "Sorry, but I think I'm losing you. I'll call later."

It was a few minutes past eight when I pulled into the office parking lot. Mateo's car was parked in a visitor spot. I adjusted the rearview mirror, put on lip gloss, and tucked my hair behind my ears.

When Darla saw me, she jumped from her seat and rushed toward me.

"You have visitors," the receptionist whispered. She took my hand and leaned closer. "In your office. I tried to keep him out, but he insisted."

I couldn't imagine Mateo ignoring Darla's request unless something was urgent. "It's okay," I assured the agitated woman. "I can handle it."

It wasn't until I rounded the corner, that it registered. The receptionist had said I had *visitors* not a *visitor*. And sure enough, visible through the open blinds, there were two men waiting in my office: Mateo and my former fiancé.

Mateo sat in the leather chair directly in front of the desk, hands firmly gripping the studded chair arms, legs apart with thigh muscles tensed beneath his tight jeans. Lance must have been the one Darla had tried to keep out as he sat in the smaller, less comfortable chair. He tapped his right foot up and down in a frenetic beat. Neither man looked at the other; both turned when I entered. Mateo rose, prompting Lance, who never stood when women entered a room, to do the same.

I struggled to find the appropriate protocol for introducing the two, something gracious and polite that wouldn't make either man feel awkward. I didn't have to worry about Lance's delicate ego anymore, and if the grin on his face was any indication, Mateo wasn't the least bit uncomfortable. I walked past my ex without looking at him, set down my briefcase, and stood on tiptoe to kiss Mateo on the cheek. Only then did I acknowledge Lance.

"I don't believe we had an appointment, and I'm extremely busy today. Maybe you could schedule something with Darla on your way out."

I leveled my gaze directly at him, pleased I felt nothing stronger than irritation. I was, however, shocked at his appearance. The Lance I knew never went longer than two weeks without getting a ridiculously expensive haircut. Not only was he overdue for a trip to the stylist, but his normally lustrous hair was greasy and uncombed. He maintained his bronzed look with regular visits to the tanning salon, but today he looked pale and drawn. His suit was wrinkled, his tie was crooked, and his pricey Italian loafers were badly in need of polishing.

"Come on, Lucy," Lance began, stepping closer. Mateo countered by moving in front of me and holding up his hand.

"I think she was pretty clear about not having time to talk to you."

"This is between Lucy and me." Lance thrust his chest forward but side-stepped halfway around the larger man. "Please," he begged. "Just a few minutes."

Surprised at the desperation in his voice, I sighed and said, "I can give you five minutes, but first you'll have to wait in the hall while the two of us discuss some things." I expected him to protest, but he shrugged, then strode out of the room. I closed the blinds.

"You don't have to deal with that asshole," Mateo said in a voice loud enough to carry into the hallway.

"I know and I wouldn't if it weren't for the things Janelle hinted at involving him. Maybe I can get a feeling for which one of them is the bigger liar."

"It's possible, but I don't like the idea of you being alone with that guy."

"I don't plan on it. I'll hear him out and get rid of him." I opened my briefcase and took out the towel-wrapped baggy with the glass. "If your friend can run this fast, I think Janelle's past might give us some insight into her involvement with the doctor."

He unwrapped it and removed the plastic bag. "I'll ask him to bump us to the front of the line. In the meantime . . ." He put his free hand on my shoulder and squeezed lightly. "Don't do anything crazy, okay?" Before I could respond, he leaned down and covered my lips with his, softly at first, then more demanding. I pressed my body to his and melted into the kiss.

He broke away and headed to the door, looking back as he opened it. Lance catapulted past him and into the room.

Mateo gave him a disgusted look, then strode away without saying goodbye.

"Thought he'd never leave." Lance flashed his old smile, the one that used to make me want to run my fingers over the charming dimple on his right cheek. Today, his scruffy beard disguised both dimple and charm.

"Five minutes, Lance, starting thirty seconds ago." I punched the button on my Fitbit and watched the seconds ticking off.

"Okay, okay." He slumped into the nearest chair. "Can we at least sit down?" he asked, in his *let's be reasonable about this* tone. In the past, his request might have come across as a soft plea with the power to lull me into compliance. This morning, it reminded me of Doris whining behind the bedroom door. Only the pup was more appealing. I leaned against the desk and glared.

"All right," he began. "Babe, I hate the way we left things between us. I've wanted to stop by a million times to apologize, but I was afraid you wouldn't want to hear me out. Last night, though, I couldn't stand it any longer. I had to see you, to make things right. I knew if I called you wouldn't agree, so around nine, I got in the Porsche and drove straight to your house. When I got there, that bitch's car was parked out front. I didn't know what to do. Knowing you were alone with her, well, to be honest, I was scared out of my mind." He paused and took a deep breath. "Because that woman—Janelle," he spat her name between clenched teeth, "Lucy, that woman is very dangerous."

Funny, she said the same thing about you.

I decided to treat him as a hostile witness, using his own tactic of creating an uncomfortable silence. That technique, he told me over drinks, went a long way in getting people to open up about stuff they didn't want you to know.

I kept my gaze fixed on him and said nothing.

"I wanted to bust through the door, but was afraid that might make things worse, especially if she'd been telling you a bunch of lies about me. Was she? Telling lies about me?" This time the whine was more pronounced.

"How would I know, Lance? I certainly can't trust you to set the record straight when it comes to telling the truth, now can I?" A wave of rage crashed over me, shocking me with its intensity. It wasn't anger about losing him or the life I had envisioned with the man, though. No. I was relieved to have dodged that bullet. The source of my fury came from the realization this jerk thought he still had some hold over me, could still manipulate me.

"Please, Lucy. I know I was a terrible fiancé, but I can't believe you're willing to give up on us because of one stupid mistake."

"Get this straight. There is no us. And Janelle wasn't a mistake. She was a choice. Your mistake is your thinking you could talk your way back into my life." I looked at my watch. "You have three and a half minutes left."

He stood abruptly and grabbed my arm. "Forget about the goddamned watch." His face twisted into an ugly mask of something I couldn't identify, not exactly anger. No, it was more like fear, maybe even terror.

I dug my nails into his wrist. "Let go of me. Now."

He released his hold. "I'm sorry, babe. I just get so worked up when I think about what that woman might be telling you about me. Everything she says is a lie. You have to believe me." A vibration from his suit coat interrupted him. He thrust his hand into the inner pocket and squinted at the screen. I once thought it was cute he was too vain to wear reading glasses. Not so much now.

His myopic stupor transformed into a portrait of panic as he deciphered the text.

"Shit!" He ran his fingers through his oily hair. "She knows I'm here," he whispered. "I've got to get out of town. I'll call when it's safe and explain everything."

"Wait a minute," I called out as he scrambled toward the door. "You can't just run away. Not if you're involved in what happened to Dr. Johnston." I caught up with him. This time I grabbed his arm.

He shook off my hand and maintained his grip on the doorknob as he turned, wild-eyed.

"That was all Janelle. She introduced me to the doctor, said he was a prospective client. Told me he had a lot of money to invest if I was interested in starting my own firm. But it was all a load of crap." He leaned against the door and covered his eyes with his forearm for a moment. Then looked at me. "If you know what's good for you, you'll keep your mouth shut about the doctor, especially if the police come around. Promise me, Lucy. No matter what you think about me, the last thing I want is for something bad to happen to you. And if you keep poking around in this shit, that's exactly what will happen."

. . .

I tried to put his desperate warning aside but ended up staring at the computer screen for I don't know how long. A little after nine Hugh came lumbering into my office.

"Darla tells me you had a busy morning," he said before sitting.

"It was definitely interesting." I summarized everything from my request to Mateo to Lance's frantic exit, emphasizing how frightened he seemed of Janelle.

"He might have good reason to be scared of that one." Hugh filled me in on his visit to the police where he shared my suspicions about Janelle's possible involvement in Dr. Johnston's death. He also told me the police had ruled out suicide.

"There's something else fishy about your boyfriend's ex-squeeze. The cops discovered a woman named Janelle Ragsdale graduated from Georgia State and passed the bar six years ago, right before she married Bart Vernon and moved to Texas. I spoke to the real Janelle on the phone, and she was surprised at what a successful attorney she'd become since she never practiced law. Instead she's home raising three kids under the age of five." He shook his head.

"When I described her alter-ego, she said it sounded a little like a roommate she had her first year in law school. Elaine Hendricks or Henderson, but they only lived together a few months before the girl moved out. She might have an old picture of her somewhere. She promised to look for it and send it first chance she got. From all the caterwauling in the background, though, I'm not expecting anything real soon. Three kids under five. What the hell was she thinking?"

"Let's hope we have more luck with the prints," I suggested, ignoring Hugh's commentary on overly prolific women.

"Whatever, but I don't feel like sitting around waiting. Think I'll take a pass at Johnston's other neighbors."

"Are you sure you're not making up an excuse to check on Maisie?"

"Very funny, Princess. Between you and me? It wouldn't surprise me if that woman has Mr. Whiskers stored in the freezer beside Mr. Gutteridge ." He eased out of the chair. "Might be a good idea if you stayed put for a while. You never know what our mystery lady might be up to. Maybe you could run some background on the other woman in the doc's life, Roberta Whatsername, the nurse."

"Garrison, Roberta Garrison." I had almost forgotten the hostile RN.

I agreed to, and Hugh left me with instructions to call him as soon as I heard from Mateo or found out something useful about Roberta, whichever came first.

With over nine hundred women sharing the nurse's name, I wasn't optimistic about finding the person who'd been so nasty over the phone. I narrowed the search by adding "registered nurse" and "Atlanta" but was disheartened when I realized Roberta Garrison might not even be her real name.

Remembering the photos of the doctor and his wife, I opened the Johnston file. Since I'd never seen Roberta, I wasn't sure what I was looking for but hoped something about the picture or the gala itself might give me some ideas. I visited the gala site, relocated the photo, and began scrolling through other pictures from that evening. The background from the photo was a mural of Van Gogh's *Starry Night*. In one of the most prominent images, groups of people beamed at the camera from underneath a banner reading *Stars of our Night*. Either Johnston wasn't one of the stars or he'd been late for the line-up, but he was missing from the group shot.

Discouraged, I was about to turn away when I noticed a familiar face on the edge of the dance floor. I zoomed in as close as possible on a woman wearing a standard catering uniform: black pencil-skirt and vest, tailored white blouse, dark stockings, and sensible shoes. She'd tamed her fluffy blonde hair by pulling it into a tight bun and modified her make-up but hadn't ditched the signature blood-red lipstick. Janelle Ragsdale, or whoever she was, had worked the gala attended by Johnston and his wife.

That meant two years ago, instead of practicing law in another state, Janelle had been serving drinks to a bunch of self-congratulatory physicians. It also signified she wasn't as new to the area as she claimed and advanced the theory that she might have known the doctor long before Lance met him.

Before I had time to consider additional implications, my cell sounded, and Mateo's name flashed on the screen.

"How busy are you now?" he asked.

"I was running background on Johnston's nurse and found a picture of Janelle at the same party the doctor and his wife attended over two years ago. But I have no idea what to do now, so I guess the answer to your questions is I'm not too busy."

"I want to hear all about what you found, but first I need to tell you what I learned about our girl Janelle. My friend at the lab identified the prints and they don't belong to Miss Ragsdale. They belong to a woman named Elaine Hendricks. She was—"

"The real Janelle's roommate."

"I'm not even going to ask how you knew that. But anyway, it seems Elaine spent more time running cons on old guys than studying law. She charmed some old coot into investing in a non-existing spa or bakery or daycare center, then disappeared. She was good, though. Only got arrested once when the vic's daughter went to the cops. Even then the mark wouldn't press charges. That was over five years ago. She showed up in Atlanta around the time of the gala. Where she was between those times is anybody's guess."

I stood and began pacing. "The big question for me is how did she go from catering to Lance's law firm."

"Agreed. I have some business to take care of but should be done by one, so we could meet around 1:30 at El Encanto. Sofia mentioned you to my aunt, and I'm in deep doo-doo for not bringing you back."

The idea of meeting another member of his family was both pleasing and intimidating. An aunt was close to a mother and meeting a mother was serious business, but I said I wold.

After making copies of the enlarged shot of Janelle at the party, I closed the file. Hoping Hugh might be finished with the neighborhood interviews, I tried his number, and ended up leaving a message that included a detailed explanation of what Mateo and I had discovered.

The unfinished paperwork in my inbox was decidedly dull. It reminded me of Elsie, and I was tempted to snoop through Hugh's private files for clues as to what he might recommend to the court regarding the case. He kept handwritten notes on everything, but most of them were either illegible or recorded in some sort of secret shorthand I hadn't been able to decipher.

I gave up on getting anything productive done and began the tedious process of going through my junk email. The company filter was effective, but occasionally something worthwhile was incorrectly labeled. I scanned through messages promising interest-free loans or a greatly improved sex life. I made the mistake of clicking on a video of a cat nursing three newborn piglets and watched it five times before vowing, once again, to give up bacon.

After killing approximately an hour, it was now 12:45. This time of day the usual twenty-minute drive to the restaurant could be anywhere from thirty to forty-five minutes, so I gathered my things and went to reception.

"I have a 1:30 lunch appointment with Mr. Sullivan," I informed Darla. "But I should be back before 3:00."

"Are you planning on dessert?" she asked. "Because that will definitely take longer."

Unable to frame a snappy comeback, I rolled my eyes and walked out the door. A whirlwind of leaves swirled around my feet. Dark clouds hung low over the skyline, muting the brilliance of the red and gold trees bordering the parking area. Heavy drops of rain swept in and peppered the asphalt. I should have believed the weather guy when he predicted thunderstorms. If I went back for an umbrella, I would have to endure another snarky comment from Darla, so I draped my sweater over my head and made a run for it.

The sudden shift in weather threw off my routine of always having keys in hand at least a car's length away. My makeshift rain bonnet kept slipping as I rummaged through my purse. Just as I located the key chain, I heard the steady hum of a running engine, followed by the rustling of sudden movement from behind.

Before I could react, a blinding buzz of electric static flashed in front of my eyes. My spine stiffened as a sizzling sensation traveled through my shoulder blades and chest, constricting my breathing. I was immobilized by a searing pain, followed by a complete loss of muscle control.

CHAPTER 19

What seemed like hours but could have been minutes later, I was leaning against a cold metal surface, struggling to open my eyes, fighting against heavy darkness. Too exhausted to move, I swallowed a scream when I realized my eyes were open, but there was no light at all, only black so thick it threatened to suffocate me. Then I was suffocating, breathing in not air, but something dense and wet. Desperate guttural cries filled my ears, and I was overcome with terror upon recognizing the gurgling came from me.

"There, there." A muffled voice frightened me even more. My body shook uncontrollably as I tried to identify the familiar scent hovering all around her, a funereal blend of lilies and vanilla.

"I . . . I . . . can't breathe," I gasped, fearful the chattering of my of teeth might drown out my words.

"It's just part of the residual effect of the stun gun. If you promise not to make a fuss, I'll take off your hood."

Hood? No wait, stun gun?

I was connecting the dots when someone grabbed me by the shoulders and brought light back into my world. A shape, blurred by the halo-like fog of my semi-conscious state, appeared. That dim glow faded, and there, dressed in black from her cap to her jeans, was Janelle.

I blinked, trying to bring my surroundings into focus, but a stabbing pain brought tears instead. I concentrated on the rolling sensation beneath me and determined I was in a moving vehicle, possibly the one I heard when I was looking for my keys.

"Take deep breaths," the woman urged. "You'll start to feel normal soon."

I obeyed and did feel better.

"Where are you taking me?" I realized I was in a van, maybe *the* silver van. When I leaned away from the interior wall, I slid sideways, my bound hands useless. "And why am I tied up? What do you want?"

"Always with the questions," Janelle sighed. "You know, that's your problem. You can never leave stuff alone. You have to keep digging and digging." She held up a roll of duct tape, smiled as she ripped off a piece, and grabbed my chin. Then she stretched the strip over my mouth. "That's better. Now you sit tight. It won't be long before you get your answers. Of course, you may not like them." Janelle climbed over the gearshift. "Ooh, I love this song," she squealed and turned up the radio.

The van filled with the latest Taylor Swift song saying farewell to her latest discarded boyfriend.

• • •

When I came to, both the music and the van had stopped. I heard Janelle talking softly with someone and made out the words "office" and "key." The driver's door opened and shut, as I squinted my eyes, trying to identify my other captor, who, like Janelle, was dressed in black from head to toe.

"All right, Miss Curious." Leaving her companion behind, Janelle stepped into the van and yanked me to my feet. "I really don't want to zap you again, but if you don't cooperate, I will. Then we'll have to drag you and you're heavier than you look."

I stumbled forward, allowing myself to be helped from the vehicle. My legs buckled and I would have tumbled back into the van if Janelle hadn't steadied me.

I swayed, then regained my balance. I peered around Janelle and got my first look at the driver, whose black cap was pulled down low. Taller and thicker than Janelle, her cohort wore a boxy leather jacket and loose-fitting jeans. In one hand was a gun aimed at me.

"Did I forget to mention my friend will shoot you if you try anything funny?"

A wave of nausea hit me. Oddly, it was the thought of humiliating myself by barfing into the duct tape rather than the obvious danger facing me that snapped me out of my stupor. I straightened up and looked away from the gun and directly into the pale gray eyes of the person holding it. Despite the angle of the hat, I could tell my captor was female. Her skin was smooth and tight. A slack spot above her dark turtleneck, hinted at the imminent arrival of a double chin. For some strange reason, this made me feel better.

"Let's go," Janelle said, leading me by the arm. "Don't want to keep your friend waiting."

This announcement put an end to my short-lived feeling of hopefulness. Which one of the people I cared about had these two insane women taken? It was one thing for the women to endanger me, quite another to put someone I loved in jeopardy.

Still disoriented by the jolt from the stun gun, I had trouble keeping up with Janelle as we crossed the parking lot to an elevator. My thoughts had unscrambled somewhat, and I wondered who the unnervingly quiet woman was. Thankfully, my vision had returned to normal, and I was able to read the sign directing visitors to the fifth-floor offices of Stalwart Medical Consolidation.

Before we entered, Janelle ripped the duct tape off my mouth. "In case we run into somebody." She reached into her back pocket, removed a knife, and freed my hands. "Remember, if you make a sound, we'll have to shoot you here."

Here? Was that what it came down to—a choice of where, not if, I would die?

Watching the lights as we ascended, a thread of thought like a loose end in a ball of yarn began to unravel.

"Why are we going to Dr. Johnston's?"

Janelle gave me a playful shove. "What did I tell you?" she asked her companion. "Nosy little bitch, isn't she?"

The woman responded by jabbing me with the gun without speaking. I bit back the pain, determined to show as little weakness as possible. For the first time during this ordeal, I was angry and consciously directed that anger at the woman behind me. The elevator shuddered to a stop, and the door opened into the ghostly gloom of an empty reception area. Stiff-backed chairs lined the walls and a few tattered magazines lay in lonely clusters on end tables.

Once again, my stomach turned, and I resisted Janelle's insistent tugging. I had the dreadful feeling if I got off that elevator, I might never leave this place. But the woman shoved me forward, propelling me into the darkened waiting room.

"All righty," Janelle chirped. "We should probably pick up the pace a bit if we're going to make our flight." She wrapped her arm around my waist in an imitation of intimacy and led me through the reception doors into the inner office where it was even darker.

The pressure from the gun in my back disappeared as the woman moved to my right and flipped on the lights.

Her easy familiarity with her surroundings suggested she had been here several times. She pushed me toward the narrow hallway and stopped outside the first door.

"Here we are," she announced, opening the door.

I stepped into the room, larger than the typical exam room. A closet labeled 'Supplies' was to my right. At the sight of the man strapped to the table, I came to a complete halt. His ashen face was purpled with bruises, but there was no mistaking that square jawline and thick blond hair. It was Lance, and I couldn't tell if he was dead or alive.

"What did you do to him?" I whispered.

"Robby just gave him a little whiff of chloroform, and the big goon fell flat on his face. He wasn't supposed to be out this long, but that stuff can be tricky. That's why we went with the stun gun for you."

Robby? I turned to face Janelle's accomplice.

"You're Roberta Garrison."

The nurse took off her cap, and her short dark hair, powered by static electricity, crackled. "Smart girl," she glared while Janelle shut the door behind us. "But not as smart as you think, or you wouldn't be here. Right?"

From the corner of my eye, I thought I saw the closet door inch open. But a low moan from the exam table grabbed my attention before I could verify the movement.

"Oh, goody!" Janelle exclaimed. "Now we can get this party started." She moved closer to Lance, who had begun to struggle weakly against his bonds.

"Janelle?" he groaned, lifting his head. "What am I doing here?"

"Don't you remember, darling? We were going to have one last fling before I left town. But I guess I forgot to tell you it was going to be your last fling, period." She laughed softly as Lance glanced away from her, his confused gaze landing on me.

"Lucy? What's going on?" He placed his head back on the paper pillow.

"You never did get it, did you, Dickhead?"

Roberta's voice brought his head abruptly up from his resting position. "Good God, Janelle. I told you that stuff was too rough for me. And no way Lucy will go for it."

Janelle giggled, and Roberta grunted before saying, "You idiot." Then she turned to me. "Move over there by the asshole. And don't try anything funny." She waved the gun in Lance's direction.

I walked toward the table but stopped before I reached it. "I'm not doing anything until you answer some questions." I surprised myself with the sudden burst of courage.

Roberta lunged at me, but Janelle grabbed her arm.

"It's okay, babe," she said.

Babe. So more than a casual friend.

"You know what your problem is?" I jumped at Janelle's brittle shift in tone, like glass shattering on a tile floor. "You ask too many questions. For example, you couldn't just act on what I told you about Lance and his involvement with Andy's death. No, you had to start poking around in my background, calling my old roommate."

My face must have reflected my shock. How could Janelle have known about that?

"That's right. The minute the real Janelle hung up after talking to your snoopy old boss, she gave me a call. You see, she and I were a bit more than roommates. She wasn't thrilled when she discovered I was using her name, but she would never want anything bad to happen to me." She shook her head. "If only you'd left it alone," she sighed, "we wouldn't be in this mess."

"I don't understand." I was pretty sure I did but needed more time. Because while Janelle or Elaine had been talking, Roberta had been totally engrossed in what the woman was saying, giving me the chance to scoot closer to Lance and, keeping my hands out of sight, loosen his left arm restraint.

"I don't either," Roberta spoke up. "What do you mean 'more than roommates'?"

"Now's not the time to get into all that, babe." Janelle waved her hand in the nurse's direction.

"I disagree," Roberta replied. "I think now is the perfect time."

Janelle rolled her eyes. "That was a long time ago. Can we deal with these two first? I promise I'll tell you all about it."

Ah, Roberta's the jealous type. Could be helpful. "Just a few more questions, please." I continued before the women had time to refuse. "I know the doctor was removing and selling organs. And I'm guessing the two of you were helping." I looked directly at Janelle. "But why did you need Lance?" I could hear the rustling from behind as he worked on the strap and raised my voice. "Unless he was the one who got you involved. Or was the whole thing Johnston's idea?"

Roberta snorted and Janelle laughed out loud. "Dr. Andy Johnston come up with a scheme like that? Get real. He was small potatoes until we came along. Running two-bit insurance scams. He had no idea what a gold mine he was sitting on—all those illegals with two healthy kidneys. Plus, he had access to the organ transplant database. As for that fool on the table, we needed someone to handle the paperwork, fake consent forms for the hospital and shit like that. I could have done it myself, but I didn't want to call attention to the fact that Janelle Ragsdale never practiced law in Atlanta. Okay, now."

"Wait, please. That's something else I don't get. A woman as smart as you, why didn't you finish law school?" I hoped flattery would keep Janelle talking.

It worked. "Because I am smart. Everybody thinks lawyers all make the big bucks, but that's only if you get on with a high-class firm. Then you work your ass off, and if you're a woman, forget it. Most attorneys go under before they finish paying off student loans."

She paused and I held my breath, fearful Janelle had sensed Lance had partially freed himself. But she was looking at her accomplice, who had been staring lovingly at her during her entire speech.

While the two of them exchanged googly eyes, I checked the status of the closet door but saw no change. I returned my full attention to Janelle, who had resumed her explanation of how brilliant she was.

"So, instead of spending time with a bunch of losers in some dusty lecture hall, I decided to help my fellow man, or I guess you could say fellow old men, right, Robby?"

The two shared a glance, and Roberta nodded. Her previous annoyance seemed to have dissipated. I needed it to return.

"You mean you had sex with rich old men for money?"

Janelle frowned. "Not nice, Lucy. I offered love and companionship to the elderly. But you knew that, didn't you?"

"Not exactly. I know you were involved with several older gentlemen, but the years right before you came to Atlanta are a blank. Was that when you and Roberta hooked up?"

"You make it sound so dirty. We met after Emerson's liver transplant. Robby was my husband's nurse during his recovery period. Unfortunately, he took a turn for the worse. Poor Emmy."

I suspected his post-operative care might have had something to do with that turn but didn't think it was a good idea to broach that theory now. So, I asked, "Is that what gave you the idea about the whole organ thing?"

"Pretty much. After my husband's sad demise, we had enough money to resettle and look for a more lucrative enterprise. We did a little research on doctors whose practices weren't booming and found a few prospects. In a way, we have you to thank for helping us discover Andy."

"Me?"

"Yes. You see, we checked the records for physicians involved in insurance claims. We came across your company's investigation of Andrew Johnston, and voila! We had our mark. Greedy and potentially in trouble. The plan was to run a few deals, take the money, and check out. But Andy was a moron. We told him not to make cash deposits and thought he was listening. Then you and that Neanderthal boss of yours went through his garbage and ruined everything." She shook her finger playfully at me, but the look in her eyes didn't match the light-hearted gesture.

A tap on the arm I still held behind me signaled Lance had broken free. But what good would the use of one hand do? I had to create a diversion if we were going to get out of this unharmed.

"That's enough," Roberta spoke up. "We need to get moving."

I didn't want to know what it might look like to 'get moving.'

"Wait. Can you just explain a few more things? Like the pictures. Did Lance take them? And who stole them from my apartment?"

"Those damn pictures," Janelle sighed. "It seemed like a good idea at the time. Robby would follow you and take photos so we could see your reaction to the rose and the email and the doll."

"So, it was you? But why?"

"We thought it would freak you out enough to get you to take a break, maybe a vacation. Or at least back off from the case until we could wrap things up. But no. You had to keep on digging. I tried to make you think it was Lance you had to worry about."

"But why steal them back? That was you, right?"

"That wasn't part of the original plan." Janelle turned to face Roberta. "Robby, why don't you explain that?" I detected a discordant note in her tone.

Roberta's face turned a shade of scarlet. "How many times do I have to tell you? I didn't see the van was in the picture. The screen on my phone is too small. And remember." Her voice rose, reminding me of the nurse's wild rant on the phone. "You're the one who was in such a hurry you didn't even look at the pictures before you stuck them in the envelope."

Janelle stiffened, the muscle in her jaw twitching. "We've been over this, dear," she spoke through clenched teeth. "You were in charge of taking the pictures. I can't do everything."

"Really? I thought you liked being in charge. Weren't you the one who wanted to give good old Andy that farewell party? *It'll be easy*, you said. Get him drunk and tell him it's just another one of our games. Oh. wait." She waved the gun wildly. "That was just an excuse to give you a chance to get in bed with him again, wasn't it?"

Janelle threw her hands up. "For the last time—"

"Don't tell me you didn't like it. Me, watching you and that . . . that . . . that man!" She shuddered. "You like making people suffer. And Doctor Creepy got into suffering, didn't he? Sometimes I think the two of you made a better couple than we do."

I could see tears forming in the woman's eyes but couldn't tell if they were from sorrow or anger.

Janelle took a deep breath. "Honey, you know that's crazy. Whose idea was it to get rid of Andy in the first place?"

Janelle's confession, intentional or not, sent a chill up my spine. Admitting you'd committed murder in front of hostages didn't bode well for the hostages.

I shifted the topic. "I guess that whole thing with you and Lance was for show. There was nothing real between the two of you?"

"Me and Lance?" She burst out laughing. "Honestly, Lucy. I know he's pretty, but that man is duller than dirt."

Roberta joined in with the laughter, but hers sounded forced.

"And in bed?" Janelle snorted. "I think I actually fell asleep in the middle of what he considered some of his best moves. Remember that night?" She asked Roberta.

"I remember." Roberta had stopped laughing. "You came over late, stinking of that girly- smelling cologne he wore."

"Girly?" I jumped at Lance's thick, groggy voice. "Tom Ford doesn't make girly perfume."

That's right, Lance. The masculine integrity of your cologne is what's important here.

Apparently, the other two women had forgotten about his existence for a moment. Janelle snapped her head in his direction, and Roberta bolted toward the table. Her rubber-soled shoes caught awkwardly on the tile and she stumbled. Janelle reached out to steady her, but Roberta threw off her arm.

"That's it!" she screamed. "I'm done with this shit. It's time to end it." She released the safety on the gun and aimed it directly at Lance's head.

"Wait," Janelle ordered. "If you shoot him here, it won't look right. Remember?" She lowered her voice and continued in a soothing tone. "We have to make it look like a murder/suicide."

"Wait!" I interjected. "How's that supposed to work?"

"Everyone knows Lance has been desperate to get you back. Or at least, that's what I've been telling everyone." Janelle beamed. "When he found out about the hot new guy in your life, he lost it. If he couldn't have you, blah, blah, blah."

"Do you really think anyone will believe someone like Lance would care that much?"

"Oh, did I forget the part where he wrote the note explaining how he and the doctor were running an illegal organ ring? And how he found out Andy was holding out on him, so he killed him and planned to take you away with him? And when you wouldn't go, yadda, yadda, yadda." She pointed her index finger at Lance. "Then bang!" She blew imaginary smoke before pointing to me. She rotated her hand toward Lance and added, "Double bang."

"Please, Janelle. You don't have to do this." I hated the note of desperation in my voice.

"Shut up!" Roberta shouted, still leveling the weapon toward Lance, who was shaking so violently the table had begun to rattle. "I'm sick of looking at these two." She took a step forward, and Lance closed his eyes.

"I know, baby," Janelle cooed. "But we need to get it right."

Roberta lowered the weapon, her grip on the gun visibly loosening.

"That's good. Now give it to me and we'll move them to Andy's office, just like we talked about."

Roberta held out the gun, but before Janelle could take it, a silver haired woman burst from the closet.

"Grab the gun," Elsie shouted, hurling herself at Janelle. I reached for the pistol and missed, careening into the nurse and sending the weapon flying in the opposite direction. Roberta fell back across the exam table. The gun landed hard near the door and a blast reverberated around us.

Elsie held onto Janelle's arm and slung her around in a circle, then released her. Propelled by fury and momentum, the younger woman slammed headfirst into the edge of the counter and collapsed onto the floor.

High-pitched howls filled the room. At first, I couldn't determine their source. Elsie sat quietly with her back to the wall. I turned to Janelle, who lay on the floor, also silent. The shrieks grew louder and more frantic, and I realized they came from the table.

Locked in a savage embrace, Lance held onto Roberta's hair with his bound hand and maneuvered into a position that allowed him to squeeze her throat with the other.

Her face turned a deep shade of purple, and her screams stopped. Eyes rolled back in her head, she went limp, but Lance didn't release her.

"Let her go!" I screamed, but he ignored me. I grabbed a metal tray from the counter planning to use it to get his attention.

Before I could follow through, the door burst open, sending splinters flying.

CHAPTER 20

"It's over, Lucy."

"Mateo!"

He dropped to his knees. "Are you okay?" He touched his forehead to mine, then whispered, "I heard the shot, and I was, I didn't know if—"

I threw my arms around his neck. "It's okay. I'm okay." I released my chokehold, and he helped me up.

Elsie sat cross-legged in front of us. Pale and shaky, she extended her arm. Mateo took it and eased her to her feet.

"Thank you, young man. I don't believe we've met. And if you don't mind, I'd rather not be here when the police arrive."

Before we could react, she slipped from the room.

. . .

It was after midnight by the time Mateo turned into my drive. I was still riding the adrenaline high that had surged through me when he rushed into Dr. Johnston's exam room. I explained Roberta and Janelle's plans and submitted to an unnecessary examination by the EMT guys. Other than a few nasty bruises, I remained unscathed. They pronounced me fit enough to go to the station to answer questions.

Seconds after Elsie made her escape, the police arrived, followed by Hugh. Roberta revived and demonstrated her fitness by screaming obscenities at me and Lance, who was also pronounced well enough to accompany the police. We would give a statement. He, however, would be remaining as a guest of the state until blame could be sorted out. As for Janelle, she showed no signs of regaining consciousness.

Framed against the navy night, the golden dome of the capitol building shone like a guiding star. This view of the Atlanta skyline grounded me. Although I remained unnaturally exhilarated, I grew calmer.

I noticed my purse in the backseat and wondered who had found it.

I stared at it for a second, then asked, "How did you know where to look for me?"

"When you didn't show at the restaurant, I called your office. Darla said you left over an hour ago. She saw your car in the lot, and we knew something was wrong. She called the police, and I called Hugh on the way over. We found your purse but not your phone, so Hugh activated the GPS locator and we tracked it to the van in the parking lot. It must have fallen out when they took you. From there, it wasn't hard to figure out you'd be in Johnston's office," he concluded.

Momentarily indignant Hugh had never told me he had installed a tracker, I had to admit it was foolish to be annoyed about something that had probably saved my life.

I thought of the way Elsie bolted from the scene and decided not to mention she was there. If it came out later, I would claim I was in shock.

At the station, Mateo waited in the reception area. Hugh sat by me as I gave my account of the last few days. Occasionally, he filled in details. I left Elsie out when I described the chaos in the crowded room. The detectives in charge of the investigation finished their questioning. Hugh remained behind, and I joined Mateo in the lobby.

As soon as I entered the waiting area, he jumped from his seat and bounded to my side. Holding me close, he said, "When I think of what could have happened."

"But it didn't. I'm fine. I'm better than fine. I'm great. I feel like I could leap tall buildings with a single bound, stop a locomotive with—"

"I get it." He laughed and draped an arm across my shoulder. He nuzzled my neck, then whispered, "What other superpowers do you have?"

Before I could answer, the double doors burst open, and Hugh moved toward us. "It's looking like you might be a hero, Princess."

"Hero?"

"Yep. A bona fide hero, or should I say heroine? Anyway, seems like those two gals were something else."

Hugh spent the next ten or fifteen minutes sharing the story of Roberta Garrison and Elaine Hendricks, a.k.a. Janelle Ragsdale. Janelle had been telling the truth about meeting Roberta after her husband's transplant. She had neglected to mention, however, that poor Emerson's death hadn't been caused by rejection of the new liver. It had been officially ruled a heart attack, but his daughter insisted Janelle's insistent and perverted sexual demands had killed her father.

"How would the daughter know what was going on in her dad's bedroom?" I cringed at the memory of my own brief insight into my parents' private life.

"Seems she caught them in the act one day. And by them, I mean Janelle, the old man, and his nasty nurse, the one and only Roberta. They had him happily hogtied while they performed, according to the daughter, *unspeakable acts.*"

"Not a bad way to go," Mateo offered.

"Gross," I said, punching him in the arm.

"Wait." I turned back to Hugh. "When you said hogtied—"

"That's right," Hugh nodded. "I meant tied up. I'm guessing the sadist sisters have a Girl Scout badge in knot-tying, including the same kind of running knot they found on the noose around the doctor's neck. The doc's blood alcohol came back well over the legal limit, and there were traces of Ambien in his system. Anyway, it looks like our ladies have a history of using their special set of skills to charm old guys out of their money. Probably started out that way with Johnston before they got him to expand his business. There must have been a falling out between the doc and the girls, and he came out on the short end of the rope."

"So, the police are positive it wasn't suicide?"

"More like a sex game set-up. The rope was long enough he could have touched the ground if he'd stayed conscious. The right amount of pressure to the carotid artery, combined with the drugs and alcohol, would have made it easy for our girls to make sure he didn't. It's hard to prove since the party girls can claim it was an accident— he was alive when they left him or some other shit. But the body part business is a slam dunk, which means by the time they're up for parole, it'll be damn near impossible for them to find any older guys to prey on."

"And Lance?" I asked.

"Jury's still out on his level of involvement. He handled the paperwork for the transplants and had to know they weren't kosher. As for the doc's murder, my guess would be he didn't know about it but probably suspected something was off. Either way, looks like his ass is grass." He paused and gave me a stern look. "You need to get some rest."

With my mind racing a mile a minute, I couldn't imagine resting but didn't argue. Mateo rose and held out his arm.

"I don't want to see you until Monday. Got it?" Hugh commanded.

When we reached my apartment, Mateo killed the engine. We sat quietly for a moment before he asked, "Still feeling like Super Woman?"

I thought of Janelle cheerfully sharing her murderous plan, and a surreal feeling came over me. It was as if I were seeing someone else fighting for her life in that cold, gray room.

And in a way, I supposed, it had been someone else. I was still the same person who demanded honesty from people I cared about and who couldn't be in a relationship without complete trust. I was, however, no longer the Lucy Howard who felt the need to apologize for refusing to accept less.

"Not so much," I admitted. "When I think about what might have happened if you and the rest of the troops hadn't shown up, I don't feel quite so invincible."

"From where I stood, it looked as if you and grandma had things under control."

"Maybe." But what would I have done if Lance hadn't let go of Roberta? Because as bad as the woman was—murder by sex, illegal organ removal, kidnapping, and general bitchiness—I hadn't been comfortable watching Lance choke the life out of her. And while shooting my ex might have provided some satisfaction, I doubted I could have done it.

"Don't underestimate yourself." He took my hand and touched it to his lips. "I think you even managed to impress Hugh, and that is most certainly not an easy accomplishment. Speaking of your boss," he sighed, "if I don't let you get some rest, I'll be in big trouble." He opened his door, and I watched him in the shadows as he came around to help me from the car.

Patches of moonlight shimmered through the branches of the willow. Only fifteen or so hours since I left home, and less than two weeks since Mateo had come into my life. But it seemed much longer. Buddy's predicament, a stalker, Dad's health scare, my kidnapping—so much crammed into such a short space.

Once during college, I made the mistake of dating a math major who became obsessed with teaching me the basics of Einstein's theory of relativity. Despite my best efforts, I drifted into my own alternate time and space continuum while he droned on and on.

The experience soured me on mathematics and math majors, but maybe I hadn't been fair. It made sense to me now that the concept of time did relate to the speed of movement. What else could explain how hours felt like days and that the short time I'd known Mateo was, in fact, a lifetime?

I unlocked the door.

"Would you like to come in for a drink?" He shifted from one foot to the other, then shook his head slowly. "If I come in, I'm not going to want to leave. And I'm not sure you're ready for me to stay." He kissed me lightly on the lips, turned, and walked away.

. . .

A persistent buzzing on the bedside table woke me from a dream in which I'd been trying, unsuccessfully, to navigate a maze-like passageway through an unfamiliar building. The lights kept going on and off. I reached for the clock and was shocked to see it was after eleven. When I picked up my phone, my mother's face beamed from caller ID.

Shit! I never called Mom back. Hopefully, escaping from kidnappers who planned to murder me would count as a good excuse.

"Hey, Mom."

"Thank God! I just saw the news and you're all over it." She broke into violent sobbing, which faded into the background amidst crackling and shuffling, culminating with Dad's voice.

"They said you and Lance had been held hostage by two accused murderers." The fact Dad had taken over the call emphasized how upset Mom was. "Your mother almost fainted." He paused and, for a moment, I was afraid he was crying, too. "Good God, honey. We're too old for this."

"I'm sorry, Daddy." Tears formed in my eyes. "But I promise I'm fine. It was crazy."

"Hold on while I put you on speaker."

I struggled into a sitting position, discovering tender spots on my back and upper arms. I heard my parents fumbling around. "Where the hell is that damn speaker button," Dad mumbled.

Normally, I found their technological inaptitude amusing. Today, it was painfully endearing. The thought I might not have been around to hear their voices in any capacity threatened to overwhelm me.

"Okay," Dad commanded. "We're ready."

I gave them a sanitized version of the events. When I finished, Mom tearfully insisted on bringing lunch over immediately and had only been dissuaded by my promise to come for dinner.

It wasn't that I didn't want to see my family. I wanted to see them more than I could remember, even more than the time I came home from that horrible two-week Bible camp where the counselors terrified and titillated us with the horrors that awaited teens who gave into the sins of the flesh. For years, even the mildest erogenous pleasure carried with it the faint scent of burning brimstone.

Today, however, I needed time to get myself together so I wouldn't fall apart when I faced my parents.

I swung my legs over the side of the bed and winced at the sharp pain in my hip. With one foot on the ground, I lifted my nightgown. An enormous dark maroon bruise started on my right butt check and traveled down the length of my thigh, stopping at my calf. I inched the other leg across, stood slowly, and hobbled to the full-length mirror where I stopped to examine the extent of my injuries. Blackish spots dotted my upper arms, the remnants of rough hands yanking me out of the van. A lavender blue spot on my face suggested I'd slammed into something solid along the way. Grabbing a hand mirror from the dresser, I discovered more bruising on my lower back. I wrapped up the tour where it had begun, taking another look at the side which had sustained the most damage. The bruising suggested an outline of the state of Florida.

I wriggled out of my nightgown and dropped it on the floor. Bending to pick it up proved to be too much effort, so I left it and limped to the shower. I ran the water as hot as I could stand it and stood under the soothing spray until it became tepid. As I stepped from the shower and reached for a towel, a sharp jolt stabbed me between the shoulder blades, and I had to stop for a moment before moving back to my room where I eased onto the bed.

Who would have thought being kidnapped would take so much out of person? On TV rescued victims seemed a lot perkier than this. After taking a few minutes to recover, I dragged myself out of bed and got dressed, then trudged to the kitchen for coffee and a bowl of cereal.

Standing at the window, I rinsed the dishes and looked out at the wooded area. The sun shone brightly, highlighting the layer of leaves covering the ground like confetti. One of the many reasons I loved this place was the illusion of being in a forest, far away from the clamor of the city. Today it made me feel isolated and uneasy. I hoped my recent brush with the very real specter of mortality hadn't ruined living here for me.

It was after one when I thought to check my messages. Hugh and Darla had left early morning voicemails. Both were checking in and didn't require responses. Uncle Buddy had seen the news and called Mom in a panic. He was unbelievably relieved I was okay and asked me to get in touch as soon as I felt like it. Bethany and Mateo had texted. My friend had also seen the televised account of my ordeal and was desperate for details. Mateo wanted to know if I needed anything and asked if he could stop by later.

I reread his message, looking for clues about where our relationship was headed. There was no denying the heat between us, but so much of our interaction had been influenced by outside forces. Did my gratitude for helping Buddy and possibly saving my life play too much of a role in my feelings for him? It was impossible to gauge how much of the pure excitement of so much unexpected and atypical danger and intrigue contributed to the thrill of being with him.

And there was Lance. Now I could see that much of my attraction to him had been based on what other people thought. Had I ever really loved him? My heartbreak at losing him had been genuine. But it was also impossible to separate the loss of Lance from saying goodbye to all that he had to offer: financial security, social position, and getting Mom off my back.

Suddenly, all the handwringing over whether I was ready to start something with Mateo made me feel like a reality show loser. I picked up my phone and texted.

I'd like that. I have dinner with the parents at 6:30, though. Can you make it earlier?

I hit send and poured another cup of coffee. Before I added creamer, I received a response.

My afternoon is open. Is 2:00 okay?

That gave me less than an hour to do something with my hair and cover up the bruise on my face. Difficult, but not impossible.

Taming my curls proved to be particularly challenging because of my limited range of motion. After unsuccessfully trying to wrap the curling iron around several unruly strands, I surrendered and pulled my hair into a ponytail. Even that amount of pressure produced excruciating pain in my back and shoulders, but I deemed the result acceptable. Not so much with the concealer, however. After applying three coats, my face began to look distinctly asymmetrical, so I washed it off and went with a light dusting of powder followed by blush and lipstick.

When the doorbell rang at 2:00, I avoided the hall mirror and invited him inside, ignoring his look of shock.

"Can I get you anything?" I asked, leading him into the combo office and den.

"I should be asking you that question" He brushed a kiss across my forehead; then we sat on the sofa. "How's my little Super Woman this morning?"

"Not feeling too super, I'm afraid." I looked down as an infuriating little lump of emotion began to expand in my throat. I swallowed it away. Was this a delayed reaction from my wild adventure, something like PTSD?

Mateo traced his fingertip lightly along the outline of the bruise on my cheek. "I keep thinking about what might have happened to you, and it makes me sick." He ran his finger over my lips and down the side of my neck, then rested his hand on my shoulder.

Even though the pressure from his hand was slight, I winced, and he drew back as if he'd been burned. "Did that hurt?" he asked. "That's a stupid question. Of course, it did. I'm so sorry."

I hated to see him looking as if he were in more pain than I was. "It's not that bad, really. I'm just a little sore."

He leaned against the back of the sofa and closed his eyes. "I keep seeing you trapped with those sociopaths."

"Other than some bumps and bruises and being a little shaken up, I'm fine." I took his hand.

Eyes open now and focused on me, he shook his head. "Right. But I'm not so sure I am."

Uh, oh. "What's wrong?"

"This whole thing between us hasn't exactly been the way you start a relationship. Trying to keep your uncle out of jail at the same time everyone's half-crazy worrying about your stalker and—"

"I get it." I released his hand and looked away. "It's hard to separate what's real from the thrill of being caught up in something bigger and exciting. I feel the same way." I did not feel that way at all but was determined not to show how disappointed I was that he wanted to end our relationship before it had even begun.

"You do?" He frowned.

"Of course," I lied. "I'm not denying I'm attracted to you." Big understatement. "But I'm not like you. You deal with dangerous stuff all the time. For me, this whole experience has been so . . ." Life-changing? Terrifying? Fantastic? Unfreaking believable? ". . . out of the ordinary."

"Out of the ordinary," he echoed. "I guess that's one way to put it. Not exactly what I was going for but interesting." He stood. "What

I was going to say was because so much has happened in such a short time, I thought we might slow things down, hit the reset button. Maybe go out on a real date, not some business lunch or rescue mission. Take our time and get to know each other. Things like whether you like the beach or the mountains. Your favorite movie or color or book. But you're probably right. All that ordinary stuff might not cut it." He stepped away from the sofa. "I'll head out and let you get some rest."

Scrambling to my feet, I reached out to stop him. "Wait. Please. I didn't mean out of the ordinary. I meant spectacular, remarkable, incredible. And it's the beach and *The Jerk*—mostly because my dad loves Steve Martin and we watched it together at least a thousand times before I moved out—and my favorite color is teal blue or coral if it's spring and sometimes fuchsia—and *All the King's Men*. My high school English teacher made me read it the first time, but I've read it at least five or six times since then. Don't bother with the movies, though. They suck." I paused for breath. "And yes, please, let's take it slow."

. . .

After several attempts, Mateo and I discovered ways to avoid the more painful areas of my injured body. This allowed us well over an hour to discover an assortment of more intimate items on my list of favorites. He learned how the slightest touch of his tongue high on my neck made me shiver and that trailing his finger from my collar bone to the top of my breast elicited a groan from deep in my throat. I discovered nipping his ear lobe caused his breath to quicken and his eyelids to flutter.

By the end of this exploration of mutual preferences, we knew a great deal more about each another than when we started.

"I guess that's one way to hit the reset button," Mateo said, trying to untangle himself from sheets and blanket without letting go of me in the process.

"Definitely my favorite way." I snuggled closer to him, and he gave up on freeing himself from the bedclothes. "Not exactly slowing things down, though," I sighed.

"Hey, we're just getting started." He smoothed my hair from my forehead. "I promise I'll do better next time."

I poked him in the chest and laughed. "That's not what I meant."

"I know." He kissed me on the tip of my nose. "But I'm serious about the getting started part. We can take things as fast or as slow as you want. We can hold hands at the movie or rip each other's clothes off every night or even have dinner with your folks."

"Shit!" I sat up, taking the sheet with me. "I'm due for dinner in less than an hour. If I'm late, Mom will send out the Highway Patrol. As for having a meal with my parents? Be careful what you wish for."

I moved as fast as I could, which wasn't fast at all, to the bathroom, turning to watch as he crawled out of bed and began retrieving his clothes from the floor. Unlike me, he didn't bother covering himself with a sheet or anything else, providing me with a lovely view as he tugged his jeans on.

"Okay, no parents for now. But what about a real date tomorrow night? Dinner? Maybe even a movie. Unless you have a better idea." He crossed the room and tugged on the sheet. I slapped at his hands and laughed.

"Dinner and a movie sound great. Now go away while I clean up and try to look like a good daughter."

"You're good all right." He grinned before kissing me. "I'll call later."

On the way to dinner, I smiled and sang along with the radio. Sitting in the driveway at my parents' house, I checked my reflection in the visor mirror and tried to rearrange my expression into something a little less . . . less, uh . . . what the hell, less satisfied.

After trying on a few solemn looks, however, I decided it was a lost cause. I wasn't worried about Dad guessing the reason for my happy glow. He was blissfully and intentionally ignorant when it came to associating anything remotely sexual with his daughter.

But Mom had this crazy sex-dar. In my teenage years, whenever I came home from a date, Mom could tell if there was a make-out session involved. Rather than address the problem directly, she would relate some dire tale of a friend of a friend's daughter who soiled her reputation and descended into darkness. Purposefully vague about exactly what that condition was, she warned me about how easy it was to fall from grace. This tactic had been frighteningly effective, causing me to associate warm tingly sensations with impending doom. Hopefully, the years had dulled this Spidey-sex-sense of Mom's, but I doubted it.

Dad greeted me before I had a chance to ring the bell. He threw his arms around me and pulled me close, releasing me when I groaned.

"Did I hurt you? Are you okay?"

"I'm fine. A little sore, that's all.

"Sorry, baby, but you scared the hell out of us." He took my hand and led me toward the kitchen. "Your mom went all out."

The aroma of fried chicken and cinnamon filled the air. Standing in front of the stove, Mom supervised a skillet full of hot chicken, occasionally dodging droplets of popping oil.

When she turned to greet me, one of the deadly little missiles splatted on her neck, and she swatted at it as if it were an attack from some pesky insect. "I'd give you a hug, but I don't want to get flour all over you," she said, brushing a wisp of hair off her forehead with the back of her hand.

How many times had I walked into this kitchen to find Mom in the process of frying or flipping or icing? After I left home, I found her refusal to take advantage of some of the miracles of the modern world—store-bought fried chicken, pre-decorated birthday cakes, Trader Joe's—sweet, but old-fashioned. I tried to explain how much easier life would be if she joined the 21st century. Mom dismissed my suggestions.

"God only knows what they put in that stuff," she would say. "Besides, I like cooking for my family. It relaxes me."

Whirling and twirling around the kitchen, fighting the constant battle of making sure everything was ready at the same time, Mom never looked relaxed. More like frantic and frazzled. Today I sensed an underlying tension behind the usual frenzy.

"A little flour won't hurt me." I threw my arms around her shoulders and hugged her. Holding the spatula in one hand, Mom patted me on the back with the other.

"Careful, honey. You'll get splattered." She broke away from the embrace and returned to the chicken. Over the sound of sputtering grease, I heard a sniffle and handed her a paper towel. She dabbed at her eyes, then stuck the towel in her pocket.

I worked with Dad to set the table. When he brought out the wine glasses, I arched my brows. "Wine on a weeknight? Pretty fancy."

"It's not every day you get to celebrate your baby girl being a hero."

"I'd hardly call myself a hero."

"That's because you didn't hear about it on the news the way we did," Mom said as she put down the platter of steaming chicken hard enough to dislodge a crispy leg. She scooped it up before it rolled onto the floor. "On the news, Lucy. The first time we heard that our only daughter had not only escaped the murderers who kidnapped her but had overpowered them." She continued loading the table, becoming a little more forceful with each additional dish.

"I wouldn't say *overpowered*. More like–"

"*Overpowered*, Lucy. Those were the newscaster's exact words." Mom slapped her hand on the table, then sat in the same chair she had occupied for as long as I could remember.

"Now, Annie," Dad began.

"Please do not 'now Annie' me." She gave him a dark look. "Let's just try to enjoy our meal."

He sighed and sat down, motioning me to do the same. For the next few moments, except for the rattling of dishes being passed and the clanking of serving spoons on plates, no one spoke.

I broke first. "How's Uncle Buddy doing?"

"You'd know if you'd taken the time to call. But you were too busy overpowering killers." Mom stabbed a green bean and began cutting it into tiny pieces.

"Buddy's good. Isn't that right, Anne-Marie?" His use of Mom's proper name typically meant he was done with his peace-keeping efforts, and it was time to wrap up whatever conflict she and I were having.

"He's fine." Mom didn't look up.

"Didn't he say something about wanting Lucy to stop by?" Dad encouraged.

"Yes." Mom sighed deeply, possibly a sign she was willing to begin treaty negotiations.

"I'm planning to get by the store tomorrow," I offered, piling mashed potatoes onto my plate. In the process of passing the bowl to Dad, I caught him give her a quick glance and a nod. I experienced a nervous twinge. Why were they so eager for me to visit Buddy? He rarely took sides in conflicts in the Howard household, and when he did, he was usually on my side.

"I'm sure he'll be glad to see you." Mom maintained a neutral expression, but I still had an uncomfortable feeling. There was, however, no reason to question either of them. If there was some sort of emotional ambush planned, I would have to wait until Buddy sprang it on me.

We spent the rest of the meal engaged in typical family small talk. Dad happily described his plans to harvest the cabbage he planted mid-summer and promised to save the best for me. Mom warmed up enough to share bridge horror stories including the break-up of one long-term partnership because, no matter how many times she was told, one of them continued to open with less than thirteen points.

My favorite dessert, apple crisp topped with real whipped cream and a dollop of guilt at causing pain to the mother who made it, was served in the den where we watched the national evening news. I was thankful my adventure hadn't made the broadcast.

After the program, I helped with the clean-up before announcing I was tired and had to make an early evening of it. Unlike my last visit, my parents seemed genuinely disappointed to see me leave.

"Dinner was great," I said and kissed Mom on the cheek.

"Any time, dear." She returned the gesture and placed her hands on my shoulders. "I hate to see you so exhausted. But I suppose when you have such a demanding job, it gets in the way of family."

I let the remark pass and followed Dad to the car where he checked the oil and tires.

"Maybe you could keep your mother a little more in the loop, especially if you're going to end up on the news." he said, closing the hood. "You know she worries because she loves you so much. We both do."

"I love you guys, too. And I promise to keep you more up to date on my life. But you don't need to worry because I'm not expecting to be involved in anything remotely dangerous in the future."

. . .

I woke to a clap of thunder. Sinking deeper under the comforter, I listened to the steady beat of the rain hitting the roof. I opened my eyes and rolled over, careful not to put pressure on my bruised hip. The bedside clock was flashing, indicating the power had gone off sometime during the night. Dim light from the slits in the blinds cast a filmy haze throughout the room as if I had been thrown into one of the gloomy, yet glamorous black and white movies Buddy and I loved.

Remembering my promise to visit him, I groaned and reached for my phone to check the time: 6:38. Normally, I would have stayed up reading or watching television the night before an unexpected vacation day and slept well past ten the next morning. Dinner with my parents, however, took its toll, and I crawled into bed a little before nine and was out minutes after my head hit the pillow.

I rose and opened the blinds. The deluge morphed my backyard from a crisp, autumn pastoral into a melting Monet. The chill in the room suggested the rain brought with it a warning of winter. I rummaged through the drawers, pulled out a pair of sweats, and went to the kitchen for coffee.

Unable to remember the last time I exercised—grappling with Janelle didn't count even though it had exponentially increased my heartbeat—I finished my coffee, got out the mat, and attempted a gentle stretch. Halfway into it, my battered body sent out a distress signal, and I abandoned the attempt.

Housework fell into the same neglected category as exercise, so I brought out cleaning equipment and attacked the kitchen first. After a bit of half-hearted scrubbing and sweeping, I made another cup of coffee and cheese toast.

It was after eight-thirty. The rain was more drizzle now than downpour. Since Buddy didn't open the shop until 10:00, I had plenty of time to get cleaned up and be at his place before lunchtime when things got busier.

The front of Past Perfect was festooned in skeleton lights. Their faint glow emphasized the gloom of the morning and reminded me next Friday was Halloween. I recalled how much my level of excitement increased when I was a kid and the holiday came on the weekend.

The last few years, I had joined Buddy and Norm at the shop to pass out candy. Buddy used the occasion as an excuse to don his Marilyn Monroe outfit, seams shiny from multiple alterations. Norm accused him of trying to fit ten pounds of mud into a five-pound sack, but ended up alongside him, wearing his Yankees jersey with DiMaggio's name and number on it. One year somebody complained the duo set a bad example for the neighborhood children, but the complaint had no adverse effect on turnout and the local homophobe hadn't been heard from again.

Walking across the small parking lot, I noticed the unusual window display. The bottom two-thirds of a thick-trunked tree took up most of the space. Its branches drooped slightly from the weight of the objects dangling from them. As I got closer, the markings on the trunk came into focus. They were the eerie features of a deeply deranged woodland creature: hollowed eyes, deep wrinkles, and a gaping down-turned mouth. It was one of the talking trees from *The Wizard of Oz*. Those damn trees had scared the shit out of me for weeks after I saw the movie. And time hadn't taken away all that much of their power to terrify. Instead of apples, it held brightly colored Halloween-themed ornaments. The grinning faces of ghouls and goblins did nothing to ease my anxiety.

The little bell over the door tinkled, and Buddy popped up from behind the counter, his arm still in a sling.

"Lucybird!" he called out. "Norm, get out here. It's our very own heroine."

The discordant Chihuahua chorus signaled Norm had opened the door to the back of the store. He strode up the main aisle in a red-plaid flannel shirt and a pair of well-worn jeans. His broad grin spread to his eyes, crinkling them with the kind of wrinkle lines that suggested a lifetime of smiles.

"We are so proud of you!" he exclaimed, smothering me against his thick chest.

I squirmed out of the hug and kissed him on the cheek. Before I could explain their pride in me was misplaced, Buddy joined us, trapping me in a one-armed embrace.

"It was a slow news day," I said when he released me.

Buddy emitted a dismissive little grunt. "Don't be so modest. The way you faced down your kidnappers and exposed their organ stealing? That's headline news any day. Including today. Show her, Norm."

Norm handed me a newspaper, folded to page four where I saw where I saw *Local insurance investigator foils illegal transplant ring*. The first paragraph provided the basic story of how I had gotten the upper hand on two women suspected of multiple crimes including the transport and selling of organs for profit. Mateo and Hugh were credited with helping take the women into custody, and Lance was listed as a kidnap victim who was being held for questioning. The rest of the article included a brief explanation of how our company had become involved in the case and background on Roberta and Janelle.

I felt as if I should acknowledge Elsie's contribution to the take down but doubted she cared about getting credit. I would, however, explain her involvement to Hugh in the hope it might make him more sympathetic to our aging con artist.

"See, there it is in black and white. Norm and I are going to throw a big party for you and that yummy friend of yours as soon as things calm down a little."

"I'm not sure that's such a good idea."

But he wasn't having it. "No arguments! When we want a party, we get a party, right, Hon?" He tapped Norm on the shoulder.

He shrugged. "I'm afraid you're going to have to suffer through a party. Don't worry, though. I'll do my best to keep it low-key."

We both knew low-key wasn't in Uncle Buddy's vocabulary.

"Fine, then." No reason to put a damper on their festive mood. "But let's keep it to family and really close friends."

"Absolutely, sugar." Buddy beamed. "I promise to run the guest list by you."

Norm rolled his eyes, and I laughed.

"But that's not why I asked you to stop by." The two men exchanged glances. "Would you mind watching the store while Lucy and I have a little sit-down?"

"Not at all. I'll just run through yesterday's receipts."

Following Buddy to their living quarters, I heard pitiful high-pitched whines and frenzied scratching from another room. He ignored the dogs and led me to the kitchen, where he began heating the copper tea kettle.

"You know I don't like to butt into your life," he said as he brought down the rose and blue floral cups and saucers from the cabinet.

Although interfering in my life was one of his favorite pastimes, I didn't bother disputing him.

"And normally, I think your mother has a tendency to overreact." He placed the saucers on the table. "But this time, she might have a point." The kettle whistled.

"A point about what?"

"You know, honey. About your job." He filled the cups and brought them to the table. "When your daddy recommended you to the company, he and your mother thought the insurance business would be a solid career opportunity. I doubt they expected you'd be chasing bad guys, gals, I mean."

I hadn't expected it either. "This whole situation doesn't exactly represent what I do on a daily basis."

"I know, but your folks are worried. That's why the timing's so good." He stirred his tea.

"Timing for what?"

"For the Atlanta History Center." He smiled. "You remember my friend Walter Green?" He gave me an expectant look. "You know, Wally? I asked him about openings when you were job hunting, but they weren't hiring? Anyway, they are looking for an assistant director of their educational program. And Wally wants you to come in for an interview."

I knew he expected me to be excited. After all, I had talked about getting a job like that ever since declaring my major. And six months ago, I would have been crazy out-of-my mind thrilled by the possibility of my dream job. So why did I feel, so, well, underwhelmed?

"Did you hear me, honey? The Atlanta History Center."

"Sorry." I put on a happy face. "I just can't believe it. The Atlanta History Center." Repeating it didn't make it sound better. "Thanks so much. I really appreciate it."

"You don't have to thank me. Not after the way you and your friends helped me." He stirred another spoonful of sugar into his cup. "You know I couldn't stand that man, but he didn't deserve to go like that. Nobody does."

Well, maybe a doctor who sells other peoples' organs or two depraved con-artists who murder him. "No, nobody does."

The clitter-clatter of canine toenails announced the approach of Norm and his pack. Paco leapt into my lap while Pepe jumped up and down in doggy delirium. Doris sat on Buddy's foot and began licking herself.

"Come here, you bad boy." Paco managed to plant a few wet kisses on my face and neck before Norm swept him up in one arm and Pepe in the other. "Sorry about that."

I wiped my mouth with a napkin. "No big deal. I kind of like being the object of adoration. But I better get going."

Buddy walked me through the store, stopping at his desk to pick up Wally's business card and handing it to me.

"You'll be here next Friday to hand out candy, right? This year we're going with a Dorothy and the Wizard theme. Of course, you can be whoever you like, but we're currently in need of a good witch, a Glenda, that is. I think I've talked your mom into being the wicked one." He grinned from underneath four cutouts of musicians in black cat outfits from a 1930s-era scat band. The shelves to his right were filled with colorful Majolica pottery embossed with flying witches and jack-o'-lanterns. Like Buddy and his store, they were a combination of the ridiculous and the sublime.

"I wouldn't miss it for the world." After kissing his cheek, I promised to set up an interview with Wally, then I stepped into the damp October air. The skies had completely cleared now, and the sun glinted off the leaves giving them a jewel-like quality. It was only a little after eleven, and I had the rest of the day to do whatever I wanted. I could take a long walk in the park or get a pedicure or pick up that book I had been dying to read.

But instead of heading toward the park or the nail salon or home, I drove in the opposite direction, directly to the office. If Hugh's car was in the lot, I would keep driving. But if it wasn't, I would slip in, grab a few folders, and take them home.

Hugh's spot was empty, and Darla was away from her desk, so I speed-walked down the hallway, feeling a little silly at having to sneak into my own office. Surprised to see the lights were on and the door unlocked, I eased open the door.

A familiar head of silvery white hair popped up from behind her desk.

"Elsie?"

"Lucy!" Elsie Erikson said, hopping up from the swivel chair. "I didn't think you were coming in today. Darla said it would be okay for me to work from here today while the tech guys set me up in the office down the hall."

"I don't understand." Elsie looked stately outfitted in a beautifully cut cream and black suit and her hair newly cut in a becoming bob.

"Mr. Farewell didn't tell you? I guess he didn't really have time. We should sit, dear. The story's a bit complicated."

It seemed I didn't need to use our adventure to convince Hugh to go easy on Elsie. Apparently, he had never been fully committed to putting our diminutive con-woman behind bars. Explaining that news coverage of a poor little old lady being hounded by nasty old insurance companies might be bad for business, he persuaded the higher-ups to drop the charges. In exchange, Elsie would pay back a portion of the money she owed in installments. He convinced the local prosecutor that, without formal complaints, prosecuting the case wouldn't be worth the trouble, especially not when the defendant looked like an ad for Grandmas Are Us. They worked out a deal and the judge signed off on it. In addition to making financial restitution, Elsie would work as Hugh's assistant, helping to identify the very scams she once pulled off.

"That means you and I will be working together. I'll be like your gal Friday," Elsie concluded, face glowing. "I hope you're okay with it?"

"I think so, but I have a few questions. Like what you were doing at the warehouse."

Her face lost some of its glow. "I thought you might. Do you remember the quilt on my wall?"

"The quilt? Yes, but what has got to do with anything?"

"Patience, dear. I told you a dear friend made it for me, but I wasn't being completely honest. Sylvie was my dearest friend, but she was also my sister. She had an antique shop in North Georgia, where she kept our grandmother's quilts with some older ones she collected over the years. She came down with bladder cancer, and running the shop got to be too much for her. So, she turned the day-to-day operations over to her son. Good-looking boy but if dumb was dirt, he could cover an acre. Anyway, this slick-talking dealer came along and offered to take the entire set off his hands for a fraction of what it was worth."

"Darrow," I said.

"That's right, that scum-sucking bastard. Sylvie died before finding out all those beautiful heirlooms were gone. But I wasn't about to let that jackass get away with what he'd done. I started checking local shops and found two of them at the Past Perfect. When I asked your uncle's partner who he bought them from, he gave me Darrow's name and told me that thief still had the majority in his warehouse. I did some research, located the warehouse, and let myself in through a broken window. I was on my second trip loading the quilts into my car when the crazy guy in the uniform and your uncle came barreling in. There were sirens in the background, and it looked like Prescott was losing it, so I knocked the cabinet on top of him and took off."

"That means you've been an unsung heroine twice."

"I'm not sure the cops would see it that way. They might consider my reappropriation of goods the same as stealing. I didn't see it like that and thank the good Lord, neither did Mr. Farewell."

"Wait. Hugh knew about the quilts?"

"He saw me leaving the warehouse and stopped by my house later. We agreed nobody needed to know I was there and that you can't steal something that was stolen from your family. Speaking of the boss. You're supposed to be home resting. He isn't going to be happy if he finds out you're here."

"I'm fine, and what Mr. Farewell doesn't know won't hurt us."

We spent the next hour discussing Elsie's role with the company and deciding which cases she should start with.

"I was going to take some work home, but with my Gal Friday, I don't need to worry." I made a mental note to Google 'gal Friday' and started for the door, but Hugh was blocking it.

"This is a surprise," he growled. "Aren't you supposed to be home resting?"

"I'm on my way out the door. Speaking of surprises." I inclined my head toward Elsie. "When were you going to tell me about our new intern?"

He shuffled his feet. "It's strictly on a day-by-day basis. One screw-up and she's out."

"Don't worry," I said, leaning closer. "I promise I won't let anyone know what an old softie you are." I slipped out before he could reply.

On the way home, I stopped for groceries and a nice bottle of wine. Mateo and I hadn't made any specific plans, but the way we left things, I was confident I would see him soon. Unless I misread him the way I misread Lance.

Stop it! I'm not going to let that asshole ruin whatever it is Mateo and I might have.

More than that, I wasn't going to let our relationship change me. I allowed Lance to enroll me in the Society for the Training and Subjugation of Successful Attorneys' Wives. From what I wore to the wine I drank, his preferences became my mandate. This time would be different.

I finished putting away the last of the groceries when Mateo called to say he had been called out of town for the weekend and wouldn't be back until late Sunday. He promised to make it up to me on Monday evening, and I embarrassed myself by giggling into the phone like a middle school girl.

While changing into my stay-at-home sweats, Walter Green's card fell out of my pants pocket. Images of the history center with its panoramic view of the city came to me as I remembered how much I had wanted to be the one in charge of protecting all those original documents, making sure they were properly admired from the safety of their glass cases. I thought about arranging exhibits carefully placed behind velvet ropes far from the grasp of sweaty little hands.

The image of Hugh focusing his flashlight on the greasy invoice I dug from the doctor's garbage crossed my mind and I smiled. No one at the history center would ever expect me to dig in someone's trash.

EPILOGUE

A little under four months and the view from my new office still amazed me. Unlike the history center, there was no panoramic view of the Atlanta skyline with the cool majesty of Stone Mountain in the distant background. Nor could I see rooftop gardens or the glittery dome of the Capitol Building.

Instead, my upstairs office in the renovated bungalow near downtown Roswell overlooked a pond surrounded by willowy reeds and creeping jenny. Branches of the cherry tree outside my window sported tiny buds that would soon erupt into pale pink blossoms.

Hugh had chosen this location as the home for Farewell Investigations, the firm he established after an amicable separation from Idleman's. In a surprise move, he asked me to join him as the head of the field team. I was the only one on the field team, but Hugh promised they would soon be expanding.

My life had expanded in other ways as well. Enrolled in Georgia State's Criminal Justice department, I began work on my masters. I learned that Elsie, who had come onboard as Hugh's assistant—both in keeping with the terms of her probation and because she was having "one hell of a good time"—was a valuable source of information on scams other than the slip and fall. While she hadn't participated in them, she'd run into other con artists along the way and was happy to teach me the difference between a pigeon-drop and a badger game.

As for Mateo, we were taking things slowly, the way I promised myself we would. Although we were gradually spending more and more time together, we weren't rushing toward a lifetime commitment or even cohabitation, though he was at my house more than he was home. He also frequently worked with the new firm as a free-lance investigator. And I still thought he was the kindest, sexiest man I had ever known.

When I thought of my life a year ago, it was like traveling through a scrapbook filled with photos and mementoes that belonged to someone I used to know. The chaos of that last year forged me into a stronger version of myself.

This new and improved model no longer wanted to keep a dispassionate distance between myself and the real world. I had come to accept that truth isn't always clean and absolute. Sometimes it's a big blurry mess. I thought my feelings for Lance were true. But that was an illusion, fed by deception. Even a man like Uncle Buddy wasn't always completely truthful, but that didn't mean he wasn't a good person. And what about Elsie? A person who had made a livelihood from dishonesty but was one of the most forthright people I knew.

The new Lucy still valued honesty but realized what a cold companion it could be. For me, truth was no longer the harsh measurement of motives and actions. It was the way Dad kicked my tires every time I visited and how he sat a little taller whenever my mother entered a room. It was the way Mom took off his glasses when he fell asleep reading in bed. It was Norm wiping my sleeping uncle's chin and the way Elsie's eyes misted over at the mention of her husband. And it was when Mateo twirled a strand of my hair the second before he kissed me.

I learned that truth alone is a finite force people can twist for their own purposes. But with love, truth becomes infinite with possibility.

ABOUT THE AUTHOR

Katherine Nichols is the award-winning author of *The Sometime Sister* and the sequel, *The Substitute Sister*, family sagas with suspense, heart, and humor, as well as *The Unreliables,* chosen by *Strand Magazine* as one of the top 25 mysteries of 2022, and *Trust Issues*. A vice president of The Atlanta Writers Club, she also serves on the board of Sisters in Crime Atlanta. As a strong proponent of women authors supporting each other, Katherine is a co-host of the inspirational Wild Women Who Write Take Flight podcast. When she isn't spending time with her children and grandchildren, Katherine loves to read, walk, and travel. She lives in Lilburn, Georgia with her husband, two rescue dogs, and two rescue cats.

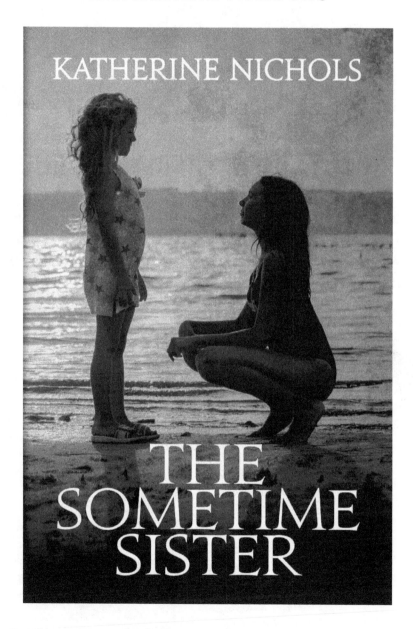

KATHERINE NICHOLS

THE
SOMETIME
SISTER

NOTE FROM KATHERINE NICHOLS

Word-of-mouth is crucial for any author to succeed. If you enjoyed *False Claims*, please leave a review online—anywhere you are able. Even if it's just a sentence or two. It would make all the difference and would be very much appreciated.

Thanks!
Katherine Nichols

We hope you enjoyed reading this title from:

BLACK ROSE
writing™

www.blackrosewriting.com

Subscribe to our mailing list – *The Rosevine* – and receive **FREE** books, daily
deals, and stay current with news about upcoming
releases and our hottest authors.
Scan the QR code below to sign up.

Already a subscriber? Please accept a sincere thank you for being a fan of
Black Rose Writing authors.

View other Black Rose Writing titles at
www.blackrosewriting.com/books and use promo code
PRINT to receive a **20% discount** when purchasing.

Printed in the USA
CPSIA information can be obtained
at www.ICGtesting.com
LVHW090325151123
763992LV00002B/136

9 781685 132699